U.P.

For: FALLING ROCK

Remember M...

BILL HART
VINMU-TV

Thanks from ABC 10

Hart & Bones

UP Power! Catie Rosemurgy

Stay True North — John Amtner

Marquette Forever! Tyler R. Tichelaar

U.P. 4 EVA

Dianna Patrick (Snowbound)

Thanks for the support, man! — Jonathan Johnson

Nancy Dwyer (Falling Rock Cafe & Bookstore)

WNMU-FM Public Radio 90

Cathy Seblonka / Peter White Public Library

Missing Marquette!

To Ron — Thanks for all you pretty cool! — Gary Kmet

Ron — You Rock!

Hi — Linda North

Go Miners!

To Ron! Thanks...

Dan Ames

Ron,
Thanks for
making a wonderful
program happen in
Gwinn!
Kathy Holman, Forsyth Twp Library
Gwinn

Thanks! James Love

U.P.

A Novel

R.A. RIEKKI

Thanks, Ron!
Island Bookstore, 7/9
Lake Bean

Ron,
Thanks
Eric Enger

Russell Magnaghi
Great idea
and beer

Thank you!
Scott M

gay books!
Mike Inley

Library of Congress Cataloging-in-Publication Data.
U.P.
Ghost Road Press
ISBN (Trade pbk.)
13 digit 978-0-9796255-6-5
10 digit 0-9796255-6-4
Library of Congress Control Number: 2008935981

Layout: Sonya Unrein
Cover design: N. Riekki

Ghost Road Press
Denver, Colorado

ghostroadpress.com

Thank You So Vre Much For All Yo Doing For U.P. Literature, Nancy! Here's A Collection Of People's Autographs From The U.P. Book Tour 2011,

Frank

1: Hollow

A cousin of mine, Craig, says nothing good has ever come out of the U.P. No one from the U.P. would ever get interviewed by Johnny Carson. No actors or comedians or pro athletes (skiers are not athletes) come from the U.P., although my father could list an obscure 5.00 ERA Brewers' pitcher, and my mother knows a neighbor who worked as a Hollywood extra on a no-name motion picture, inconspicuously walking by with an umbrella and playing a stomach-sprawled film noir corpse. One film was shot here, *Anatomy of a Murder*, which no one has seen, a true story set in Marquette and Big Bay. Craig's study hall teacher says he was in it, but no one believes him.

Up here are plumbers and miners and nurses, jobs with no awards, no Grammys or Heismanns or Emmys. I asked my father who our most famous person is. He said, "Dominic Jacobetti." You have not heard of him and neither has anybody else except for my father and all of the other Yoopers. Jacobetti is a Senator or a mayor. I forget.

Yoopers are people from the U.P. It stands for Upper Peninsula, which is the top part of Michigan. Occasionally it is omitted from maps. Antony says the U.P. looks like a gun. Craig says it looks like a turd. But the universal sign for the U.P. is a flat left hand with palm up and fingers held together parallel to the ground with thumb pointing up, so Sault Ste. Marie is at the tip of the middle finger.

When I tell people I am from Michigan, they ask if I live in Detroit. Ishpeming is an eleven-hour drive northwest of Detroit. So no, I am not from Detroit. I grew up in Germfask (three years, none remembered) and Ishpeming (the rest of my life), but I was born in Ironwood, thirteen hours from Detroit. Like Iron Mountain, Ironwood is one of the U.P.'s bigger cities. The biggest is Marquette, our metropolis with 15,000. Ishpeming has 7,000, but it is growing because our neighbor a block away on Second Street is the town hundred-thousandaire and he keeps building more gas stations. Thanks to him we have two more Exxons at the furthest east and west areas of town. You drive in on US-41, get greeted by those double XX's, leave town, and get a neon "so long!" If you keep heading west, on the way to Michigamme you get greeted by the triple XXX's of the Evergreen Theater—the only adult movie drive-in in the world, the pride of the U.P. Craig has stories about that place, but they are disgusting.

Ishpeming has as many gas stations as churches. With all this gas, I want to know where everyone is heading. Duluth? Ottawa? But more important than gas or God are the bars. The U.P.'s greatest export is drunk drivers; its greatest import is cold weather.

Our house in Ishpeming is next to a Shell station. The S on its sign is burning out. For several years, no one has replaced it despite the nonstop static blinking.

Two years ago we lived in Palmer, on the Suomi side, for a month. With my parents' red Honda packed so neither my brother nor me could move (ski poles pointed at my head, sofa cushions blocking the windows), we were on the snaking back road from Gwinn. M-35 was ice and two times we slid into the wrong lane. I said, "I wonder if there are accidents out here." My father said, "People have been killed on these roads." "Well, not us," my mother said as we pulled around a bend, and there it was—Palmer, in its isolated splendor. The town skyscraper is a two-story firehouse. Above the village is a massive dirt pile, the lingering constant presence of the Empire Mine, and this site could be perfectly viewed through my mother's bedroom window: a sky full of dirt, that keeps getting taller. My mother lasted a month, then she had us move back to Ishpeming.

I would tell you how many people live in Suomi, but it is not in either atlas my parents own. Palmer has 820. And Suomi is smaller than Palmer is. It has ninety, maybe. Half of its people are polite alcoholics whose annual income is less than $11,000; the others are their beanpole kids. ("Suomi" is Finnish for "Finland.")

This is about that undiscovered treasure: the U.P. 'Someplace special,' as TV6 reminds. But, as Craig says, 'special' is a term reserved for the retarded. This is also about another undiscovered treasure: my cousins. I have a lot of cousins. I have at least fifteen cousins.

Families in the U.P. are a competition of kids, armies of children. The Thompsons have nine. The Ruuvinens, ten. The Corts, thirteen. The Corts are Native American, and one way to ensure nobody messes with you is by having twelve boys. I feel sorry for the sole daughter. Their youngest is Matthew Cort. Remember that name.

That size creates two types of family environment: either dens of bored Christians or asylums of future felons. Either way, people in the U.P. beget like the Bible. That is what Finnish Lutheranism and vodka does. There is not much else to do in the U.P.

The theory that nothing good has come from the U.P. does not change if you apply it to my cousins, or to the weather. Year round it is cold except our two-month summer when it is nice, or what we call nice. Because of Lake Superior winds, the average June temp for Marquette is 59.8 degrees. We have Pioneer Week, reunions and cakewalks, and everyone wears shorts for the first time in an eternity, except J, who always wears pants, even swimming. On a freak eighty-degree day he still wears faded razor-ripped acid-washed Levis with so many holes he might as well have worn shorts.

Four of us hang out—Jason Seppukunen, Antony Seurat, Craig Leannes, and me. They call me Hollow. As far as similarities between Craig and me, he shares my last name and that is all. Craig is on my father's side. J and Antony are cousins on my mother's side. J's parents divorced, but my grandmother said to ignore it, so following her orders J and I are still cousins.

The four of us were best friends, if best friends can be family members. We all live in Ishpeming except J. He is in Negaunee. But Negaunee and Ishpeming are the same anyway; the two towns bleed into each other on M-28 and the dividing point is the highest peak, Suicide Hill. Across from Suicide is the town dump.

My childhood photos have at least one of those three in it. Antony is in the majority of them, because he has always been a Yooper; whereas Craig has lived all over. And J lived in Sudbury, which he calls "the Canadian Palmer." J said Canada is clean except for Sudbury. Mining towns are always dirty. Soot has to land somewhere.

I have a scrapbook I started but quit. It has four photos. On the cover is a black-and-white of J and me. We poured a five-pound bag of pastry flour on our heads to pretend we were ghosts. My mother said it was so cute she could not be mad. She shot it with Super 8, posing us in the middle of the napalmed white pantry floor. I am so young in the film my body had not developed to the size of my head. I look like a Q-tip.

There is a colored photo with Antony and me, our hair teased up like electrical socket victims from an overdose of his sisters' hair spray, two hours of life spent holding frozen while his sisters treated us like experimental rag dolls. Antony insisted no makeup, but you can see liner raccooned around my eyes. I let them put lipstick on me. Finished with Antony, they concentrated on "perfecting my beauty," giggling. But I turned out more monster than rock star. It felt good though, tingling, their fingers close to my mouth, me puckered, hearts pulsing, wishing they would lean in, kiss me, both of them, the drawing of deep purple to the most delicate skin on the human body, our lips.

There is a black-and-white with Craig and me on my rooftop after a school-canceling blizzard, leaping into snowbanks—a favorite U.P. pastime, roof diving. My gray hood's strings are pulled so tight you only see nose. "Watch the fence," my father warned; it was hidden, under snow, waiting. Craig is in mid-air, arms spread holy with diabolic thundering face, aware and uncaring. Flash-rewind two winters before the photo when Craig landed on our arrowhead fencepost, leg impaled, a blood formation in the snow, like devils' art, his skin punctured. Diving in front of our picture window, I shielded my eyes to the glass, banged, to get my almanac-scouring father to see my desperation. Speedily shoveled out, Craig limped proudly, awaiting stitches, no tears, to our car, dad revving the engine. "Damn," Craig said, "I was shish kabob-ed." Yet twenty-five months later, Craig ignores the memory and is back to having fun, knowing my father tore up the fence last summer, so now it is safe, or as safe as diving into the unknown ever is.

The fourth photo is blurry, crinkled.

I have to tell you about those three cousins in order to tell you about the biggest event this town ever forgot. It happened in our neighborhood and it had never happened in the U.P. before. And I do not think it ever will again. It would not have happened if my cousins had not lived here. And it would not have happened without Craig.

Craig is youngest of us four. The shortest of his class, his nose ran with snot around the clock. I cannot remember a time at Lakeview Elementary when his nose was dry. His parents never knew when he was sick, only when he was injured, which was often. Craig collected wounds. His chin sports an eleven-stitch scar from using his bed as a trampoline when he was five in Colorado, landing hard on the tile, splitting it open, and getting his first experience of hospital-attention. The scar never healed correctly, because he picked at it, liking the blood. Ten years later, when Craig was fifteen, his older half-brother, Dick, another blood lover, moved out. Until then, Dick beat the snot out of him, which explains things. Watching Rowdy Roddy Piper's "Piper's Pit," they reenacted the screen in their living room. Dick said, "Hey, yous guys want me to beat up Craig?" We cast votes. To this day, Craig hates democracy. But we loved it—and so did Dick. In a whiny wimp voice, Craig pleaded, "No, vote no, please." Usually we voted yes, because you should always be positive. And because, as Antony says, everyone loves a good pounding. Several sports are dedicated to good poundings. Boxing, hockey, football—like watching your family on TV, but with padding. Sometimes we voted no, say, if he had an upcoming birthday; he reminded us, "Come on, Monday is my party. I will not invite you." We said to pummel him so he changed tactics, "Guys, seriously, I can give yous the presents. Vote no and yous guys can come and I will have gifts for everyone." We laughed and voted no, but sometimes, bored, we voted yes. His brother grabbed Craig by the hair; he called it "Three Stooge-ing." If Craig squealed, his brother suffocated him under sofa cushions. He called it "Baby-sitting"; Dick sat on Craig while we watched *Chiller Theater*. He impersonated Ned the Dead, "Vhere iz Craig? Haz anybody zeen heem? Boy, zhese cushions zure are zoft but zo lump-y. Ha, ha. Ah-ah-ah," his laughter vampiric. Craig got a bloody nose, which combined with his runny nose to become a waterfall of yellowy, blood red snot. Craig complained of a couch-induced sprained arm and banged his eye on a chair corner so he went into mini-Hulk Phase, blindly throwing a sofa pillow, a saliva-wet dog bone, and the remote control. The remote broke, which meant lectures from his mother: "I cannot have anything valuable in this house, can I?" After that we got up to change channels. It was common to see Craig's mother's feet propped on the coffee table and Craig cramped by the TV switching channels, complaining, "My legs hurt." His mom's answer: "Then sit different. Now put on Oprah."

If I had to trace the root of their fights, I would blame bus stops in winter. Dick would tiptoe behind to give a swift strangling yank to Craig's grand-mother-knitted turquoise scarf in the stillness of a February morn at the bottom of our Third Street hill—afterwards no griping from Craig, just retaliation. Dick was just keeping warm. He grew tired of chattering teeth and late busses and pulling his collar over his ears, so he settled on the blood pumping warmth of brawling. Snowbanks were wrestling mats. Dawn-lit slugfests were continual from brutal December until March marched in and out like a lion. This, combined with Craig's mother's stinginess with the thermostat, and I have a feeling Craig and his brother were attempting to beat sunlight into each others' veins. If those two had grown up in Daytona, they might have had a shot at an honor roll life. But up here, it is tough to study when you keep thinking about how much your throat hurts.

Craig fought with his mother after Dick left, which meant fewer fists and more yelling; Craig was often pep rally hoarse. Craig talks a lot, a trait inherited from his mother, and that is why I know him so well, even if his talk is never about what matters. When someone keeps talking, you have no choice but to stare, memorize their face, their quirks. Of all of Craig's talents, the most remarkable is his ability to walk towards the door as an argument with his mother reaches crescendo, and spit out one final curse as he slams the screen door, the timing of an expert. He does this in front of grandparents, pastors, virginal nieces. He saves up his f- words for just the right inappropriate moment.

Then when Craig did fight his brother, it was not fun and there were no votes. From Superfly Snuka horseplay, it developed into barroom eye gouges, cheap shots with week-long bruising, fingernail scars to the cheek. They tugged shirts over their heads and gave each other sleeper holds until one tapped out and the other would let go and run. Twice Craig choked his brother unconscious, which is bizarre to witness, like watching someone die for a few seconds—then came resurrections of hate. Their biceps got vein-y, competing for the scariest body. Craig won. Although with his Finlandia bloodshot eyes and marks from lost fistfights, his brother's face was the scarier; Craig called Dick "Prison-head." He was the only one brave enough to say it. When they fought, and even when they were not fighting, I looked in their eyes and saw pure red hatred, like ghouls.

Secretly, we loved their fights. It was in their house or outdoors, so no one cared if they broke chairs or noses. It was better when they did, more dramatic. If you missed it, you felt jealous of those who had front row seats. Spectators took pleasure in whispering recounts, emphasizing words like boxing commentators. "Craig killed him." "His eye was bleeding." "You see when he bit his ankle?" Then Craig got too big.

The fights stopped and his brother rarely visited, moving, wisely, into one of Ishpeming's countless cobwebbed second floor vacancies, attic rentals for unemployment recipients. Once people frequent jails, their sense of humor leaves and they become frightening, uncomfortably dangerous, dark, gaunt. At least Dick did. But before he could do any serious damage to society, a couple years later, he died in what Craig calls a "drunk-driving accident." Dick was stumbling along Business 28 drunk off vodka shots from Hickey's Bar when a sober librarian from N.I.C.E. Community Schools named Molly Pytomaki hit him with her Nissan Turbo at 45 mph. I remember when Craig told me, a casual fact. I hugged him and he said, "What the hell you doing?" I said, "I thought you might be down about it, kind of like affected." He said, "Screw him."

Like a mutation, Craig grew: a teenage mutant. Antony explained, "There is nothing like repeated poundings to get you motivated." He must have been right, because Craig became a mammoth, a beast. Antony said, "Eating a ton and sleep is not enough. For weightlifting to really work, you need to have plenty of hate." We all laughed.

But let's begin at the beginning of the end, which, really, was a year ago, eleven months, an eleven months that whizzed by like trees through a car window. Sometimes I woke up and did not know what month it was, only that school was that much closer to ending. J and me were going into senior year of high school. Antony and Craig were becoming juniors. And 1989's summer was fading like the final hanging notes of a Don Henley ballad.

Iran-Contra and Tiananmen Square were the news, constant television replays ingraining images on our minds. A green uniformed Ollie North has his hand raised, swearing to tell the truth and nothing but. And, meanwhile high schoolers bored with their parents' news programs did what to them truly mattered—

craig crawls all over the pyramid like a apeboy
august
autumn
the fall
the long long fall of north northern michigan
& still that faint chill in the air, like a warning
summer up here is 2 months long—june, july
although long aint really the appropriate word
its in the high 50s for the last day of the year
so we get a crew of us to ball down at miners
& heres craig all actin like a gorilla but dumber
at miners park in negaunee theres this 9 foot pyramid monument jus off the
highway that people try to climb on but you cant. too slippery. but not for craig.
go swimmin at swede & hell dive from rocks no one else would even try. &
make it. usually. & when he dont, man, thats enterfrickintainment. last week
he rode his bike off lakeview elementary. school. his idea. not mine. though i
supported him as friends do. he went e.t. from the roof & it looked peter pan
magical til his body hit the concrete & that looked peter painful wit his lip
yibberin away wit enough blood to paint a entire picket fence. now his face is
all mummy bandaged hilarious. the kids always bleedin. people say i talk like

craig. but he talks like me! this fat chick was hangin out wit my sister & my sister started gainin weight so i was like, "that friend of yours must have the Wide-ass Touch cuz everythin she touches turns to fat." craig stoled my shit. sayin my line. thats my frickin line. & i was the 1st to quote Back to the Future & now bonehead craig is doin flux capacitor Doc Emmett L. Brown impressions i started

not only do we talk alike, though we dont really, but our lives are bout the same. like whenever i get in a fight with my parents, i call him up & sure as hell he got in a fight wit his. im surprised were not related, though we are both cousins of hollow, but everyones a fuckin cousin of hollow

people get me & craig confused though we look nothin alike cuz for the last 2 school years we swapped yearbook photo spots. the picture guy comes & craig says hes me & i say im him. funny shit. specially the dork expression on my face wit "Craig Leannes" printed under it. pure genius & all my idea

anyway theres 7 of us. jus minutes to dusk

7 of us playin ball

im a jock if you consider a jock someone who quit babe ruth, got kicked off the wrestlin team, & signed up for football but then never tried out

other than boxin i play sports only when begged. cuz if you ask me a sport aint a sport unless someones hit in the face. everythin else is a fancy faggy hug-me waste of time

so theres 7 of us

7

messed up number for baseball. 3 gainst 4 waitin for another to show to save you cuz youre runnin for fouls all day & no 1 can catch so the batter swings-n-misses & gets it his self, a good hike to think bout the strike 1 gainst you

it helps to get a all-time pitcher. thats hollow

hollows a skinny borin westwood patriot wannabe starve-faced frickin brainy bookworm senior athlete bonehead whos my cousin and whos not really a ath-lete but he is a bonehead cuz he does the 3 big wimp sports—cross country in fall, basketball in winter, & tennis in spring. damn, might as well do ballet in summer. & how can you be a jock when you dont like to compete, but thats hollow. he gives fair pitches, slow midlevel lobs you poke out on the highway, though sometimes he throws outside & someone strikes out & bitches & throws

the bat. all-time pitchin sucks cuz they try to line drive you—at least i do—&
it happened too, to hollow, once, in the cheek. hilarious. a real riot cuz he was
groggy & toothached & bean ball drunk, which is even funnier to see from a
lanky tall freak like that boneface. imagine manute bol flailin. but now sleepy-
eyed hollows healed & its moosehead craigs turn to be blood-faced

    me? im smiley. im smilin check swingin over by the water fountain which
is a pipe stickin hacked outta the ground. negaunee craftsmanshit. craig puts
his thumb on the end & gives me a good spray so i tell him try again & i swing
away at the water like a friggin summer new york bronx kid fire hydrant-ed.
im hittin homers wit water

    cloudless, the sun steady

    today is baseball & nothin but. except maybe dad earlier gettin happy-drunk.
pops closed the basement door & i dunno what he does down there but i heard
him sing frank snot-ra in this cry-y voice, but whatever. today is sunshine. grand
slams. me. sky

    somethin bout the sky. lookin up at it, i pretend like im in a auditorium &
like all the angels up theres lookin down on me waitin for me to bus a rhyme
like im in concert as a openin act for P.E. & im frickin holdin the bat like a mic
bout to rap into that thin imaginin what its gonna be like when im so famous itll
be like i jus float up into the sky & am gone from this borin life forever when

    along comes "big nose matt cort"

    cruel ass matt parachute pants wannabe scumbucket cort. or as craig calls
him "big nose cort." cuz he got a schnozzle like scottie pippen & barry manilow
combined, elephantitis of the beak, fat chick massive, larger than the planet
sagittarius

    & big nose rides up on that piece o crap no brake bike of his & this tard drags
his no soled shoes & hes no-shower greasier than a welcome back kotter johnny
travolta. he comes to a fred flintstone foot-draggin stop & looks like a fool fallin
on his face in the dust crushin his thick nostrilosos, seriously, you could fit a han-
dlebar up that snout, & kids laugh on the inside cuz big nose is a cigarette-arm-
burnin freshman-hallway-trippin notebook-knocked-outta-your-hands rockhead
& they cant laugh on the outside or hell do his whole schizo routine, a real live
negaunee township nutcase who biked all the way from the airport jus to ruin
our lives. he wants to play. course he does. & id let him if he wasnt so penisless

without lookin up, i say, "already we got teams"

sidekickin beside him is u.e. corts got his bully buddy, u.e., thats the mongoloids nickname, u. friggin e. & that kid got brakes on his bike but no horizontal crossbar which means the dikehead is ridin a girls bike, which im sure of cuz its also pink. "then re-pick," cort says, not lookin at me. big nose grabs a sloppy duct tape handled aluminum louisville slugger & swings like sasquatch golfin & big nose turns to u.e. & says, "watch this" & the cockhole cocks back swingin full tilt nailin me smack in the shoulder. hard core shit there. shot of collapsing numbness through my whole left side. that quick. like thunder lightnin

that quick i go from a happy-go-loser punk-ass who watched his tongue to bein one sufferin cocksuck. that quick & i go from baseball & runnin into the road dodgin cars to steal homeruns, & next you know—im fucked wit a capital -uck

big nose matt corts like, "oh, wha-what happened? did i hit you? im so sorry." like this moerfucks hands slipped. i get up, weak, not wantin to fuck wit this kid cuz hes cuckoo like coco puff mad & i start walkin, home, i guess, not knowin where, jus away, to sort shit out cuz this is sudden

i decide to walk to the clinic, shoulder outta whack, caved in front, the pain joltin like a headache in my stomach

& thats never good

never

left my bat & glove & bike & all

cort walks alongside goin, "sorry, anthony. really i am."

i hate when assheads call me anthony! i look from the side of my eye, goin, "dont worry." & my voice changed. im quieter, afraid. cuz if youll do that, youll do anythin. anythin

cort fades

standin beside him, u.e. fades, away

cort is watchin me walk cringed, & he goes back to the game to see if he can take my spot. no soul in that soulless soul. theres so many of that type in the world you cant count em. a trillion cuntheads stuffed in 1 planet

i look at negaunee goin, "wheres the clinic?" seen it dozens of times & now its hidin

a light evil wind & i could not find that clinic cuz i know ishpeming more

18

than negaunee & my heads down, eyes on the ground like i dont want eye contact wit the world & a empty queasy stomach feelin like im gettin motion sickness jus from walkin. hollow runs up wit my bat & craig rides up wit my bike. as big nose probably catches popups wit my glove

craigs shirts ripped & his chest is cut. hollow says craig fought big nose. "they broke it up," craig says, "or i woulda killed him"

we walk a block, craig kickin his feet along, seated on my bike

"that doesnt look good," i hear hollow whisper to craig

i say, "can you believe that?"

"whats that, antony?" hollow asks wit this gentle look, like a woman, like i was on my deathbed & he was worried id croak

i didnt want to talk. i jus wanted the clinic. "wheres the damn hospital?"

"this way," craig says, "ill run up, let em know youre comin." craig hands my bike to hollow & takes off like nothin. he runs like craziness, fence hurdlin, flower tramplin, like he got a license to anythin cuz an emergencys underway, fun, adventurous, somethin happenin more interestin than baseball & he got to get in a fight & all that unleashed burstin fuckin energy from that & mine was drained, jus drained, realizin baseball was over. & bikin. was over. & boxin. was over. so bein happy. was over. for good

3: J

When I was nine, all three of my remaining grandparents died within a one month timeframe of each other, all from different causes. Death comes in spurts.

Because the same year, Sid, ten and a half years ago, to this day, died.

Greatest human ever, Sid.

February 2, 1979, Groundhog's Day.

Dead.

Of what? What else?

The '70s, as far as music is concerned, was one long dead decade of death. Dad told me how the sixties were a great beating pulse of heart, just life, man. Then the seventies came along and in the first year we lose Jimi and Janis. Then more true poets falling like autumn's carcinoma leaves—Morrison, Elvis, Skynyrd. Man, the list is a void of longing, lost names turned to flat words. And to close the decade out, the final slam of the sarcophagus—Sid. '79.

I remember Johnny asking, "Where would you like to be right now?" This was after Nancy died. Sid replied, "Under the ground." Under the ground. And he felt that.

Don't we all?

If I was placed on a desert island and I could have only one song to listen to from now until the world gets atom bombed, it'd be "Bodies."

Why did Sid die?

Y

. . .

If I was on a desert island and I could only have one movie to watch from now 'til the Russians invade, it'd be *Elephant Man*. Lynched.

Same thing really.

Song or movie.

Or life.

It's all the same.

In the end—you die.

In the meantime, you're lucky if you can find something worthwhile.

Dad. Dad loves bikes. I call him Papa Wheelie.

Dad loves bikes, Hogs, to talk about fat boys, full dressers, sportsters, low riders, choppers, super glide, built his own from individual pieces, sweet motor, striker kit, so the pistons go faster, the crack of a fistful of throttle, zero to sixty mph, front tire off the ground, sixty to 120, burying the speedometer, short pipes lighting up the whole road at night like he's a meteor, a star, the sun, big tanks, smooth traveling saddlebags, pushing it to the limit, life, howling cleansing wind, like a sauna of cold, stretched out, leather vest and chaps, radical, talks to cops to get outta tickets, and loud, so loud you can hear him two miles away, no joke, mufflers cut right out, taught me how, how to set up a decoy muffler to trick the police, the most important part is the muffler for that flaming eagle roar.

I know the mechanics' ins and outs. And I can't even ride the damn things. Unless he's there by my side.

My Dad loves Harleys.

Me, I love my Dad. And I'd be just like him, if it wasn't for my legs.

Chapter 4: Cräig

Here's the blah blahblah blah:

I live in the U.P. 'You pee,' as in piss.

Ishpeming—my hometown begins with "ish." It's like being from Yuckville.

Hollow told me Ishpeming's Indian for "Heaven." If that's true, heaven sucks. There have been times our house was so covered with snow I had to dig a tunnel for my dad to get to the mailbox. That don't happen in heaven.

The only thing to do up here is get in trouble. Or ice fish.

It's like the houses are made of boredom. My mom says it's peaceful, but death is peaceful.

Which reminds me. I was born in Germany, lived in Colorado, down state, and now here, by Negaunee. Hollow looked up 'Negaunee' in the dictionary and it means nothing 'cause it's not in there. He said it would be between 'negativity' and 'neglect.'

I grew up in Detroit. Or as Antony calls it—Destroyed, Michigan.

We switched between Detroit and the U.P. Ishpeming, Detroit. Detroit, Ishpeming. When the mines had layoffs, we moved to Detroit. When Detroit's auto factories had layoffs, we'd move back to Ishpeming. If Michigan isn't building cars, it's digging up shit to make 'em. At one point nobody anywhere was hiring, so we moved to Colorado. 1977. I don't remember anything about Colorado except hate. My mom says we're up here for good now. I'm not sure that 'for good' is the right term.

Between Ishpeming and Detroit, you'd think Ishpeming is safer, but I talked with this crew-cut cop. I said, "Must be nice being up here." He asked what I meant and I said, "In the U.P. Not all that crime." He said, "You'd be surprised." He explained in Detroit you knew backup was minutes away. But here in the U.P., on a call you could have to go back in the redneck woods of Champion, to some isolated deer camp driving out on dirt roads with bumps deeper than Detroit potholes, skull-rattle bumps that knock mufflers off, and you'd realize if you needed backup, it'd take hours for them to get there, if they could find you at all. Plus all these people out in the woods, you know they have guns. These are northern hillbillies, ice hicks, snow Confederates. Some can't afford heaters, so they light candles until their shacks smell like shrines and haul firewood until their backs cave in, but the fireplace doesn't heat all the way to the toilet so every time they sit down, they get more and more ornery, and if it's an outhouse I don't even wanna talk about it. They definitely don't want some troll pig coming around messing with them. That's why they live above the bridge. The Mackinaw Bridge separates the U.P. from Lower Michigan, so anyone that lives, or lived, "below the bridge" is a troll. And the only thing worse than a troll is a damn pig cop troll. He said he felt safer in Detroit, the cop said. I never looked at my hometown the same again.

My mom prefers it here though. She says the cold keeps out the riffraff. We don't have any homeless, because if you are, you die. I told her it doesn't keep out all the riffraff 'cause Antony's up here. She laughed, which is rare 'cause she's one of those moms who have mastered the crabby face—baggy eyed, beady eyed, black eyed, like decades of anxiety gone straight to the eye sockets. Antony's my bud. We're cousins. My mom hates him 'cause he says the f-word in front of her. A lot. I use other words in front of her, but not that one. Once it slipped out and her eyes glared up like *Clash of the Titans'* Medusa, like she was going to strangle me with the spaghetti. Makes no sense, I said 'cock' in front of her before and she never even flinched. She even sort of smiled. Maybe it's an inside joke. God, I don't even want to think about it.

Antony's short but stocky. He's one of those ripped up cut Pygmy shrimps. He'd look impressive if he wasn't such a midget. But don't call him that 'cause he'll flip! And I mean, flip. Like a lunatic twig, Antony snaps. This sixth grader with one slaughter of a name—James Upton Eaton—called Antony a "cock-schmock" in fifth grade, so Antony held him down on the cement hopscotch recess area and punched until Upton "I-want-to-be-a-politician-when-I-grow-up" Eaton needed corrective dental surgery. Antony was like, "It's no big deal, his dad's an orthodontist." Antony got suspended four weeks and got taken to court. He kept bragging, "Man, I'm getting sued. How cool is that?" The suspension was a vacation. "It's like being in jail and stabbing someone and the warden goes, 'For this infraction, we're letting you out of prison for the next four weeks.'" America's biggest problem is it doesn't know how to punish people. Upton's family realized this 'cause they moved back to England; those lopsided tooth Brit bastards won't know what to do with an orthodontist. To this day, we call Antony "Cockschmock." No one knows what that shit means, but Antony says it means, "Will you please give me a thorough beating?"

Antony's the perfect high school jock type pack-a-week smoker you'd think would have all the girls, but his attitude is so crappy they stay away, wisely. It's like he could screw them, but when they want to put out, they do their little girl oh-don't-move-so-fast horseshit and Antony says stuff like, "You whore-ass bitch, get your trout-cunt outta my face." And they do. It completely destroys the mood.

When he's bored, he shaves his head. Even in winter. Which is stupid. Body hair and fat keep you warm. That's why so many Yoopers are ugly. It's the smart thing to be, fat and hairy. Bigfoots and lumberjacks never get cold. Beards are so prevalent in Palmer it looks like a North Pole ZZ Top convention.

Antony shaves his head 'cause of premature male pattern baldness. As a teenager, that's gotta suck, to look like Gandhi's evil twin. Antony does it solo, his head. A pair of scissors, a razor, and 'H_2O.' That's the way math teachers say 'water.' Playing Atari today, Antony said he had to take a dump. Twenty minutes passed and I was so sick of Kaboom! by the time that cockhole came back out—and there he is, top of his head bleeding and watery red droplets dripping down his cheeks like blood tears—and not a hair in sight, including eyebrows. And he did it all one handed. He hates hair. But I suppose if anybody should hate hair, a kid going bald is the perfect person for the job. If anyone needs to get laid, it's Antony.

Antony was going to this record shop in the Marquette Mall with covers from rap albums, saying, "I want my hair like that" and it'd be something like dreadlocks, which he doesn't realize is impossible for white people to get, especially bald white people. Jesus X. Christ, if he had a brain on his shoulder he'd get a wig of one of those Bon Jovi perms that chicks spread their legs for like scissors.

I used to think opera was the biggest horseshit music ever invented until rap came around and stole the crown. Antony's one of those types that takes rap way too serious, like he forgets it's just music, and shit music at that. So he acts black, when truth of the matter is he's white as the pissed-on snow. I'm darker than he is 'cause I'm twenty-five percent Greek. And seventy-five percent Finn, which means I'll drink the country of Ireland under the table and use their flag as a beer coaster. And since I was born in Germany, I'm basically German.

Antony's Italian or Polish or some crap like that. Which means he wishes he was me. But who doesn't?

Antony really does though 'cause he's a lowly IGA bottle boy. Sucks to be him.

He's been employed there longer than is legal in this country. Antony's dad knows the owner, so he got him the job when Antony was like, I forget, twelve, thirteen. Bottles rattle down on a fossil conveyer belt with metal parts like a thousand tambourines to make the day as loud as possible, and you sort them. Or he does. Pepsi goes in the Pepsi pile. Coke in the Coke pile. Diet Pepsi in the Pepsi pile. Mountain Dew in the Coke pile. A&W has its own pile. Antony said it makes no sense and he's right. He used to think it was by company, but it's not. Mountain Dew goes in the Coke pile and that's that. He sorts from eight to close Tuesday and Thursday and if bottles are stacked to the ceiling, he comes in Sundays. But he only works once a month despite anything he says. I helped a few times. For free. Actually four times and I'm like, "Man, you owe me." He goes, "Yeah, yeah."

Last night, after they closed the place, we hid in the basement 'cause Antony said if they weren't giving him the day off when he was in the hospital earlier that week, then they could at least make a donation to our stomachs. Antony brought a jacket 'cause U.P. nights are iceboxes. I sat there shaking a good hour, tucking my hands in my groin for warmth like coach taught. I didn't care about the crazy cobwebs, the dark peering corners, the collected rubbish in the one-foot gap under the stairs where snakes, rats, bugs lurk. I wanted warmth. After we were ninety-nine point nine eight percent sure no one was there, no footsteps, no creaks, we looted the place. Antony knows there are no security cameras. It was ghost-dark in there with the occasional headlight coming from US-41 causing us to duck like paranoia-heads. We grabbed Copenhagen and jerky and pop and anything we could put in those cheap thick paper grocery bags, which I swear they make cheap so you can't steal large amounts. But we still hit that place like *Price is Right*. Antony said to not take too much, just a bit of everything. I stuffed Twinkies in my pocket, and we nose-held passed the shack size garbage bins, up the dirt bike hill, and crept the back streets to his house carrying Ragu and Bubblicious and Cookies & Cream and the shit was heavy and dripping. Going through Antony's backdoor, we put the stuff to be kept cold in this second freezer Antony's dad keeps for venison. Antony's job's cool, but I always thanked the high god above that Antony was the only one working 'cause nothing good comes from having a job. That blessing worked for quite the while.

Until now. Lemmy explain.

I was antsy and bored, hating the summer, which was thankfully ending, when my dad did something cruel and unusual he thought was nice, but wasn't. He got me a job.

I work at Ishpeming Cemetery. This would have been my dream job if I had convicted a felony 'cause I would be doing the only job I can stand: landscraping. That's what the convicts from Marquette Branch State Prison do—landscrape. I've seen them.

Instead he got me a "respectable" job. I sell burial plots. The cemetery hires locals to go door to door frauding people into buying property. Good-looking kids that seem trustworthy cash in on old Yoopers. The owner tells me that!

Ishpeming Cemetery used to be first in the region. Now we're last. He needs attractive guys and girls to sell plots. That's me, the Corey Hart of tomb selling. I know I'm a stud 'cause I lift like a son of a gun and have enough hate in my gut to feed Ethiopia. My motto: 'It's not the weight, it's the hate.'

After the job news, I lifted. CC in me. Fifty CCs of DeVille. At Harley's Gym on Main Street, I had a satanic power surge. The biggest logger in the U.P., Michael Salonen, is in his forties and benches 550. I go up and say, "Spot me."

No one asks him for a spot 'cause he's focusing on a screaming 125 lb. dumbbell bench. But I didn't ask, did I? He's like, "Look at this punk." I put on 400. A 400-pound bench. And I never max. Maxing's for fags with tight shorts to their ass. I breathe heavy. Mike says, "Let's go, Cräig." He knows my name. Hulking, breath to kill a rhino, old Sal. Slayer's in my head. Slay-hair, the opening, the scream, "Force is like avenue rocks frozen minds for your life work human minds for angel a death four hundred billion wanna diiiie!" The lyrics aren't printed. I hate that. I hate when they aren't printed. Pisses me off. Banging my back on the bench, I grind my palms on the bar like a motorcycle, winding, then touch my nose to the bar. Mike drips sweat. It falls in my hair. He steps back, "Get it, get-it getit." I bar-bang my forehead, think of fire, of the throned goat on the *Reign in Blood* album cover, commanding. If Picasso could draw and had talent, he'd have done the Reign cover. Red goat speaks and I listen, "Cräig, if you don't get this, your soul is mine." I lift, Uh! The world falls, flames fly flickering like sex tongues. The gym radio plays Journey which I won't have in my hell this inferno of orange yellow red larvae lava veins 400 lbs I control easy 'til a sticking point curve my back eyes slam shut heave last lyric line of "Necrophobic" and the word 'control' is locked in my mind. I slam-drop the weight, open eyes to see Mike's wrinkled nodding flab-head. I ask if he helped. "No." "You didn't touch it?" "No." He guided it. He leans, counts, too fast to be correct, says, "390." A little off. "Put that on the board," he says. I go, "Yeah, that goes on the board." Yeah. 400. Not 390. 400. On the board. 400. On the board that lists maxes. When Sal hit 550, they made a board just for him, SAL'S BOARD. Now my name's up there. Now I can die. Now I can do anything.

For one thing, I can sell burial plots along with a bunch of NMU Greek letter Wildcat sales gigolos he hired, but you never see 'em 'cause the boss either gives them motivational one-on-one conferences in his secluded rattrap office or he's got us out giving presentations to dying fools, hitting up every crusty aging family member we know, calling up aunts in Dollar Bay we never met or even knew existed until mom says the words "just got a goiter" and we ask, "What? Who?" Or dad tips us off that some cousin to Uncle Leo's brother lost all his hair, and no tip's greater than mass hair loss 'cause that always spells gold, chemo gold. Unless you shaved that shit off to be a USMC jarhead or you're Antony, your ass is about to croak. Somewhere a busty blond saleschick is driving lake shore late night to Au Train to stumble through her reading of, "Whether or not cremation or traditional disposition is chosen, a memorial service is one of the very most important aspects of the coping process for the friends and family left behind." I asked the prick boss what 'disposition' means and he said, "It's okay if you don't know, you'll relate to the public more, similar lack of education."

He's one of those types that tells you about your faults so he doesn't have to deal with his own.

"We're also going to do trade shows, seminars, and malls," the boss 'tard says, "Selling crypts at the Marquette Mall. But the heart of our sales come from the door to door presentation." This takes fifteen minutes, no more, no less. We give a rehearsed speech we're supposed to memorize, but I write it in ink on my palms, in longhand. Boss makes us recite in his office, eyes piercing into us like Zulu warrior lip spears. How can you concentrate under those conditions? I always forget the part about pet memorials. "Craig, let's take care of this here and now, okay. Repeat the phrase 'our ceramic marble pet urns are truly a work of art.'" I do.

"Our ceramic marble pet urns are truly a work of art."

"And smile, remember, their pet just died. You care."

I do. "Our ceramic marble pet urns are truly a work of art."

"Stand up straight. Think 'presentation.'"

I do. "Our ceramic marble pet urns are truly a work of fart."

I do know how to stand with my arms behind my back with both middle fingers pressed against each other so boss can't see. Christ, it's like I have a brand new dysfunctional father, a worse one, another one ready to explode at the drop of a vase. Except this one's always around. Then after the incorrectly memorized speech with improper posture, we show the client a video of an elderly couple grinning Miss America hideous. I can't stand happy old people 'cause they look crazed. Sure, when they're frown-faced I can handle 'em 'cause that's understandable, they know they're about to die from constant knee pain. But Christ, when they smile, it's like Jesus smiling on the cross; you feel gross. So these happy-go-dumb-ass washed up vaudeville seventy-something actors turned cheap business video whores walk up to the camera hand-in-hand through a graveyard, mind you, if that isn't enough to give you the creeps, and it cuts to an ex-con comb-over round-faced used car salesman type who is too enthusiastic about life. He runs through prices so quick you have to rewind to understand how much money he's talking about. There's a lot of decimals and nines, and worse, the guy says "free" every other sentence. Free this, free that. For a few thousand dollars, you better get a lot of "free" stuff. He explains it may seem expensive, and he hung on the word "seem" for a half-year, stretching the e out like a dollar. He goes into how death is one of the most important parts of life and he uses the words dignity and plan and remembrance and security and simplicity and care and eulogy and pre-payment and loved and thousands and no interest. And if I could sum it up in two words, it'd be "no interest." No interest whatsoever. I avoid eye contact with customers 'cause I'll crack up or tell them, look, this is bullshit, start planning for death and you're heading full tilt for the grave. It's when you look down that you fall off the tightrope. That's how I see it. Then we chat. No choice, have to. This is where boss says to take interest in any nearby photos. Give their kids a good three minutes each, but ten minutes max, the boss says. Ask about: what college their kids go/went to; if they have/want grandkids; if it's a guy, talk about the Lions and how I play for Mr. Puletti; if it's a woman, compliment her house "even if it's a sty." Then go in for the pitch. Start with a joke. "Say we have 'lots of lots,'" the boss says, "Folks like simple humor, nothing complicated. No swearing." Stress how important it is to buy now. Prices only go up. They're low but won't stay that way. If sales are upcoming, never tell them. And last, the best answer if I don't know something: "Here's our card. My boss, Richard, can answer that more specifically." Always end sentences with a word at least three syllables long; 'specifically' has four so it's perfect. Above all, stress that "prices go up annually." We have a chart. Show the chart. Its edges are bent to hell from hauling it all over Marquette County. But sure enough, the chart shows that the prices do go up annually. Just like every price on the goddamn globe. Christ, on my allowance I can't afford Butterfingers anymore. Tell the customer that if they unwisely wait until they die, the price could double or triple, maybe quadruple. If the wife is in the room, ask the husband, "Do you love your wife?" and lead in to how if they want to get spots close to each other, they need to act now. Love is expensive. We sell affordable cremation services and nameplates, top quality gravestones, plastic and real flowers, more than fifty types of flags and vases, "majestic" statues, even mausoleums. Boss says, "You'd be surprised how many people don't want to be buried in the ground anymore." I have to memorize the headstone types. Flat Marble. Upright granite. We have this one cheap—well, cheap for a couple hundred—headstone where they take a nail and scratch the person's name in tinfoil. I saw the boss do it and I'm like, "What's that?" He's like, "It's our new Cursive Model." One hundred fourteen types of engraving. Full packages include everything from the lot and tombstone to the Guaranteed Family Placement Program including choice of casket, "not coffin, never coffin, it's always casket." Even thin expensive lace books with blank pages to put "important thoughts to be remembered, recollected, cherished, fostered, and shared for generations to come," including "MY FAVORITE PLACE," "I WISH I WOULD HAVE HAD MORE TIME TO," and "MY FAVORITE PLANT IS." Who has a favorite plant? How about "MY FAVORITE METAL TUNE" or "THE HOTTEST CHICK IN THE WORLD THE YEAR I CROAKED WAS." I get six percent on crypts, nine percent on niche, and thirteen percent on full packages. And zero percent on "at needs." At Needs are people with no money who want whatever the city can give them, the absolutely cheapest thing available. "Burying At Needs is like burying garbage," boss says. When At Needs leave his office, I hear the boss call them 'cunts' above his breath.

So far I haven't sold a thing, except one At Need. I'm rich. Yeah, right.

The only bonus I get is a family discount. If anyone dies in my family, I get fifteen percent off anything listed in the catalogue. I wonder if the boss realizes he's encouraging me to go on a killing spree.

I remember when dad came in my room and asked, didn't I want a job at the cemetery? I did. I wanted to be a gravedigger, my calling. Last year I went to the public offices by the library and cop station and climbed the steps to talk with some mustache of a guy who "works" for the city on the third floor behind a wooden desk chopped down from a gigantic Redwood and I said I wanted to dig graves. He joked I'd have to commit a felony first 'cause that job's for prisoners on work release. I asked if there was a felony he recommended. I went home and cranked "Mandatory Suicide" off *South of Heaven* 'cause what else was there to do?

Dad says he knew a guy who knew a guy who knew a creep who works at the graveyard. My mom told dad I wanted to work there and things are shattering to pieces quicker than my mom can open up her pie-hole. Dad drives me to Ish. Cemetery. Conveniently, the bowling alley is across the street so dad can kill time by renting clown shoes to underhand balls into the gutter that is his life. We walk into a shack. Dad smiles and I smile and the boss guy with his shiny gold tooth smiles and my dad says he's gonna look at grandmom's tombstone while I talk with my new boss and new boss smiles and I smile and dad smiles and dad closes the door and I look at the boss and he's not smiling. "Take a seat." I do, but he motions that it's not the right one. I move to one closer to his desk and he lets loose. I have to work hard, get out there, I look like a hard worker, but I gotta get out there. He knows about my "past police incident," a vandalism joke from a year ago that got blown way outta proportion. He says he doesn't mind, he likes kids with energy, kids with get up and go. All I hear is he likes kids. And I sure the hell wanna get up and go. "What does this say?" he asks, points to his WE SELL nametag. "Weasel," I say. "We sell," he says, "This is the selling business. Our dream is to sell." His weasel head yammers away. I daydream about digging ditches, if I can work my way down to it. He keeps on the sales, how he was made for sales, how I look made for sales, and I wish a gale force wind would come through and blow me the hell out this hate shack, twirl me outta there like Dorothy and Tonto, up up and a-goddamn-way, but the U.P. has never had a tornado and never will have the luck to get one vicious enough to destroy this death shack. A diploma is misplaced on the wall 'cause it can't be his. Gogebic Community College. Sales. I'm thinking, "Sales? This is a cemetery. Isn't rotting free?" It's sure the hell not. America's got a price for everything. I try to make out the certificate, careful not to let him catch me. Hotel Management. All work and no play makes this guy a nutcase. He says I start right away, and the most important thing is this . . . He doesn't say anything, so I look at him. The gold tooth flashes. "This. This is the most important thing"—he points to his smile, his constipation face.

I have to smile. On command, I can't. Every family photo has me with my eyes closed, wincing. I hate to be told what to do. Even if it is just to say "cheese." Especially to say cheese. If a K-mart cameraman said, "Say 'pussy'," I'd have a grin the size of a fist on my face, but instead boss goes, "Come on, if you can't smile, you can't work." Promise? Dad opens the door—the alley's closed—and as he does a burst of my prayed-for wind kicks in ten minutes too late and

31

papers go up in the air like young employees wanting to escape. Boss slams his forearm on the table, the most work he's done all day, protecting his piles of shit and this makes me smile, seeing old gold tooth's work disorganize, this makes me smile big. Boss looks up, sees me, and says, "Better!"

Christ.

I wish I had the jobs ugly people get. Ugly people never have to smile. What would be the point? Ugly people get to work in great scummy bars and have the freedom to dig graves. That's what I want. Graves. Dig graves. With my walkman on. Listening to Slayer. In heaven.

Ugliness. Disfigurement. I should look into that.

5: Hollow

At the haggard basketball courts at Jackson Grove, two-handed, Craig chokes
Jeffry Thompson, doing his best to look like he is giving him whiplash.

"Quit laughing, Vagina Breath" Craig says, "Make it look real, dumb-ass."

A blue car with a ski rack passes. Jeff flips it off as Craig keeps choking him.
The car disappears over a hill.

"Where are the cops when you need them?" Craig says.

This is our cure for boredom. Usually it is Craig and Antony, but Antony
is laid up at home. So instead Craig and Jeffry stand by a roadside pretending
to fight. When a squad car pulls up, they run. We never get caught, because a
huge picker bush attacks your pants the second you get in the woods and the
police always stop short. Of course every time we do it, our feet hurt. Getting
home, we put our shoes in Craig's laundry, but the pickers never come out, so
my feet always itch.

Police rarely come, so most of the time we point at any passing car and run,
to see if they will at least stop and chase us. The good part is if you get caught,
you were not doing anything wrong in the first place. But usually no one both-
ers, so all we do is stand around talking and choking.

"College looks like it might be out the window," I say.

To get out of Craig's chokehold, Jeffry grabs one of Craig's fingers, bending
it back. Craig slaps Jeffry in the face. They get in a staring match.

"I said college might be out the window."

They keep staring.

"College. Hello. Craig?"

Craig's face slowly transforms into an insane alien. Jeffry does not laugh; instead he punches Craig in the chest, then Craig chases Jeffry around the court. A fence is nearby and they both hurdle it. The fence is half built, ends suddenly, there being no reason for its placement in the first place, extra fence just thrown here, left. Ishpeming has a lot of these fences, started, incomplete, tucked back in the woods or at the side of roads.

Craig is supposed to be at work, but he called in saying he had pink eye, which for some reason he finds to be the funniest lie he has ever told. For all the complaining Craig does about work, he never seems to do any.

My grades are my job. As long as I have a "B" average, I stay free of French-frying at Beef-A-Roo. I had the easy life, until today. My mother hinted at college and I said I had intentions of going, until she asked how. I said I thought they would help pay, but she sat down and gave me a Beef-A-Roo pep talk. I would rather die than go to Northern Michigan during the day and work at Beef-A-Roo at night.

Needing to talk, I wait while Craig kicks out Jeffry's feet in the middle of running. Jeffry falls to the rocky basketball court gravel and the knee of his pants rips open. Adjusting the hole, he tries to see if he is bleeding when Officer Stegnowitz sneaks up in his squad car and suddenly the three of us burst into dead-on sprinting straight for the briar patch. I, of course, wear shorts.

Running behind the hooting and hollering duo, I feel the prick of dozens of thorns burying in my skin.

6: antony

i hate matt cort more than i hate life itself

doc fit a figure 8 brace round my shoulders. bulky bindin reminder, pins my shoulders back. painful hug. like Christ on the cross. cant sleep. i cant sleep on my side. cant sleep on my stomach. so i cant sleep. gave me aspirin. i complained so they upped it to tylenol codeine. all cuz of cortfuck

sweat soaks in the brace so it stinks. so i stink. which means comments from craig. all cuz of cortfuck

i stay in. go nowhere, do nothin. craig calls but i tell ma to say im not in. hollow comes over, watches bosom buddies, mash, win lose or draw wit me. some smirkin old guy from the carol burnett show tries to draw "hope," but time runs out

me & hollow dont say 10 words the whole time hes here

after he leaves i struggle one handed makin a chocolate sauce banana split wit nestles quik. then go to the couch to put my feet up on 8-ball, our dumb poodle whos real names tiffy, but i aint callin no dog tiffy. 8-ball gets up & leaves

i couldnt stand my collected sweat smell so i took my first shower in 2 weeks. ma partially helped take the figure 8 off & i headed in the bathroom, wit the furry kleenex box watchin me groan doin the rest myself. felt weak, brittle. washin off one armed i felt like the bone was re-breakin. i was whimperin like a bitch. poundin the door, ma askin "you all right in there?" yeah, yeah yeah yeah-yeah i dropped the ivory soap & didnt bother searchin for it. showers over.

i looked in the mirror when i got out. body dont look the same. my legs, chest, everythin looks wilted, broke. my shoulder, the skin, its swollen black, blue, brown—a fuckin rainbow of pain. all cuz of cortfuck

"you able to move your arm some?" the doc says when we get to the hospital. "hows that brace?" the doc says. "hows the pain?" doc says

in front of the doc, im a mute. id shrug but i cant do that so i dont say shit. ma comes in so shes the answer man, shootin me dirty looks, not understandin why i wont speak. it aint my fuckin fault im like this. i told you a trillion times, its cuz of cortfuckinfuck

after proddin and pokin and pain, docs final verdict comes. "its not bad news but its not good news," doc says. i wanna know when the brace comes off, i want it to be soon. doc says, "normally itd take 9 weeks or so"

normally. but i have a "displaced clavicle fracture." my bone splintered like a twig. chards stickin down toward my lungs. lungs are right under the collarbone. a little harder & a lung coulda been punctured. attempted murder, if you ask me. cortfuck

get home and all dad says is, "lucky he didnt hit you in the head"

no wonder no one hangs out wit pops. no wonder hes solo in the basement cleanin closets wit old style in hand listenin to ernie harwell tiger radio games cursin to himself & hummin "thats amore." the only thin close enough to actual people that can stand him are coats on hangars

every time he comes round, i got nothin to say. nothin

nothing but lifes a bitch. period

a bitch on her period

you wanna learn bout my moerfuckin life, listen to Ice Cube's ameriKK-Ka's Most Wanted. thats my life, motherfuckwhore. cept set that moerfuck in the u.p.

yeah bite the dick you ho-ass bitch-ass ho-bitch

im the white boy you love to hate

& i dont need to tell you shit bout my life

fuck you prick

7: Cräig

My favorite thing about people is when you get to have sex with them. That rules, especially if they don't have AIDS. That makes it even more special, and romantic.

I love girls. I really, really love girls. Really. It's all I dream of. Happy dreams of females in fields with poppy seeds floating down from seaweed green skies landing on rounded mounded buttocks, and girls in frocks on beaches with waves of milk and sand gently massaging their gentle dripping nipples like grand hands. Swimming in women.

Females are like coke, like Coke, like cocaine, like I want to shove them in my veins, drink them, eat them, like eggs, like fish, like KFC chicken breasts, like Hostess Hohos—three oval meals a day, shoving my face. In. My last girlfriend, I used to tell her that. I want to cook you, chomp on your arm, swallow your fricking flesh like a horny cannibal. I can't get far enough inside them. If I could crawl in, I would. Tent out. Live. Cave. What's it called when you go in and out of caves? Spunking?

They calm me. Chicks do. In the hallways, between wood shop and study hall, there are these moments, after I've closed my sock odor locker, and I'm walking down the hall, where one of these sixteen year old goddess's asses walk by and I'm left in the smell of them, this sweetness, basking, the best drug in the world—perfume— and I inhale, hold it in like a pot toke, their bodies entering my lungs. Women!

In class, if one goes to the sharpener, I ass-stare, memorize, photographic, especially when they're going off on that pencil, churning, hips swaying, grinding that lead. Walking down the hall on the way to the bus, I'm weaving in and out in and out so I can keep an eye fixed on Sandra Wrezsinaski's ass. I love Polish ass. I love the way Polish asses make elegant hearts and lovely Ws, and erotic apples and perfect pears, and they swishswishwish. Move. Smooth. Ass. All ass ass ass ass asssss. Lovely, lovely ass. Listen to those s's. That's the sound of asses swishing.

August 14th is my birth date. A nothing day. Empty fall. Today. Classes started, so I was nauseous. I vomited on the boys' room mirror, left it as a memento, and got a tardy slip 'cause I refused to tell Mr. Sanderson where I was. Then I went home and had my birthday. No one was invited 'cause I don't like people. I asked my parents to change my birthday to June 30, but they ignored me as usual. Dad bought a cake at IGA and a generic card with homo calligraphy that read, "Happy birthday wishes," which is probably the most meaningless sentence in the history of existence, especially considering he didn't even take the five seconds to sign it. My mom tried to hug me but I escaped by stubbing my toe on the end table. It was worth it too 'cause birthday hugs are suffocating. Ma needs to realize the umbilical was knifed years ago. I went to my bedroom with ice for my toe and tried to sleep with the light off, shades drawn, pillow over my head. Ma came in and asked what was wrong, but I kept perfectly still like a behaving cadaver and concentrated on how dark the world really is, a sky-black that's this gaping hole that continues in my head and goes all the way out to the end of the universe like a constant death. If you don't believe me, just close your eyes right now and you'll see it. And the numb cold icepack feels what darkness looks like. You know, something is wrong with my guts, like I swallowed a razorblade and it's slowly hollowing me out, working its way to my brain. Later that night I dry heaved into a bucket mom placed by my bed and before I turned out the light, I noticed that mom had put a birthday candle she'd saved by my nightstand. Some vanilla frosting was still on it, so I licked it, then got angry for some reason and I don't know why I do these things, but I ate the candle. Wick and all. That helped me to go to bed, finally. At four in the morning, I woke up with a headache between my eyes. I went to the bathroom, no light, staring at myself, trying to exorcise Bloody Mary, and the pain made me make a serial killer face in the mirror perfecting the look until I had insanity down pat. But the pain leaped up and I had to relax my muscles, so I dry-swallowed a couple Tylenol. I picked up dad's cheap plastic blue Gillette and thought about razoring my arm a good quick relieving slash, but the blade was dull and dirty from daily sawing at his face.

Slash. Live ?!*@ like a suicide. One of these days I'll finally have the guts.

Next day, my parents give me presents. It's not even my birthday anymore and now I get presents. "Are you still sick?" mom asks.

I was never sick.

I'm always sick.

They give me the presents in the morning. Right before school. When life is at its bleakest, its dreariest, that's when they choose to give me presents.

For my birthday, I wanted ass—a fresh tight petit freshman ass. Instead I get shit—school clothes. Notebooks for doodling jagged letter metal band names. Pens for teething. My mom buys me cocksucking Kmart blue-light district fake Reeboks: "You'll need them for school." Yeah, I do, so that automatically disqualifies it as a gift, now doesn't it? I shove the shoes and other cotton fleece turtleneck prissy horseshit back in the box. So I wouldn't explode unnecessarily, it was important I vocalize my concerns: "Ma, I don't want this crap." She got all teary-headed like a goddamn wallaby. I opened the other 'gifts'—tube socks, rubber-banded pencils, a box of erasers. How much can one person erase in a lifetime? I tried to act enthused, but she didn't buy it. She bought me goddamn socks, sure, but not my acting. She gave this wounded glassy-eyed kangaroo look, like she was begging for a good smack, which I have no problem delivering if she doesn't lighten up. It was worth hurting her feelings as long as she stops buying me alligator shirts. Last birthday she got me a RELAX T-shirt. Frankie Goes to Hollywood. Frankie moved from San Francisco. My response: "Ma, you already gave me a name that rhymes with 'fag.' Do you want me to fight every human being in the school?" Actually I didn't say that. Actually I said, "Ma, come on." She said I'm not getting presents next year, I'm too old. Thank goddamn christ. Truth of the matter though is I'll get pencils and socks every August 14th from now 'til I croak.

The only good present I ever got was from Bobbie. Who's Bobbie? Only the most everything girl in the world. I told her not to come over and she goes,

"I'm coming over." I was like, "Do you have a dick in your ear or something?" And she goes, "Okay, it's settled then, I'm coming over." And the bitch hung up. She gets me horny-butterfly-stomach happy-pissed-off in three second flat. And I just met her. Women—conniving little angels. You have to learn to love their head games or else you're just another stupid cock.

Bobbie came through my window, if that isn't the coolest ever, just to give me this calendar that says who was born on what day and I learned all these athletes were born on my birthday. Earl Weaver, Mark Fidrych. Antony will be pissed 'cause I looked up his birthday and he has all these shitty people like the guy who wrote *Wizard of Oz* and some geek whose name was like Wavy Gravey or something. I shit you not. I called Antony on the phone to tell him and he was like, "Cräig, you suck, you get to be born on Magic Johnson's birthday." I told him Bobbie said that however the planets are aligned on your birthday, that's what you'll become in your life, and apparently Antony's going to become a great big zero. Which will be no change from where he is now.

But back to the women. And I emphasize butt. At twelve, I lost my virginity. Twelve and ¾. A barrette-headed sophomore took advantage of me. I was headed for greatness when I closet-fucked a sophomore at twelve. I'll talk about anything, but I won't get into the details of that. Let's just say it was wonderful, wonderful Heaven, all life's meant to be and all that. Enough said. Oh, what the hell, let's talk about it. In drafting class, Belten saw me bang my fist on my desk. My nerves were shot 'cause we were about to take a test and I'm a good solid D+ student. D for dolt. I'm no good at memorizing, except ass shapes, buttocks geometry. And that's what education is, memorizing dates that happened hundreds of years ago in the damn Stoned Ages, and names of kite-flying cocksucks who wear Whigs on their heads, when I can never even remember what day Xmas is. Hell, I'm trying to memorize who I'm scheduled to fistfight after school. Belten says, "Look, Leannes is wackin'." What? I know there's Mr. Miyagi with "wax on, wax off," but what in Helsinki does that have to do with me? Now I was playing a lot of 2600 Atari at this time and the day got done so I walked home and stuck in River Raid and out of nowhere got hard as a Chinese rock 'cause of the way I was holding my joystick. Hard-ons are painful longing struggles for girls, like magnets. Like sperm screaming, "Cräig, listen, we need to see the light of day, let us escape this hellhole scrotum, Cräig, oh

40

pretty please, we'd rather float on a ship of Kleenex in your lovely toilet ocean taking a gentle spermatozoa cruise." Anyway, Lisa Wilson, I have her on my list, is over and she's waiting her turn. I die by running into a half-inch helicopter by a bridge. Lisa wants the stick of joy, but I won't give it to her, so she raises her voice up to soprano level. Meanwhile my mom's in the garden gardening gardenias 'cause she's into tulips and sassafras peas and all that faggoty maggoty crap. I prefer weed to weeds, but my mom has ears like corn so I'm hushing up Lisa with a part of my body that has multiple uses—my knuckles. Gently, of course. I'd hit a freshman, a mailbox, even the principal, but never a girl, especially if she was hot. Or requested it, in bed. Meanwhile dad's out driving around window yapping with crotchety geezers—and I emphasize the "crotch" in crotchety. One of 'em, Dead Bill Macadaeg, rumor has it his balls hang to the floor and one time he was running naked to answer his door and stepped on 'em, on his balls, so he got sent down to Sconny where the real hospitals are. ("Sconny" is Yooper for Wisconsin.) Dad's off blabbering with Dead Bill Macadaeg about Alan Trammel's .400 batting average and about his boy who eats like a gorilla and my mom's crusty tulips. Lisa grabs the joystick. And this is the great thing, the miraculous miracle of being me. I don't know where I got this gift 'cause Antony and J sure don't have it, but I take her hand and put it on my groin, and it is this brick, you know, a nice hard solid Brick O' Flesh. In her eyes is red pupiled Satan. She knows what's gonna happen more than me. All wordless, she puts her hand down my pants. And it's screaming for Lisa. I'm . My brick's going, "Lisa Lisa!" It's going, "Cult jam!"

My hard-ones throb like Tom Araya's bass lines. I don't like them. I don't like them on the busses and I don't like them in the weight rooms and I don't like them in the Livonia Mall and I don't like them with green eggs and ham. I don't understand them. They're too persistent. Like they have their own brains. Tom's a genius. An evil mad scientist.

I'm getting a little lesson, some understanding on life and what these raging bastards are about. Lisa leads me to the closet, speechless. Among my black hole of T-shirts, I tell her to do this, show her, what I was doing when Belten made fun of me. Do that. I don't know why, just do it. She does. I feel nothing, but it feels good, in an experimental way, in a nothing way. It's hard to explain. Nothing happens. She pumps like a Detroit piston and we stare, at it, concentrating. I feel the heat of her eyes, on my testes tube, like it's from a chem. kit, a beaker of light, a magic wand, something, but then it's nothing. Looking at her, for the first time, I saw it, it, how women change during sex, become something else, mad eyes, bending, breathing, needs; a small fire was in her, revealed. Her shoulder, sun freckled, half-leopard, moving, slightly, determined. We weren't kids, now we're other. It's due to my prick, teenage budding rock hard like hard rock and boring and there I am pulling away, like this was fun, a real treat, but my mom's gotta be done gardenia-ing soon. Lisa holds tight and when someone has a firm grip on you, the best you can do is hope the gripper maintains a friendly state of mind. She goes faster and I wonder what she knows that I don't and then it happens, spurting, white gold, sex's tea. Well, the first thing you know I'm not feeling any different, the same except this white gobbledygook soars up to eye level to ensure we get a good look and we do. I'm more in shock than anything, wondering if I should tourniquet this beast so we don't flood the basement with my, what is this? Cream? Milk? Sugar? I have no orgasm. Lisa looks up. She's a fifteen-year-old and Lucifer and a fifteen-year-old all in one. I can't believe that came out of me. A door slams. I yank my pants and feel the wet press into my underwear. Hopping out the closet, it hits me, finally, this dizziness, a total loss of equilibrium, friction drunk. I could fall over and it's a joy like I could plummet into a land of licorice. Great wooziness of Lisa and earth and life and Willy Wonka.

I just discovered the meaning of wife.

Lisa says she has to go. Oozed, I'm about to tip over, when Lisa says, "Hi, Mrs. Leannes." Lisa's back is to me and she has on Levis. She walks away and my mom wipes her hands on her apron allowing me to give Lisa a good long ogle at her jean ass outline, how the stitching simulates butt crack, a 100% cotton facsimile of buttocks. Thank you thank you Lords of Levi for your century of perfecting the presentation of the ass. Her round cheeks move out the house, the perfect shifting that is women's, girls', females' asses, apples, access, smooth globes sway away like gods' creations. And red hair, her hair red, fiery, long, combed, bouncing bouncing-bouncing. This vision of Lisa is the ideal female. I'll search my mom's Sears Roebuck catalogue piles until I find the treasure of a redhead model in tight-fit blue jeans, looking away from the camera, out at some ocean buoy or at her kids on swings or over a Mackinaw Island bridge railing and I can see this sweet grownup glossy Lisa ass. And if her hair goes to her mid-back, I'll really hand it to myself. From thirteen to sixteen were the crazed years, the addicted years where I couldn't wait for my parents to go gramma's so I could be alone and try for four orgasms in forty minutes. Tom, my carpet-burnt little buddy red, exhausted, me sprawled out on the couch immobile, when I'd hear the garage door, my parents' return, their "Ritalin-tolerant" son finally, thank god, settling down.

Lisa left, moved on, to others. I got quiet, reserved, wondered if people were making fun of my hands. Excessively I used hand lotions. I'd say it was for calluses from lifting. My right hand was softer than my left, tender. My right hand was moisturized, soothed, scented like rose petals. Shaking hands, I felt awkward, like the person could tell my hand was too soft. Watching *Teen Wolf*, I vowed never again. I promised god and Satan, but an hour later I broke the promise so I'm damned for eternity, which sucks. All because of Sandra Wrezsinaski's butt. Satan did a fine job when he made that 'tocks.

8: antony

one thin i cant stand is everymoerfuckinthin

To quote Craig: My favorite thing about pot is when you get to smoke it. My second favorite thing is when you get to smoke it more.

Mom was gone to Madison for allergy testing, so that allowed me to close up all the windows and use our house as a bong. When I smoke, thoughts flow so life makes sense. And I like the way forms move, more 3-D, and.

What was I talking about?

Pot. I wish pot was legalized. Although if it was, it wouldn't change my life any. Pot shouldn't just be legal. It should be encouraged. To mellow out the assholes of the world.

The second week of school, I'm at the top of the stairs on the top floor of dusty Negaunee High. Negaunee sucks because my cousins go to Ishpeming, and I heard Westwood has teachers who care. But Negaunee is more the average, nothing, normal high school. Sitting, I'm swinging my legs when this kid comes down the hall in a wheelchair, pushing along, rolling.

I'm no Jerry Lewis freak. Easter Seals has never done a thing for me. My Dad approached the March of Dimes when I was in fourth grade and they said I didn't fit their profile. So when I see this kid coming down the hall, I actually think, hey, at least he's got a wheelchair, and probably didn't have to pay for it.

But two fuckers—one with a large nose, the other with a caveman forehead—come up behind the kid in the wheelchair. They grab him and push.

The kid looks up, his eyes, just his eyes, you know. And they're pretending with the kid it's a game. They go real fast, in circles, up on the fourth floor, away from the rest of everything in the world, the shit shit world. It's empty up there, just business classes with no real teachers around. The kid says stop, waves, stop. They take the kid and wheel him down the steps, off the steps, letting go, this crashing fall. And he's lying there, and the fuckers look at me and this is what I do. From my boot, I pull a switch, flicking the safety off like I practiced a million times on the bluff overlooking Teal Lake with the lights of the city reflected; from that height the city looks train-set fake. Repetitive relaxing motion of me with my knife whap spring tension giving, revealing eight inches, eight fucking inches, waiting and I'd love to go nuts and disembowel those fuckers. No guts. I would have, honestly, just one step at me, anything, a blink—pfhtt, knife.

They take off, cowards, down the hall, cowards, so I take care of Rich that's a poor kid Richie got primary progressive MS near total paralysis helpless just nice as fuck I pick him up and start bawling heaving me not him he stares up like I'm everything he wishes he could be or something I lose it me fucking baby bawling going sorry sorry sorry about all this sorry ass world he looks up like a statue looking just up and that tear snot comes out my nose when he laughs at me at that he laughs he's laughing fucking laughing at me saying slurred-word: "I'm . . . Okay . . . That's . . . all . . . that . . . matters."

In Principal Saarinen's office, he wants me to describe the "young punks" who did it. Describe them? I say, "They're not punks." He ignores me, insists, "Who are they?" He wants to help, supposedly. But I don't know who they are, what they look like. I mean, how many people are in the school? Six hundred? And I talk to how many people in the school? Six? And how many of them do I like? None.

Saarinen says he understands why this would concern me.

Wouldn't a kid in a wheelchair getting thrown down steps concern everyone?

10: Cräig

My mom's Victoria Secret lotion disappeared 'cause boy, Victoria knows how to produce a wonderful secret. I get a nice glide and it even arouses you when you pour it on. Bored, I'll put on that bayberry stuff or this amazing coconut lotion. Lemmy tell you, that is embarrassing shit when you go to Victoria's Secret in your white and blue football jersey surrounded by pink-purple panties and spectacled Hot for Teacher sales clerks and you buy Coconut Lotion. It's so good, I had to. Five bottles. No use frequenting the place. That'll supply me a half year. Or at least six months. The lady looked like, 'You really need a girlfriend.' Nah, she didn't say that, just gave the look. My bedroom smells like Hawaii. My mom's like, "Cräig, your room's so fresh. Do you use incense?"

But I do other stuff too, not just wack. I hang with Antony and Hollow. It's weird, but all my friends are related to me. In the boondocks, that's what you do. Inbreed. But we didn't do that. There was always a hot Italian chick to save the gene pool, keep it from getting corrupted with three eyed Finlanders. We'd play baseball. Anthony'd bat, Hollow'd pitch, and I'd go out in center and run around like a hyperactive gazelle. When I wasn't doing that or throwing desks out the school's third story window or playing tackle in the snow, well, then I was running the sink in the bathroom, wasn't I? Simple life. I'm easily pleased. At age seventeen, I'd done it probably a thousand times. That's a lot of wasted water. In math class, I tried to figure it out. Mr. Pytonnen was going on and on and on and on and on and on and on about L equaling V times H minus K cubed and I was using my calculator to estimate total number of masturbations.

M = 1,027, approx.

And I only got caught red-handed once.

It's a dangerous thing to masturbate to a Prince video. Sure, Prince may have two women kissing in his video, but right when your dad walks in, that's when the camera switches back to Prince's sedated face. Then you really have some explaining to do.

Eventually, though, things changed. I filled out. Got huge. It was a weird bizarre stunning thing. I got cut. I got the chest going, the bis, tremendous wrists, and the girls started approaching, so I ran with it. Some guys get all the luck and I'm one. At sixteen, I went sex crazy. Crazy sex. I had a drought of three years after Lisa, but then there was Beth. She was wet enough to cure any drought—Tropical Rainstorm Beth.

Oh Beth. Beth, what can I do?

I heard her calling. She was five-nine, chipper, one of those lovely, lonely cheerleaders who always reluctantly cheers, sexy half-ass school spirit, with braces, squirrelly breasts, and knew how to use makeup to hide acne—that's key—and we hung out like we were friends. I made her laugh with my impersonation of Jimmy Carter pounding his brother Billy to a pulp, and she rode me like a fucking bronco in the back of dad's Chevy Beretta. We went to Butler Theater movies: *Beverly Hills Cop*, *Adventures in Babysitting*, *Doctor Detroit*, *Peggy Sue Got Married*, all that shit. We drove into this field by the baseball diamonds, where I thought bong-head buddies might catch us to increase my bragging rights. I didn't have a license, but ma lemmy drive as long as I didn't get arrested, "One ticket and you're done, for good, you hear me?" We kissed and dry humped and dry breast caressed and finally wet humped. Nothing like a good wet hump. Except two wet humps. I said we should go in back so the horny steering wheel wouldn't get any action. It was humid D-town summer. I'd been lifting at Powerhouse Gym International on Middlebilt Road 'cause the high school weight room was weak. I wanted to show her my chest, so I took off my shirt and she liked my chest 'cause she rubbed it saying, "I like your chest," which is a good sign 'cause it's like saying, "You can come on my cleavage." It's the reason I do all the reps, for that privilege. I flexed and she about came when I did this thing where I alternate raising up each individual pec. Arnold does that. Ahnold. Conan. The barbarian. God. She clapped. Then noticed I had a cut—long, fresh, new, un-scabbed. (If I could get a tattoo, it'd be UNSCABBED across my torso, in tribute to Philgod.) Always have an injury on your body, preferably on your face, but chest is acceptable if you go shirt-less. Chicks respect two things—bruises and tattoos. They want men dam-aged. Tattoos are artistic injuries. It shows you enjoy pain, which means you know how to give it, skillfully. She said, "Oh, baby," and the way she said it . . . I'm telling you, guys don't have the power to do what women do. Women do magic. Screw Houdini. Screw Harry Blackstone. Women are the most incred-ible, I don't have the word for it. Goddesses. Especially porn chicks. And their voices. Their voices rule. How high they are. And soft. And the way women put sentences together. The words they pick. She said "baby" so nice, like I was one. Soothing forget-everything voices. So I did. I let the world drip away, like come. Then I did. She gave me head, gave me; it's a gift. She bobbed her head on mine and I looked down in the moonlight and loved that scene. It was like a Mike Angelo painting, her head bobbing up and down like a crank shaft and her not being able to see me, just total concentration, eyes closed, solace, for the both of us. Man, it was an offering from the Lord Heaven. Blonde hair the color of clouds. I put my hand in it and it felt like something they'd spin into gold in those old ass fairy tales. I kept picking up her hair and letting it fall through my fingers. This smacking sound came from her until she paused out of breath like she'd forgot to breathe. She looked up and I gave an approv-ing grin, thumbs up, this smile that said, "This is good." She went back down like a good little girl. It took awhile, but I let out an honest load of schism and she gulped like it was vanilla-chocolate mousse. She opened the door and spit. Good thing too, I'm so potent she could've got pregnant just from swallowing my shit. And you know I'm the type that's gonna give 'em triplets or worse. She kissed me. I didn't care she had the white stuff in her mouth moments before 'cause I was falling. In love. When I Frenched her, her eyes went, "What're you doing?" I must admit though, I was curious what my stuff tastes like so that is my only opportunity to find out. I mean, I try standing on my head right when I'm about to explode when I'm home soloing, but man, it's hard to aim for your face when you're in that position.

Seriously.

If you don't believe me, try.

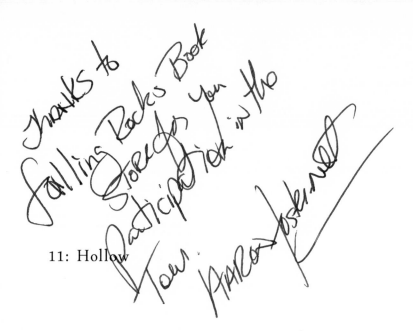

11: Hollow

After visiting the cemetery, we drive the back way from Ishpeming to Negaunee while Bobby McFerrin plays even though no one in the car likes the song. After the song ends, my father clicks off the radio.

Ishpeming is as still and depressed as the facial expression on the town center Old Ish Indian statue, the sluggish dead feel of a reservation. A twenty-year-old bearded kid walks down M-28 with his hands shoved in sweatshirt pockets. The area fashion sense is thrift store homeless.

Out of the gnaw of silence, I say, "At least he is in Heaven."

Mother says, short, clipped, "There is no heaven."

A gust of wind blows so harshly I feel the car jolt, a snap. Clear and fresh in mind I see gravestone—gray, the color of the clouds above, sad. The vision is so strong it feels like it's a reflection in the car window. His stone is next to my grandfather's WWII memorial: DANIEL 1967-1986.

"Then where is he?" I say, "In Hell?"

"There is no Hell," mother replies.

"Then what is there? Dirt?"

My father orders, "Watch the tone."

We pass day-old road-kill, skunk. The town dump is to our left, its weak chain gate locked. "So what are you saying? He is dead and is always just dead?"

"I am not talking about this," mother says, "Not now."

My father turns on the radio, searches until he finds oldies. The song is upbeat, repetitive, counterfeit, a Beach Boys rip-off. Mother turns it down.

A Santa in a sled sits on someone's roof, weather-beaten, no snow in sight for months. Below it, on a porch, a flanneled wrinkle of a man sits with an expression like Jesus Christ just died. Nothing is thicker than a family's anger.

When my grandfather died in Okinawa, my father stopped believing in God. My brother died and I feel like I should start searching.

But I hide it. As soon as we are home, I storm to my bedroom, lock the door, pull out my scrapbook, turn to the fourth photo. My brother Daniel, fourteen, is in his blue-and-red Bad Boy jersey. Isaiah. #11. Towering, high-spirited, on our back porch, having just had a twenty-rebound game against the Gwinn Modeltowners, Daniel is a curly haired Goliath who liked to call me "Dumars." He did so many things well, if I wrote them all down the entire Ishpeming Library would not have room for the books I could write.

Then, he vanished. The only person I ever cared about, disappeared.

Craig is lucky. To not care is a lucky thing.

To not care is a blessing.

To care is like rotting. Looking like an embryo, naked at the bottom of a scorching shower, fist and eyes clenched, I pray.

Then dry off, call Shelley, wearing an old towel.

In a way, I dated her to spite my parents. Some date the town hell raiser. I dated a Christian Scientist.

Lying on my bed, I ask Shelley a question I never ask, how church was, hoping my mother will pick up the phone to call grandma and get an earful of "worthy is the Lamb" or "in the beginning was the Word." While Shelley responds to "What was the sermon about?" I daydream.

Out of J, Antony, Craig, and me, I am the only one who has a steady girlfriend and I think I am the only virgin. I avoid that conversation whenever it comes around, especially with Craig. He has theories on how you go insane if you do not relieve yourself twice a day, like it is some psychological necessity. Craig is messed up, but he is hilarious, so you have to hang around with him.

Craig's girlfriend is Bobbie Ruuvinen, and she has a high-pitched voice like a little girl. She is fifteen, but sounds like she is in third grade. The school is full of Bobbie rumors and Shelley filled me in on a couple brief ones. After Spring

Fling, Bobbie was caught making out with Peggy Thompson in the men's locker room. And, her father is being investigated by the I.R.S., which I have never heard of happening in the U.P. before, because first of all most Yoopers are honest Lutherans and second of all most people up here do not have enough money for the I.R.S. to care what we do. As Antony put it, Craig is "metalhead over heels in love" with her, mostly because with a mother like Craig's, a girl can be a wench and still seem friendly. Bobbie wrote a letter to Craig saying how glad she was he was in her life, really pretty generic love stuff and Craig came over at two in the morning to read it to me with Blatz on his breath.

Shelley is one of those people who answers questions with a simple "yes" or "no," and never elaborates. She would never write a letter, and if she did it would be less than a paragraph long. She is a sophomore, green-brown boring eyes, light brown wavy modest length hair, but she fits into my arms the way South America would snuggle into Africa if you took out the oceans and pushed them together. At parties, I see boyfriends and girlfriends never by each other the whole night, but she is always right there at my side. As my grandpa would say, she is "cute as a snug bug dug in a rug."

Having a girlfriend is weird, because Craig never has had one, never for more than a month, until Bobbie. Craig gets these head cases, but he says they are better in bed. He knows Shelley is religious though, so he never rides me about it. There are certain areas he will not touch, but then you have to be like that with him too. One time I made a comment about his real father and he did not talk to me for two months. And, I did not even say anything bad about him, just merely mentioned his name. Craig left the room and I had to figure out what was wrong. With Craig, you cannot talk about your problems, you have to figure it out on your own and whenever that subject comes up, avoid it; otherwise he is a fuse-lit mailbox pipe bomb. In fact, if he were not my cousin, I would avoid him like Three Mile Island.

Lately, I have missed my brother like you would not believe. I wish I could talk with Craig, but whenever I try he gets quiet and acts guilty or he complains about how stupid his brother was and that makes me feel worse. But still every time I miss Daniel, I bike to Craig's. Craig hugs you by punching you, and I feel like I need a punch. As long as I do not talk about my brother, I can rely on Craig to have me laughing in minutes, either with him or at him.

After Shelley hangs up, I feel listless, unhelped, needing to leave. Getting up, I black out. This happens frequently, although I have no idea why, maybe because of my height. Collapsing, face to the floor, arms corpsed at my side, I breathe in the dirt smell of carpet until the blood gushed back to my head.

Craig was not home, twice. His mother said, "Look, he can call you when he gets in."

So I go to the bluff.

J told me about it. I would invite him, but J prefers to be alone. And, every time Craig goes out there with me he spends his time bending young trees in half so they die. And Antony will only come out if he can drink.

From the bluff, you can see all of Teal Lake. Its shoreline is bordered with leaves of every shade of green—yellow-green, blue-green, deep emerald, aquamarine. The blue and white sky and water make you feel peaceful. In less than a week, this will all slowly change into October's barrenness. Blood reds and dying yellows will begin to rainbow the forest.

I smuggled out a Bible. My grandmother gave me it for Christmas, '86. She had it when she was a teenager. A couple of pages hold crisp fragile leaves tucked inside like they were left from some fifties science project. I avoid those pages, worried that if the leaves fall out, some part of my grandmother will be lost. I hide that Bible under my bed as if it were a girlie magazine, afraid of my mother catching me with something religious, and have to listen to her questions. When my mother was young, the nuns hit her with rulers, so she hates churches now. But I have always loved churches, even though I do not go. I love churches, because I love quiet. I love quiet open spaces.

Out of the woods, two voices explode. Antony arrives with, of all people, U.E. I am surprised to see them together since U.E. is friends with Matt Cort, but either Antony is more forgiving than I take him for or else he is just too drunk to care. Only one can remains. The rest of their six pack is circular empty plastic rings, tossed down towards the water, ready to kill dolphins if Teal Lake had any. Antony offers one, but I hold up my hand. "More for me," Antony winks, downs his beer, nodding to U.E. to drink more of the beer he has in hand. Smaller in stature than Antony, U.E. staggers near the cliff's edge, his head back to guzzle. Antony tells him, "U.E., you know you can fly? You can. Nobody else can. But you can. Trust me."

U.E. steps forward, standing at the brink, looking, wondering if Antony is telling the truth. Maybe he can. The only way to find out is to try.

Antony creeps up behind, his push is slight, gentle, a nudge, an assisting. U.E. loses his balance, falls over the edge, instantly is gone.

chapter 12: antony

u.e. didnt die. he didnt break his shoulder. or ankle. or ribs. he didnt split his head open on rocks below. didnt cliff dive into concrete, onto boulders, into death. my mom didn't get no phone call from cops, parents, lawyers

i dont care what happened to that fuck. if hes dead or bruised or dead. all i know is it feels good

satisfied

revenge is like hot chocolate in winter

i heard paybacks a moerfuckin wigga

but somewhere down in there, in here, in me, i still got somethin to take care of

cort

cort

cort

cort cort cort cort cort cort cort cort cort cort cort cort cort cort

get rid of him

get him on my side, set him up

but every time i see him, at the circular school cafeteria tables, at the gravel b-ball court across from the hospital, in my rapid blurry fuckin dreams, all i wants to slam his face, so hard. so so hard. so so so so so fuckin hard. but i cant. not now. not til im healed. so i have to think. time to think. & thinkings bad.

cuz over time your thoughts get worse. & worse. & worse. til its like you keep seein this person, fuckin rottin

    & once you can see someone dead, i mean see it like in-depth like detailed wit grave mouth & corts crooked teeth & pit-stained shirt & holed sneakers & crazy thinness, corts metal-head hair black & uncombed & unwashed in front of his eyes, all coffined up, decayin. eyes closed, forever, lyin back, relaxin like death lets you. & me there & on my mouth a fuckin deep wide full fat-wallet smile for that bitch

    once you can see it, you aint far from doin it

Chapter 13: J

People are shit. All people. Except Iggy. And Lou. Lou, Iggy, David, Sid . . . and Dad. The rest can go to hell.

An only child, I was born December 31, 1969—the last day of the Sixties. The best days of the United States were over and the world was left with . . . me. When my mom was sixteen years old and seven months pregnant, I came out after only a few hours labor. Ten years too early for her life and two months too early for a pregnancy. I was the size of a fist. A fist. Three pounds, nine ounces. Mom said she could hold me in the palm of her hand. They nicknamed me Keyhole, because they said they could've fit me through a keyhole. They had a premature New Year's celebration in her hospital room, in the snow-reflected daylight of 3:43 p.m. New Year's wasn't the only thing premature.

'Cerebral' comes from cerebellum, the part of the brain controlling movement. And 'palsy' means paralysis, of muscles. My cerebral palsy, thank goodness, is not quadriplegia. I'm diplegic, which means it affects my legs, only.

I stutter, but it has nothing to do with my C.P., but it has a lot to do with why I don't talk much. I'm like my cousin Antony in that way. Except Antony goes on streaks of silence and then suddenly, around friends, he'll blab without shutting up; whereas, I mostly just talk in my head.

I'm ataxic—I have balance problems. I hate scientific jargon B.S., but I had a phase where I thought every term I learned would bring me that much closer to dunking a basketball. I'm six-foot. If I could stand perfectly straight, I'd be six-two. I gave up on dunking, because you reach a point where you become a realist, right around the time gnomes and God cease existing except in books.

Idiot doctors said I'd be in a wheelchair for life. Proved them wrong. Even with eight years of college, doctors are as accurate as weathermen and psychics, meaning fifty-fifty.

The cause was lack of oxygen to my brain when I was in the womb. I have a form of brain damage called hypoxic-ischemic encephalopathy, but that's speculative; doctors contradict each other like bumbling slags. One time when a physical therapist used the term "brain damage," mom grabbed the guy's wrist and said, "You ever use a term like that in front of my son again," and never finished her sentence. And never had to, because she made a call to Bell Memorial and we switched therapists that same day. Mom's a foot shorter than me, so to see her animated and pissed was awkward and awesome all in one.

Like a noose, her umbilical cord wrapped around my neck. My intro to the world. It wasn't mom's fault, and anyway it's not that big a deal. Basically it means I walk a little funny, my knees together and my feet separated apart. So, yeah, walking two miles to the IGA can be difficult. And I can't ride bikes. So what. It's not bad. Except one thing. People. They think it's a big deal. Give the looks. The finger-pointing looks from kids who don't know better and corner-of-the-eye looks from adults who do. But who can blame them? Other than *The Facts of Life*, there's never been a person with cerebral palsy on any TV show I've ever seen. There's never been a person with cerebral palsy in any movie I ever watched. And even if there was one, they'd probably make us look like idiots, court jesters, comic fucking relief, no flesh and blood person. No schoolbook I ever read had a person with cerebral palsy in it. No one with C.P. signed the Declaration of Independence. So who the fuck can blame them? But tell you what, I got so sick of it that I just went with it. I'm a celebrity, right? Famous. A rock star. So I dress in torn punk shirts and camo pants and skull sweatbands and got tattoos at age seventeen. Dad let me. Coolest guy in the world. Lives in Florida. Coral Gables. Goes to a methadone clinic daily. Told me about it. Guess lawyers and doctors go there along with him. They're on the way to the office and nobody knows because they're wise not to tell, get their methadone and go on with their lives. Course, you also get your skid row bums. My Dad's in the middle. Normal guy, biker, just a nice guy. Nice, nice guy. My Dad's tall, lanky, like Jesus, with the same personality too, as Christ—shy and perfect. He has tattoos on his arms, his back, none on his face though. Everywhere else. He got into drugs when he moved to Vallejo. After Daniel died. My Dad was Dan's godfather and it's irrational but he felt responsible. Especially after his sister,

Dan's mom, attempted suicide, sleeping pills and a nap in a full bathtub.

My Dad's like that, cares too much.

When I was eight, I had another series of surgeries—on my hamstrings and Achilles tendons—in October. Mom said, "It doesn't look like you'll get to trick-or-treat, but we'll have your father go out and get candy for you, okay?" My Dad saw my expression and said, "Oh no we don't. I have the perfect costume for Jay." Mom frowned and put her hands on her hips, because my Dad contradicted her and because the surgeries drained our money so we couldn't afford costumes. My Dad jogs into the pantry and comes out with a first aid kit. He pulls out gauze and wraps it around my midsection, arms, and head. All of us couldn't help but laugh and mom put on a forty-five of "Monster Mash" by Bobby 'Boris' Pickett & the Crypt-Kickers' and we sang along. Every time my Dad wrapped the tape around me, it was like a constant hug. My legs were already bandaged, so we didn't have to worry about them. Dad couldn't wheel me up the steps to the porches, but the neighbors were kind enough to come down and put candy in my plastic pumpkin, commenting on my mummy costume. "I'm not a mummy," I said, "I'm a car accident victim." They didn't get I was joking so Dad told me to say I was a mummy. I got so much candy we went home twice to dump my pumpkin on the floor. That was one of the few Halloweens with no snow, no sleet, no rain. In my mind, in my memory, it was sunny that night, even though it was past dusk.

That's what my Dad has always been like, magical. When he's around.

Anyway, we're at my father's friend's house, Bill, and my Dad is up from Florida. He surprised the heck out of me, always does that unannounced and boy was I happy, him showing up with his deep bass laugh, wearing his unwashed "Harley-Davidson Motor Co—1903 to 1978, 75th Anniv" cap over a ponytail. Running in the house, I changed, got out of my tattered Subhumans T-shirt and put on my RIDE FOR LIFE tee with the blazing wolverine eyes and my pair of red 'n' white Air Jordans and then wham he takes me out on his Harley and it's pure raw joy because I get to sit on the back and put my arms around squeezing him the entire ride and this is the only time I get to hug him like that and because, well, I just love to have my father in town with his steady nostalgic scent of smoky clothing and long dark split end hair blowing in my visor. Even though he doesn't, he forces me to wear a helmet. It feels like you're an astronaut. Free and enclosed all in one. Exploring worlds.

We go to Kate's, Katie Aistillinen, this girl who doesn't know I like her and I show her my father and his Harley and she's beamy eyed. She loves Dad, but who doesn't? Then my Dad says, "You can have anything you want, I leave tomorrow, wha' do you want?" He's got this kid soft face underneath the scruff and while I think, he says, "Oh I know what you want. But it'll take four years to get it." He grins proud. Without consulting me, my Dad's been telling neighbors I'm going to be the first Seppukunen to go college. Ignoring his comment, I tell him, "I can have anything, right? You promise, right?" and he says, "Oh no, what is it? Not a hooker." I tell Kate we gotta go but she wants to hear what it is, so I tell him I want a tattoo and he says, "Your mom'll kill me if I let you get a 'too." I say, "You're gonna be in Florida, Dad" and I say 'Dad' in this great tone. My voice cracked when I said it, because of puberty and because I wanted it to and he caves in and maybe he wanted mom to kill him, because he says, "We're going Bill's." He says it definitively, like he's been wanting to do this, and we're back on his bike and Michigan looks untouched and the air is flawless and unpolluted Teal Lake soars by on our right and the endless railroad tracks to the left and then we're in Rock, Michigan before you know it.

We pull up to this cabin off a side lane and it's all woods, which is no surprise, with acres of fenced field, and a stunning sprawling red maple in the center of the lawn. Dad knocks. A bit early for Halloween, the front door has a smiling skeleton hanging on for dear life. The fibula is missing and its edges are so worn you wonder how many Octobers it's lived through. There are no other decorations, as if this one skeleton is festive enough. The wait is long, but a light is on inside, even though it's midday, letting us know somebody's home. Finally, in good spirits, out comes this guy with tattoos on his face, his head, cobwebs around his neck and covering his forehead, and his head's shaved so he can fit more tattoos on his skull—if you could tattoo hair, he would—and his shirt's off as it normally is to show a great beast of a fish pounding its tail in the water on his back and out of the waves come skulls and half-clad mermaids and discolored rainbows flowing over onto his chest and it's too chaotic and psychedelic for me. Bill is a walking, breathing yearlong Halloween decoration. His pants hang low showing white underwear, which isn't so white, and words and half-words, LSD on his arm and SISU on his shoulder and GREAT SEA and JESUS

DIED SO I CAN RIDE on his back and I read him and it's a quick read and I see more skulls and intricate designs going down to his groin area and on his arm is this jarring SARA with a heart that doesn't fit at all with the rest of the . . . can I call it artwork? Hell yes, I can.

Bill's body sags. He shakes hands with my Dad, pats him on the back and in I walk. "You brought J," Bill says and gives a Hell's Angel grin that breaks right through his rough exterior so that you see remnants of dimples underneath his ten o'clock shadow and pale smoker's skin and you can tell it's taking some effort for him to be happy and we're invited in. A deer head hangs over the chimney and it's got this dumb look, like, "Fuck, I'm about to get my ass shot" and the deer head was right. It'd be a nice house if it was cleaned, but motorcycle parts cover the kitchen counter. For Bill dusting means opening the windows in summer, but the house has a flavor and it feels Midwest pleasant, like home, with more knick-knacks than the Marquette Prison Gift Shoppe: amateur oil paintings of rivers and a six-inch jagged chunk of copper from Copper Harbor and miniature woodcarvings of Coast Guard lighthouses and Iroquois canoes and dwarf humans with delicate fishing poles on bridges and it looks like it took a long time to make them, but that's what people do in the UP, kill time and deer.

I collapse on the couch and my Dad says, "My boy's getting his first 'too."

"Well," Bill says, "I'm honored."

Dad's like, "Who else would I come to?" and so he won't have to laugh anymore, Bill asks if we want coffee. Dad does and I don't. I'm nervous. Coffee would make it worse. I look for the needle.

My Dad comes over, sits down with the coffee piping warm and blows on it. After an awkward pause, he says, "So. You ready?"

I barely get out, "Guess so." Now I wish my first tattoo would have been with friends or, better yet, alone. Too bad I didn't know how to give myself one.

I should've went to The Tattoo House down by the Wooden Nickel on Presque Ave in Marquette. This 40-year-old with finely combed cropped graying hair and an adorable missing top front tooth said she would give me one as soon as I had my parents' permission. And here I was with this polite recluse named Bill asking, "So what do you want, son? A skull? Dragon? Your name, a design? What?"

"Do you have a book?"

"A book?"

"At The Tattoo House, they have a book, four books, and you can look at . . ."

"I have some photos of old tattoos I've given. That what you want?"

I nod. My Dad sips coffee while I follow Bill to look at the photos lining his hallway wall, a shrine. I ask if I'm going to be on the wall. He says, "If you want," but he isn't looking at me. He's too casual. If he was more into it, I would've said yes, but instead I keep silent. The photos are mostly guys—sons sporting military barber butchered hair with thin Navy anchors on their triceps, or high school bus drivers with hooded Ghost-of-Christmas-Future Grim Reapers across their back, or beer-gutted weightlifters with Chinese gibberish calligraphy on their chest. A few women are included—Suomi College juniors with tattoos of teeny dolphins on their thighs, or tired Big Boy waitresses with haloed long-necked cats on their calves, or even more tired mothers with silver barbed wire above their breasts. I keep lingering at those pictures. Bill centered the female photos, located them in the most easily accessed areas. Most of their breasts are small, little stocking stuffer breasts, cute, proudly displayed. The bigger ones droop straight for the floor like they're filled with eight-pound weights. It's interesting how the women didn't care. Crooked teeth lit up jack-o-lantern faces.

"Wow," I say. My Dad comes over. "She's beautiful." I motion toward a picture.

"Come on, you're supposed to be finding the 'too you want." My Dad says to Bill, "He's looking at the girls." Bill opens his mouth and moves his head like he's laughing, but no sound comes out. I look at the photos, the girls. Dad does too. "Is this Julie Maki?" my Dad asks Bill. Bill shakes his head yeah. He shook his head weird like his head was real loose, on a broken swivel. My Dad says, "I thought so. How's she?"

"Good. Lives in Thunder Bay."

"Doing what?"

"She got them kids. Bob's kids."

"Bob Maki. That's a name I haven't heard in years. What's he doing?"

"He's in Milwaukee. He was working at the brewery. Last I heard."

"Man, you ever been there?"

"Uh-uh."

"Stinks. Smells like shit."

"Old Milwaukee is shit." They laugh and my Dad has a real loud laugh so it was like the whole house got the joke.

My Dad murmurs, "Can't believe you two never married," and Bill gets real melancholy and it's one of those lessons on how quick conversations can turn if you're not careful. That's the reason I don't talk with people—too dangerous.

I wanted to go back to the photo I'd shown my Dad, but he was in the way. Five girls are in the picture but all eyes are on this one brunette. She is probably, I don't know, 25, but I don't really know, maybe 35, maybe 20. She had one of those hard to read faces, hard to gauge how much sadness it'd felt, engraved on the skin. You can tell age by the visible sorrow, like rings on a tree trunk, and age has nothing to do with it. But she was untainted, with this energy, a sparkle, not in her eyes, but in her body, her heart jumping out of the photograph. She had a tattoo of a rose and the stem was in her cleavage. You could see her breasts clearly and they were perfect, just the size you could cup in both hands, and she had a bright face with exact teeth and straight smile, and she was having so much fun getting this tattoo with her friends blurred out of frame in the background like they probably are in real life compared to her. You had the feeling for her everyday was like this, a nonstop happy event of tattoo parlors and merry-go-rounds and contact buzzes. What I wouldn't give to hold a girl like that one night. Just once.

I force myself to look at the other photos, of obese bouncers and lanky bartenders in black T-shirts reading 'The Horse and the Cow' in Harvey or 'Hickey's' in Ishpeming. I recognize Stevie Laatunen. A kid was picking on me so Stevie picked him up, feet dangling, and said he'd kick the kid's head off if he did it again. My Dad played fastpitch for Tobie's with Stevie. Stevie played first and was good at scooping balls out the dirt. Most people wince or turn their head. Not him. He kept his eyes fixed, daring the ball to bounce at his face. It never did. Just went right in his glove soft and tender, a light thud. Stevie weighs 400. When he'd hit a single, we'd put in a pinch runner. He only hit singles and homers. Panting, he'd sit on the bench and say, "I'm hungry," and everyone in the dugout would crack up. Once I bought a Fudgesicle at the concession stand after he said he was hungry and everyone laughed and he said he wasn't really hungry but still ate the Fudgesicle. They call him "Whale." My Dad told me not to call him that so I never did. Stevie made fat jokes and they were hilarious. I don't know why; he just had this way of saying he wanted to go to a buffet and everyone found it funny as Bill Cosby. I'd stay by him on the bench asking questions like, "Why don't you live in Florida?" "How come you're not married?" "How can I be as good as you?" I admired the way he made being fat funny, so one night I made up a joke and the next game I said to Stevie, "People in shape run marathons. What do people with muscular dystrophy run?" He didn't say, 'What?' like I expected, so I said, "Telethons." Everyone on the bench got nervous and a couple guys got up and left. To be honest my stomach got upset saying it. I guess you can joke about being fat but not about cerebral palsy. I don't know why, but those are the rules. Still I bet Stevie would make C.P. funny if he had it. When the team warmed up before a game, Stevie'd play catch with me until Mr. Alhainen arrived. Anyway, in the photo, he had a light saber tattoo on his arm. Stevie was a *Return of the Jedi* freak. Two months ago, the last day of July, he had a heart attack. Now half of his face doesn't move. He has trouble spelling. He's crabby now, forgets my name. I'm glad I don't see him around, because when I do I get sad and don't talk the rest of the day.

There were other photos.

I kept scanning, scanning. Then saw it—the tattoo, on this guy with a crinkled face like it was beaten with mallets and set on fire. He was in a chair and on his shoulder was a brand spanking new tattoo of a girl burning in hell. A sailor's cap covered her eyes and she looked like she was from a fifties movie but sluttier and she was riding a pitchfork like a broom and flipping her other hand back rodeo-style like it was a total blast in hell and hell was a bunch of blue flames and fang-white stalagmites and two penetrating eyes of Satan hid in the background. I pointed and said, "That's the one I want. But on my arm." My Dad and Bill exchanged looks. The guy in the picture had tears on his face, tattooed on. I remember my Dad saying one time after we ran into a friend of his who had a tear tattoo under one eye that it meant he served five years in prison. I thought it meant he was into theater. Antony said that's bullshit, that a tear means you killed someone. But how would Antony know? By listening to some rap lyric? I'm still not sure what the truth is.

Bill walks over to my Dad and mumbles and my Dad says, "If that's what he wants, that's what he wants." So Bill prepares the equipment. And this triggers something in Bill. He acts all professional and it was meant to calm me down, to let me know I was safe in his hands, but all it does is make me wish he'd stop talking. He tells me he's getting "thee auto-clave ready. That's what surgeons in the medical field use to sterilize." I ask why he doesn't just boil water and this only makes him talk more. He explains the autoclave, how it's a big oven, a glorified pressure cooker. He says he operates his parlor like it's a dental office and says he restores antique cars. The antique car area is over there and this is the tattoo area, he says, and the tattoo area is kept perfectly clean and it's not like the old days where you'd walk in and the parlor would be grimy and he never says the word AIDS but I keep expecting it and he has this whole set of instruments and he's been doing this for twenty-seven years and the main thing of tattooing is seeing the people's photos and he says there are a lot of scams in this business and he says he'd tell me more but he is afraid people would steal his ideas and he says people have photos and the main thing is to make sure it's their work and to make sure they're not showing you photos of someone else's work claiming it as their own and the entire time I do nothing to show I'm interested in hearing about this, but he keeps talking.

I stare at the photo and inside I feel sick, like I'm stepping into a world where the air doesn't have enough oxygen.

My Dad leans over and says, "So you like that one?"

I look at him serious and say, "It's not that I like it. It's that I want it." I say it so serious he backs off, sips his coffee, looks around the apartment, and walks away. I am into the photo now, staring at this man and counting the tears and it's hard to tell because he faces away turning his head backwards to see the camera, but I swear I could count five tears, possibly six, but I'm not sure if that sixth one's a shadow. I lean forward squinting, but can't tell. Five tears would be twenty-five years. Twenty-five years in prison. You could see it in his eyes— like bats'. And in his pale skin—like Bill's. And those tear tattoos guarantee stares. My eyes lock, connect, with this man, this hardened man who's a lengthy world away from the youthful boredom I've lived. Poking from between his legs, captured in the camera, is a detailed, expensive work of art—a cane. I lean further forward examining. Its top is a carved wooden bird's head and all the way down it appears to be intricately lined with tiny chunks of gold that twist around to the bottom. I love canes. And he has the pimp daddy ace of them all. I admire that. He could be beaten, maybe you know, force raped in prison, humiliated, whatever goes on in there, degraded and down and encaged for years, and still he has the class to have this priceless cane.

During this, their old men bodies framed by a doorway, Bill and my Dad reminisce about a fairy tale Rhinelander fast pitch extra inning championship grand slam.

I look down from the picture, at my legs, my knees, how they turn inward. I expose my left shoe's side, the wearing away other people don't have to worry about. I go through a pair of sneakers in two months, a month if really active, which encourages me to sit at home. They don't design sneakers for people with cerebral palsy. The shoe company doesn't think about it, how we, at least I, walk with my feet collapsed in and half the time I walk on the side of my shoe, particularly on my left side, although I shouldn't, but it feels comfortable that way. I rip through shoes like crazy. Mom broke down and bought me the cheapest pairs she could find, seven dollar sneakers from ShopKo, made in China. She stitches padding on the inside to prolong their life. Calluses line both sides of my feet from big toe to ankle. I always wanted Air Jordans and she'd tell me there was no way. I begged, told her I'd only wear them on special occasions; I promised I'd treat them like Sunday clothes. She said I don't go church and don't know nothing about Sunday clothes and I screwed up and told her I'd go to church if she got me a pair, so she bought the damn things. That Sunday we went, and she introduced me to everyone, and I mean everyone. And God knows my mother knows a lot of people. Especially at church. I hate introductions. There's nothing honest about them. Mom even introduced me to her enemies. In this town, everyone has at least one enemy.

My Dad startles me, sneaking up to my side. "You know, when you get a 'too, it's forever," he says nonchalant, "There's some 'toos I wish I never got."

"Like what?" I say.

"Well, like all of them."

"That's not true."

"For example, this one." Dad points to his arm and it's a skull that looks like it's screaming at the top of its lungs, if skulls have lungs. He has several other skulls on his arms, wrapping around, covering his body with death. Most of them he got after the divorce. On my father's back is a full graveyard scenario, several tombstones, spirits rising out of graves, an elaborate horror movie zombie resurrection scene, but for some reason he points to this one skull.

I ask, "What's wrong with it?"

"Guy drew it too fast. He was drunk. I was drunk. Never go to a drunk tattoo artist."

From the other room, Bill pipes in, "Did I hear you say, 'Never go to a drunk tattoo artist'?"

My Dad continues, undisturbed, quieter now, "Don't drink. Worst things of life happen when you drink." He stares as if letting this sink in. I give a soft, disappointed look. He continues, "You see how lopsided it is. It doesn't even look like a skull."

His first tattoo, its ink has faded, blurred, blotched. "It's not that bad," I lie.

"Could be better. Point is I have this on my arm for the rest of my life."

"Get a graft, couldn't you?" He doesn't respond. "Isn't that what it's called?"

"I'm too old. No use now. That's what I'm saying," he says, "Are you sure you want that? I mean, won't your mom say something?"

"Now you're worried what mom'll say?"

"A little bit. Yeah."

"Then I won't get it," I say loud enough for Bill to hear. He looks over.

My Dad says, "Get what you want," and walks away. It's like he's excited I'm getting it but won't tell me.

I hear the needle buzzing and Bill yells, "Ready?"

I walk over and say, "Bill," and it's weird calling a man his age by his first name, "Who is she?" I point to the girl with the rose tattoo.

He says, "Mindy?" I say yeah and he says what about her and I say I want that on my arm, her, on my arm.

I say, "Make the girl look like her and underneath put the word 'Mindy.'" Bill laughs. My Dad doesn't.

My Dad says, "You don't wanna do that." I give this grown-up look and it's a rude look, piercing and now I know I'm getting it. My Dad crosses his arms and Bill looks at him and my Dad says, "Give 'im what he wants," goes to the couch, grabs the remote, and clicks until he's on Upper Michigan Today's interview with Rufus Kempainnen about the Lutheran Church's roots to Finland. My Dad's Finnish, but I wonder if suddenly he's trying to be righteous, wondering about his boy with his girl-in-hell tattoo.

"I'm real gentle," Bill says and he's not. Bill sees it hurts and tells me this is the worst part, the outline, which makes me feel better, but he adds, "You know, the least painful place to get a tattoo is on your arm, on the outside, where you're getting it" and this makes me feel bad again. He drags the needle across my skin and it feels like he's cutting me rather than the puncturing you'd expect. I breathe heavy, exaggerated, so I ask for a break and on the third request Bill rolls his eyes and goes to get a beer. Without asking my Dad, Bill hands me one, says, "Go ahead," so I drink Pabst and don't like it. I'd ask for orange juice but Bill would think I'm a wimp even if I am getting a tattoo. When the cutting, or outline is done, it gets easier, less painful. I felt so much more pain with the leg stretches they force me to do at the clinic. This feels like a hot buzz and I'm not sure if it's from the beer or the needle. When he gets done with the flames, he goes to Mindy's photo and takes it down then tries to make the girl in hell look like her but it's hard he says and I wonder if he actually did the tattoo in the photo. This takes twenty to thirty minutes and Dad says he has to go soon. He flicks to preseason baseball with Harry Carey announcing the Tigers against the Cubs and Bill says, "Hari Kari?" and takes the needle, pretending to impale himself. His attempt to loosen me up makes me more nervous, especially since he pops open another beer. Harry Carey is in the background slurring his words shouting drooling and yukking it up about a second baseman named Ryan. Harry tells an anecdote about a guy nicknamed The Bird and my Dad says, "Hey, this guy's named The Bird. This ballplayer." Bill says, "Who?" But my Dad doesn't answer. Bill mumbles, "I hate baseball," and finishes the flames and, other than the sounds of the game, it's quiet. He finishes the girl, putting devil horns on her head, and I look but it's hard to see my own arm from the angle my head is permanently at. Bill says we're ready to put on the name and my Dad says there's no time, we have to get going. Bill says it won't take long and asks what kind of music I want on, because he wants some "tunage" and I tell him I like Lou Reed, Iggy Pop, Bowie. He asks if I like the Stones and I do, so he puts that on and asks if I heard of some song called "The Cocksucker Blues" and tells me a story about how they wrote the song to piss off their record company then my Dad says it's time to leave and I'll have to get the name put on some other time. My arm throbs. Bill says not to let the sun hit it for a month and says some people say you don't have to wait that long, but he tells me to wait that long and not to sleep on that arm and my Dad pulls me, but not before Bill says, "You know, if you want Mindy's number, I think I could give it to you" and I smile and I'm yanked out the door.

Phillip Stutz
The V.P. Book Tour
2011

chapter 14: antony

the only color in my family is the freckles on my sister tracys face

theres no blacks in the entire damn u.p! not now. but the 90s are comin. in 60 days, 90s is comin. change. i can see a lot changin

aint 1555

its 1989

1989, 4 oh clock in the a.m. hail storm assault batterin my window like moerfuckin mother nature wantin to break outta prison. feels like devils nite. & it is

howd i spend it? asleep. restin my throwin arm, restin my shoulder. not my mind though, not my mind. thinkin, words, revenge, yeah. on cort, this town, the world

been thinkin bout cort like an obsession like love except its hate

cort. punk ass cort

i checked out this jap library book bout revenge, not readin it, but jus that cover, its got this vibe, feel to it, slashin letters like fuckin samurai swords, keeps my mind focused. & combined wit Straight Outta Compton, im set. ghetto mentality. corts gonna be hard to reach so have to keep my ears open, find out if cort did that shit on purpose, if he bragged bout battin my ass, to anyone, & get ready. one at a time. chess. pawns in the fuckin game

devils nite. tonite

been thinkin bout this town

you know i seen a couple blacks in marquette, one in houghton, but i couldnt tell if it was jus a really tan whiteboy & dad kept drivin, but they dont ever come to ishpeming or negaunee or wastewood. they stay the fuck out. cuz niggaz know what time it is. they know some saltine crackerll barrel down the street in his ford four-by-four hillbilly-yellin out the window, "nig-gore your ass izz in the wroooong place"

this towns a great big dry leaf fire hazard waitin to ignite. & im jus the nigga to do it

my hometowns nothin but polocks, italians & finns. & that fuckin sucks for me boy cuz i is aaaaall bout the rap. Ice Cube in the moerfuckin house, boy. "turn off the radio. "what they hittin foe." "the bomb." oh my goodness, man, the bomb! shiiit! don even know what that nigga sayin & still, fuckin skin bumps, jus fuckin mind-boggled, shit bout controllin your mind like hitler, schizo-phrenic shit. ooooooh shit—Cube! that album ends & you be like man wha jus happened? whiteboys talk bout weak shit like "walk this way." nah. was Cube for me. did it. thats when i knew i was gonna be a rapper. i can feel it. in under a year, you watch, watch, ill be signed

but its not only Cube, man, its more. i mean, "On A Mission," "Words Of Wisdom," "The Boomin Moerfuckin System." cuz mutinyonthebountys what im all about. board that shit & turn it on up, bitch

all that shit. i loves that shit. fuck. K-N-O-W-L-E-D-G-E. buckwile moer-fucka. buck-wiile & shit

niggaz comin to this town

can feel it

niggas smell a whitetown all silentnight & they love to come agitate. fuck santa. niggazzs comin loadin up motown mercedes bentz with 5 kids & man we gonna have a good ol time wakin up saltine ass whiteboys. we know when they be sleepin. yeah. we know when theys a wake. ha. gonna be Nigaunee. hard times comin to your town

tonites devils nite

like craig says, in my book every nites devils nite

antony all up in this moerfuck

bitch

you dont know me, you will. check this shit out, you dont know me bitch you willl

unforgettable A

An-Ton-Y

& i got rhymes. madass rhymes: "yo, you know, i dont give a moerfuckin

moerfuck thats the fuckin problem, see a moerfuckin cop i don't even dodge
em"

aw-ite thats eazy e comin but i got my own. cant fade skills, boy, skiyills.
check this shi-ite . . . 'yo im finn but im in this moerfuck.' yeah boy! aint no
moerfuckin polocks get on the m-i-c. even though there a shitload of words
rhyme with "-ski"

like "bob on my knob but first get on one knee"

step the moerfuck back n Gimme dat motherfuckwhore!

been thinkin bout this world

marinate on it you 5-eyed ho-ass biiiiiiiiiiiiitch

Chapter 15: J

In spite of my continuous wearing of long-sleeved shirts, mom found out about the 'too, saw the bandage, and I couldn't lie, so she's dragging me to church. Church is the cure-all for every sin.

When she smelled weed in my room, I had to go church.

When Craig and me stole that yield sign and put it in Jack's living room, I had to go church.

When Antony said the f-word to mom, even though it wasn't me, I had to go church.

As far as I'm concerned, church is one big scam involving a lot of old ladies.

"Gladys, this is my son. You never met him because the boy refuses to step in church, but look what we have here." Gladys shakes my hand, staring at my legs. Mom introduces Winnie Karpinnen who's got a glass eye and I can't even tell if she's looking at me or not. Mom tells Winnie how I never go church, but lookee here the Devil himself has made an appearance. And mom goes to the next person and if she knew how much I hate this, a boiling cauldron of detest, she'd never drag me to this beast of a building. And for someone who never goes church, I sure go to church a lot. The only way I cope is by bonging it up in the bathroom before departing and that requires a risking of it all, everything, the possibility of a series of unending lectures and inevitable substance abuse counseling and the weekly dragging to Immanuel Lutheran that'd have me shower curtain hanging by the third week of this torture. If you ask me, pews are electric chairs.

If there's one thing I've learned, it's "Do pot in the bathroom." It's the only room where you can lock the door and spray the room with air freshener with the windows open, and no one gets suspicious. In fact, the more time you spend in there, the less likely someone will go in after you. It's perfect.

But nothing kills a good buzz like a bad sermon. And today's was exceptionally sobering. By the midpoint, I felt as antsy as a DT sufferer, so the boredom fully kicked in and I was forced to pick up a nearby Bible and skim around the pages hoping a bit of graffiti on a page might at least give me something to read.

The pastor says "Paul" three thousand times and finally lets us escape.

We stand outside and I can't wait for the moment when the church isn't in my sights, so I turn my back to it, which is the least I can do. The ladies talk about where to go for coffee like it's a major life decision. "There's always The Midway." Mom says it's too noisy. "How about Vango's?" Joy says "Elias' sandwiches?" and Gladys says "Joy's vegetarian" and mom says "I didn't know you were a vegetarian" and Gladys says "She was, then she wasn't, and now she is" and boy do they laugh over that, like it was an actual joke or something. Winnie's eye goes back and forth like a tennis match each time one of the ladies speaks. Her glass eye stays in one spot, a marble in her head, for keepsies. I watch her good eye roam then see that glass eye not moving and feel weird like it's this spiritual thing but with a lot more comedy than in the Bible. Winnie sees me looking, so I kick the ground and we finally go with my mom saying to me real loud, "Okay, you can stop kicking the rocks now." Last minute Gladys remembers we're meeting Hollow's mom at Johnnie's, so the convoy snails down County 492 at twenty miles per hour with plans to eventually, I guess, get there. In Catholic school, nuns routinely smacked Hollow's mom so she hates anything having to do with God or measuring. To her, church is the crawling black plague of death. I agree.

They talk about Hollow's mom until she arrives. And for the rest of the next four hours over coffee they keep repeating lines from earlier, "She was, then she wasn't, and now she is. Oh, Caroline, you are a dandy, you are a real jim-dandy." And "Joy Surunnen, you are a character, you are a character" and they say this shit like they really mean it.

Agony.

Then they talk about who died. This conversation lasts five days. Ed Sondhi had a heart attack "while bass fishing for trout" and Bobby Kynnenen didn't know what was wrong with Ed, even though Ed's a prime target for stroke the way he smokes and drinks and eats fish and cusses and he died on the way to the hospital because it took them forever to bring the boat in. Ed brought roses to Pete's funeral and didn't even know Pete. Fifty-seven years young. But a pill-popper. And Aunt Baker died, who is not my aunt, but they call her Aunt. Croaked from skin cancer. They discovered it two weeks ago and said she had five months to live and boy were they wrong because she died Tuesday. Andy Hill passed away during a catnap. Mmhmm. Break-dancer. I interrupt, "Break-dancer?" Mrs. Surunnen mumbles, "No, silly, brain cancer." Mom frowns, but all I can think of is Old Lady Surunnen using "silly" and "cancer" in the same sentence. They go back to acting like I don't exist, because I don't. Joy says, "I heard he choked on his own tongue." Gasps around the table, then more fork-fuls stuffed down their throats. Stuart Juodawlkis died of kleptomania and they couldn't believe it because he was such a nice sweet old man who hauled wood for us in his van and never could sell his homemade varnish at Art on the Rocks. Aino Saatanen died of ecdysone and now that was a man that loved his wife, too bad she didn't love him. Gladys whispers, "She has a gambling problem. She lost five grand at the Kewadin Casino in Christmas." Winnie says "I think it's just evil that those Indians put a casino in a town with 'Christ' in its name" and everyone ignores her and Gladys says that Georgette is leaving Arne and I'm not sure if they're talking about soap operas or real life except that no one is named Arne on television so it must be real life but at the news everyone gasps and sips coffee and orders coffeecake and cheesecake and pumpkin pie and other crap desserts and complains that Aino's wife gives gossiping a bad name and the list of the dead goes on and on—

Paul Maki—drunk driving, no seat belt, if you're going to drink you should at least fasten your seat belt, always was a knucklehead, oh Gladys, I can't believe you used that word, knucklehead, much laughter.

Kay Hill—emphysema, pack-a-month smoker, after hanging on two years, dead at Mather, Josh Makella said her last words were, "Gabe, I don't under-stand." No one knows a Gabe. No one in the U.P. is named Gabe. A real mys-tery. Just like that TV show with what's-his-face, the one eyed man, Columbus. Oh, Gladys, "Columbus," you are a character.

Stu Kuollanen--drowned. You didn't hear? Awful. Canoeing with Harold Maki on Dead River, oh the name of the river alone. The canoe capsized and

Harry wasn't much of a swimmer, I mean he could swim, but he wasn't much of a swimmer, and lo and behold the water was so cold he couldn't make it halfway to shore. I interrupt, "What would be the point of making it halfway to shore?" But I'm a ghost. A ghost of a ghost. Sad sad sad sad—they repeat the word like they're trying to conjure up the emotion, but these are some smiley cake eating Thanksgiving bonneted seniors. "Only thirty-seven. Just turned thirty-seven." Laughter, but very womanly and fake and real at the same time and ends abruptly when more cake arrives. These women eat like they're pregnant, with tapeworms.

Sue Ellen Holmes—oh, this is the saddest one. Pneumonia. At ninety-nine. Almost made it to a hundred. Close, but close only counts in hand grenades and horseshoes. Her daughter Cindy, that's Lu Ellen's mother, you know the sweet girl that does the Girl Scout thing each year, yes, Lu, yes, the cookies, well, she told Cindy that if she made it to a hundred, it'd be the happiest day of her life. She didn't. Sad sad sad. She always brought that banana bread to the VFW. Oh, it was awful. Never had the heart to tell her. She didn't use butter. You have to have butter in banana bread. A third of a cup. We had a raffle to fix our Negaunee chapter roof and Sue Ellen, of course, brings in a plate of her bread. Well, I don't know what happened, if she dropped some dye in by mistake, but it's green. The bread's green. Well, Arne Vittula wins it. That sweet old man pays fifteen dollars for green banana bread and goes outside to throw it in the dumpster. Everyone saw him through the picture window. Even me, and I'm half blind. I always thought he was sweet on Sue Ellen. Of course, he ended up marrying that Tyhmaki girl. Jo Ellen Tyhmaki. She was anorexic in 1983. Or bulimic. Anyway, her face caved in and she started collecting Cabbage Patch Dolls. She owns that craft shop near Koski's Korner. I bought a leprechaun from her. So cute. Flimsy though. In our front yard. His left arm broke. But it's more antique that way.

I pipe in. "Do you guys know Dick Trotsky?" These old ladies look at me concerned through owl eyes, shaded with age. They're waiting for me to speak. I don't, so Winnie says, "I don't believe we do." "He died last week," I say. One of them says, "Dreadful." I keep going and with careful pronunciation say, "He had the clap." And it hurts so bad to keep from laughing, but somehow I do. I'm choking holding it down and one of the ladies says, "Oh" in a playful way and mom says, "This is how Jason likes to tell me he's ready to leave," then she looks at me and says, "We'll go as soon as I finish my coffee, okay?" She pulls fifty cents out of her coin purse and says, "You like video games, don't you?" and looks off to a corner where a beat-up Ms. Pac-man game is stashed. I wander off. I'm still going on the game when she comes up and says, "It's time to go." I say, "I'm not done" and she repeats, "It's time to go."

All of this because mom finds out about my 'too.

I can't even imagine the penance I'm going to have when the bandage finally comes off and she sees the eternal flames of hell for the first time.

Chapter 16: Cräig

I banged so many chicks I had to keep a list. The List.

I have the original, all crinkled with different handwriting where you see me get older as I write. The best name on it's #19, Cory, 'cause I wrote her name right after we did it. My only Jew. Jews are never in the U.P. They're in New York and Egypt, places with colleges and guns. Cory's at Enema U. in Marquette for some foreign exchange college slummer party massacre gifted MENSA mooseshit 'cause Jews have IQs like Albert Eisenstein. She's going to Yale and I'll be lucky if I go to Jail, I said and laughed in her face. I biked there 'cause I was bored out my skull, ten miles with hills and early November's wind biting my face like Jack Frost teeth. I had to get out the house 'cause I fought with ma about porn 'cause it was the topic on Donahue and I screwed her in her dorm, the Jew, not my mom. Sweaty, I was like damn I'm a stud 'cause I am, until some two-fisted bastard knocks on her door. I go to walk out but she tugs me schizo. I was like it's just a participant in your Whatever Program and she said, "Out. Now, but not through the door," and I'm like how and the bitch made me Superman it out the second story like I'm magical or some shit. I'm not. Windows are for desks to be thrown out of, not humans. But I didn't care 'cause I dropped sperm on her bazoombas—that's hospital terminology for jism and tit-tays—and rubbed it all over like Sun Block H and she loved it 'cause women are like that, closet freaks. I knew from gym to bend my legs and roll so the ground wouldn't fly up breaking my knees Mafia style. My hands shook 'cause I was orgasmed out and tired from nearly slaughtering my ankles and luckily I keep The List back-pocketed but I had no pen so I went to the front desk ID checker carcass skull-face reading a book in Vantwerp Hall to study for his Recreation major mid-terms memorizing different canoe paddle shapes and he gave me a Bic on its deathbed. It wouldn't write no matter how hard I jabbed, so he searched around all bothered and pulled out a maize crayon and I was like good enough. So so bad I wanted him to ask what I was writing 'cause I wanted to say, "A chick's name I just banged," but he picked up a copy of Huckleberry Finlander and shoved his head in like "Do Not Disturb!" I biked the miles home and was so hungry I ate an entire pack of candy corn I nabbed from Citgo 'cause no one busts you for shoplifting until you get over the five dollar mark. It's a law. I down the bag—100 candy corns in 2.5 minutes. It's great to look in a mirror with a chapped lip freezing red winter biking face and go, "Blyaah" and see how yellow your tongue is and how insane you look. I can look pretty insane. I keep practicing.

I'm happy I did a Cory 'cause Cory Everson's the hottest chick in the Milky Way. Playboy chicks are fake, like dreams you can't screw. Muscle & Fitness chicks rule, female bodybuilders on squat machines—there's a god and his name's Joe Weider. Cory's only exception is Tawny Kitaen whose performance in the "Is This Love?" video is unequaled in music television history. Except for the Great White/Warrant video chick—Bobbie Brown. And no, not the "My Prerogative" asshole.

Here's The List. If you're on it, you're the few, the proud, the Boned.

1) Lisa – six times.

2) Beth.

3) Marian – just head.

4) Jeannie – can't remember if she was before Marian or not 'cause they were close together, on The List, not in my bed—I wish.

5) Simone – first person anally, very very good, favorite position is doggie-style alternating betwixt the vagina and the 'tocks.

6) Barbara—bitch talked about her grades a lot.

7) Katherine – What a liar. She'd lie to god and he'd believe it. She needs a new face. Plastic surgery's made for her. Last name was like Andryzrski, something ugly and Polish, like her. Perky breasts. My favorite word—perky. If I ever name a daughter, it'll be Perky. If it's a boy, Lucifuge. Tattoo my arm 'I Love Lucifuge.' Girls shouldn't worry about tiny breasts 'cause they're a turn on as long as your face isn't too messed up. Plus big bazoombas can suffocate and kill you to death.

8) ? – forgot her name, screws my List. I'd ask if people know her, but they'd think I like her and I don't. Can't remember what she looks like, but she said I was cute so I did her good 'n' plenty. Me, "cute"? Right. Said I'm the best she ever had and all that crud. Virgins.

9) Mary – we were both waaaaaaaaaaaaaaaaaaaaaaaaaaaaaaaaaaaaaaaaasted.

11) Debbie – had an abortion. She drove to Boulder for it. Why didn't she just go Marquette? She took care of it though and that's what matters. I told her I'm all for women's lib and stuff so it was her problem to deal with.

12) Sigrid – Swedes are great bobjobbers but she grew tired too fast. Stamina's key. She dumped me and wouldn't say why. How'm I supposed to improve myself if I don't know my flaws? She had amazing eyes like this dead cat I saw at the bottom of the bluff. I still see those eyes. The cat's.

13) Barbara – a different Barbara. An uglier Barbara. A fatter Barbara. (Most Barbaras are fat.)

14) Jean – first old chick. Thirty-two. Moaner and a smoker. All sluts smoke. Gotta put shit in their mouth twenty-four hours a week. I did laundry at Hollow's 'cause mom's lazy and his unemployed house-lounging aunt talked me into going in his above pool, pushing against me by the ladder so hormones took over and I was her slave. Pools lubricate. On Hollow's bed, she did me on a pile of pukewarm laundry. His sheets weren't soft that night. Only time with a whip. Overrated. Or not a whip, what's it called? A lasso?

15) Dobbins – chick's name's Dobbins. I think it's her last name. God, I hope so.

16) Joyce – did it 500 times—at the drive-in, in the old man's Ford, behind the bushes screamin' for more more more. Used sperm as a lube to get me going again. Slept like ten babies. Thought we'd wed, but she's a bitch. She'd PMS to be normal. Traced to her dad. He lisped, collected Archie comics, and did 6 years in Marquette Branch for malicious destruction for keying his father's speedboat with a pickaxe. A comic collecting dad would be enough to screw me up for life. Add the rest, you're a certified nutcase. If I was her, I'd be adopted. She had bumper stickers with "I'm a bad thing that happens to good people" on her parents' station wagon and backpack pins with "I bitch therefore I am." Wore braces. Reason

she's bitchy. Headgear feels like your face is being yanked in two. Her mom's cool though. She stunk like mildewed ashtray but she gave me free Blatz so who cares.

17) Christi – jesus would be pissed she has his last name if she wasn't such a goddess in bed. I'd go soft to straight rager in .666 seconds flat. Dropped me high off 'shrooms. Said she "saw our relationship clear," but also said the Grim Reaper was in my closet. How can you understand life if you're hallucinating? She inspired The List 'cause I was so proud I did her 'cause she stripped in Spread Eagle, Sconny. (The only better city is French Lick.) The U.P. has no strip clubs. Negaunee had one but it got banned. And Main Street is bar after bar. Negaunee and Ishpeming have what? Three thousand people each. So how can they keep 13 bars open! Think about that! But put in one strip club and Lutherans sober up and crawl outta their shacks to picket. And Yoopers love to picket. They learned that from working at the mines.

18) Sheila – said she's an ex-junkie. Liar. Alcohol swabs and aluminum foil in the back of your bra drawer mean one thing, bitch. Never shoulda did her. Smelled like Joyce's mom—smoke and moss. Don't get me wrong, I love the smell of trailers, just not hers. Wanted to tie me up. Right. Set yourself up to get pissed on, robbed, killed, raped, rope burnt, and then she'd cook crack on my stomach. Plus the bitch listened to Stryper – if that ain't ho plus mo. If you're gonna be a junkie, at least listen to death metal.

19) Cory – the Jew. Honestly, I don't know what a Jew is, except good in bed.

20) Candy – Bible teacher. Worked to get it outta her. She loves sex like strippers love poles. Nympho. That's what men want, sex addicts. She's a dwarf Olivia Newton John. Never shoulda become a bible teacher. Come on, a Bible teacher named Candy. Porn awaits. But Jesus won't let her. A waste. She don't know shit about the Bible. I'd ask questions and she'd take an hour looking it up so by then I forgot the question. And who cares if it was Simon or Peter who brought the goddamn hay to the manger. If you're gonna be a Christian, memorize the shit.

21) Etta – here's a story. She's pissing like a racehorse 'cause chicks gotta be on empty to screw, while I nose pick furious. The Holy Grail up my left

nostril digging a golden boog and she comes out near catching me. I pretend I'm Hitler saluting and she buys it. She bats her eyes and all that overdone dogshit, grabs me and, yup, licks each finger seductive like five pricks on each hand. Digit-bobbing, an ecstasy waiting for her to gulp my yellowed index and then I burst, laughing. She stopped. I had to tell her that her face was the Mona Lisa and all this bull to get her to still do me. It worked.

22) Jackie – bitch talked about choir a lot. Singing sucks dick. If you ask me, the only real singing is screaming your lungs out.

23) Susyn – pagan, so nutty. She's from Ohio, which explains everything. At night she saw ghosts when she'd take a leak. I told her not to piss. She had a bladder infection and couldn't hold it. I said keep a cup by the bed. Only had sex twice 'cause of that bladder. Woulda kept dating her, but only if she won a game show supply of antibiotics. The ghosts she saw were from LSD, which is why I can count the number of times I've done that drug on two hands. My brain freaks out enough when I watch Freddy Krueger flicks. Christ, if I did as much acid as Susyn, I'd go machete loony.

24) Linzy – my breasts are bigger than hers, but I'm broad-minded. She asked a balillion times if I mind and the answer you needy bitch is no. Women don't know how hot they are. Why do they got such low self-esteems? Jesus Cockchrist, have all of 'em been pounded by their dad since pre-school? Lemmy speak to the females right now. If you have breasts, just got 'em, you're hot. And every male with a working pair wants to pump you and what more could you ask for than that? Linzy's the hottest ass on The List. Angular. Tremendass. Fourmendous. Curvature of the spine. An ass beyond asses. Jutted. That's the word. Her ass jutted. That's good.

25) Martha – Jesus, she died of leukemia a little under a year ago, so I shouldn't really say anything about her, except christ I hope she didn't get it from me.

26) Leslie – our first date was at the circus and boy that was fun he said sarcastically. By the way, no chick's easier than one whose dad recently died.

27) Anne – Her dad's an orthopondist cockhole who makes braces for feet or some shit. God, I hate when families talk to you.

28) Tammy – mother of my baby. She wanted to get married, but she's the reason why the groom is never the best man. She thinks we were married six weeks and how do you argue with idiotic bitches in their fantasy worlds? Nothing more needs to be said about her. Ever.

The following chicks I did in Lauderdale. How many Ishpeming sophomores go Spring Break, real Spring Break, not Milwaukee? I hitched with Hollow's bro before his yearbook photo read "Football 1, 2, 3; Death 4." In Lauderdale every girl is a slut and nothing's better than sluts; hence, therefore, Florida is a glorious Heaven. If I ever die, that last sentence goes on my tombstone. But I'll never die! A friend, Rod, if that isn't the best name, plays flugelhorn or whatever down there in the band Massacred Sacred Red. They're black metal and white rap, "def metal." He threw me spare groupies 'cause even polka bands get chicks, even if they are crusty scags. I groupied the groupies condomless 'cause it was too warm down there for a jacket. Who can afford condoms? And if there's anyone I know who won't get HIV, it's me. My dick's Kryptonite to AIDS.

29) Rosa – at her DJ boyfriend's turntables, she walks up and puts her crotch against my hand so I tickle it stroking her and she introduces me to her boyfriend Romero while I do this. Sa-weeeeet.

30) Tricia – blah blah blah likes cats blah blah.

31) Doris – I didn't know they still name chicks "Doris." I thought that name went out with Herbert Hoover and the cotton gin and Texaco ads.

32) Satish – Nothing on the face of God's bounteous Earth is like the tans Indian chicks have. Bangkok must be packed with tanning booths. And I don't mean tomahawk Indian, not a mascot. I mean Indian chicks from India where they hate McDonald's and God is a Cow with a capital C. In order to screw, we had to light candles. Nothing gayer than that.

33) Rachel or Raquel – Rod's parents' friend's parents have a beach hut where bikinis walk by all day and she stumbled in drunk, saying, "Anyone wanna screw?" We raised hands like students and took turns draping her over a tub. Awesome. A room full of flesh. Women are princesses. Especially girls like that. She's my first chick with a condom. I'm not dumb. She had to have AIDS. If she didn't, she does now.

34) Geneen – know nothing about her other than that's the stupidest name ever. Apparently her dad can't spell. I didn't come in her so don't know

if she belongs on The List. It's not sex unless you come in them without a condom.

35) Katelyn – from Ireland. Last name was O'Connell, but I called her Ho'Connell and she thought it was cute. Chicks are messed in the head.

The List returns to the U.P. over the last school year and summer.

36) Nancy – said she was pregnant, so Antony calls her "Pregnancy." I wanted a test. Pull a dead rabbit out of a hat, something. She's either bluffing or, well, she's bluffing. And chunky. Maybe she's always pregnant. A guidance counselor told me to take responsibility for my actions so I made an oath not to shoplift unless I need it, you know, like a boom box. I dunno, I might be . . . not sterile, but, you know, I don't get chicks pregnant very often, which is good. Sometimes I pull out and put the white stuff on their tatas so that helps. Breasts don't get pregnant.

37) Rebecka – screw her, I did. Her boyfriend's a poet and poetry's for fags.

38) Steph – she's from Kuntucky, now lives on a Gwinn chicken farm, same thing really. She's a redhead so I did her in the sewer. Their hole of a house smells like elephant ass. Walk in to rows of heat lamps lined up for baby chicks. Like that's normal in a hallway. I guarantee Steph-y has body cancer by the time she's a hundred. Humped in my car at four in the morn. Her parents 911ed my ass 'cause I dropped her off at 6 and they were up way before then raping the pigs or whatever farmers do. I thought I was going jail so bad, but she never snitched. She's thirteen. Just turned.

39) 'Poo – bitch farted in my car, so that's her name for the rest of eternity.

40) Sewer – blonde, but not down there. She's 'Poo's youngest sister whose name is actually Sue. I alternate between calling her Sewer and Sooooey.

41) Candice – incredible, grandiferous. Why? Her favorite song is "Madhouse" off Anthrax's *Spreading the Disease*, back before they sold out rapping. She left me for the lead singer of this shit band named Sue Saint Marie who play songs like, "Oh Darling Your Eyes Make My Heart Smile So Wide."

42) Bobbie – amazing. Whore-ific. She screwed my brains out. Girls, if you're listening, hold your boyfriend down and screw his brains out. Nothing's better. God, she screwed my brains out. Good job, Bobbie. Screwed my brains out. Was stupider after I met her 'cause she screwed my brains

out. Girls, this is a plea—tonight hold down your boyfriend and screw his brains out. Please, if there's a Lord in sweet Heaven above, hold your boyfriend down and screw his brains out. Even if he's tired and would rather go bed, just give him this little treat, hold him down and . . . oh, you know the rest.

That's it. My look-who-I-did List. Almost fifty. And lovin' every minute of it. Dar-nar-nar-nar.

Those names represent the best times of my life, moments where the dull existence of sitting on stairs at a party gabbing blah blah about Pantera's new album blah Hollow thinking of joining the Marines blah. And you don't look at the geek you're talking to. You look at this voluptuous heeled tart walk by in skirtless miniskirt. I love skirts. The inventor of skirts should be crowned king. I wonder if his name was Skirt? Jack Skirt. Another passes drink in hand and vein purple lipped smirk and accidentally upside-down crucifix earrings, and one of those glorious women plucks you out of thick air 'cause it's never the male who decides. And you're off to a car or trailer or park and you get to be in them, they invite you inside them!, inside their panties or ass or pussy or life or mouth. Being in them feels like swamp. I love swamp. Lovely lovely eyes, every one. I've never saw a woman who doesn't have gorgeous eyes. Fall in. I remember Sigrid's. Green, reflective, could see yourself inside, see your soul, sometimes even see your penis. She said, "You seem wistful when you look into my eyes." See, only women say lines like that. Guys don't have the language, the allowance to be that poetic, that . . . eloquent. Holy shit, if that isn't a homo word. Eloquent.

And the names women have—Mandy, Jazz, Nancy, Susyn, Debbie . . . Compare those to Craig. Ugly Craig.

Jesuits' Christ, I just saw. #10 is missing off The List! Shit.

You know, a few of these women I loved. Christi, Lisa, Candice.

Bobbie. We pounded cans of Red, White, and Blue so bad I couldn't walk and in the parking lot of that whacked out triangular church across from the Jailhouse Motel I dropped to the ground like a drunk noodle staring at the black ceiling of a sky and KISS T-shirted Bobbie crouched down, kissed my upper lip and said, "You remind me of my father."

Bobbie.

Christ.

You know, when I'm nice, I'm treated like ten acres of Palmer manure fields. But when I'm evil, drunk, then I'm God with a capital G.

Bobbie. #42. On the list, #42. The only one that belongs on it. She is The List.

In the kitchen, I shovel drawers until I come out with a Villa Capri matchbook, and go back to my room. I figure, "If you love her, do it." The list, all these names I'll never remember the order of again. I open the matchbook. No matches. In the kitchen, I see the oven, turn on the heat, stick my head in, reach in and it lights. Instant orange, I put the letter to the flame and it turns black. The flames spread up until they get to my fingers and I don't mind the heat a bit. I let go and the paper drops on fire to the ground, charring tile. Smoke causes cancer but like the rest of America I don't care. I go to the fridge and drink some grape juice spilling down my chin, on my white shirt, thinking about what I just did for Bobbie.

Bobbie.

Like fingernails-on-blackboard, the front screen door slides open and my mom is frowning. She's back from her Pap smear or what the hell ever.

Chapter 17: Hollow

Craig is delusional.

He was born in Germany, sure, because his father was in the Marines, but that does not make you German. He puts an umlaut above his name, because bands do, so when I give him a card, for birthdays or what have you, I include one to keep him satisfied: HAPPY BIRTHDÄY.

Antony has strange rap music quirks, like wanting us to call him MC Antony X. Craig said, "If you want me to call you Antony X, then call me Carlos Satana!" Antony shortened it, so every once in awhile, Antony calls Craig "Satan."

It fits.

Chapter 18: antony

on the phone doc told ma i could take my brace off tomorrow. see how that feels

how it feels is weak. i took my brace off last night anyway. left it off. so its good doc confirmed what i already did. im tender as elvis wit that fucker off. walkin round wit my good hand nearby protectin it. & the skin white as glue. fuckin wrinkled too. like my arm got old

woke this mornin to vacuumin. is ma celebratin somethin?

no

a bitch is comin over

a hag ass cort bitch comin over

ma tells me to put the brace on, back on. the one thin i never want to do again. ma wants me to look injured

why? so we can talk $ wit a bitch. ¢ with a bitch. about a male bitch that took battin practice on my body

& then soon enough punkass cortfuck sits right cross from me in my livin room

in my livin room

the guts, balls, nerve to sit cross from me wit his head headrestin wit his big mouth under his big nose suckin on a big flavorice my motherfuckin mother gave him, his lips turnin more & more purple so he keeps lookin more & more like a corpse

you are 1 cold-hearted lizard of a fuck to want a popsicle in the middle of december

behind him the only light in the house comes from bruised strings of Christmas lights distract turnin green-blue-red-green makin the room as inappropriately festive as you can get & i wish instead i was seein jus blue, steady blue, lights, sirens, cops comin, haulin his ass away, like it should be

next to him, spread out like jabba the slut is his hag ass bitch-ho "mom," mrs. richards-cort. a regular blob wit a cottage cheese neck, shes one of those feminist bitches wit the hyphen. nothin more romantic than a fuckin hyphen. & hocuntfuck says she has a very very good lawyer & ma backs up sayin we can settle outta court if they agree to pay my med bills & matts whoremom scraggly-ass smokers cough fuck voice says she could very well arrange that. matt 'settle outta' corts ho-moms tryin to talk educated when you know this bitch aint done nothin but smoke marlboros & pricks her whole life spreadin her map colored legs for fuckheads like ted cort, matts high high school flunkin garage mechanic punk drunk dad who cant hold down a job or his vomit. fuck her & slap her & call her the skeezer she is. & wheres my motherdickhead pops durin this fiasco of a meetin of the corts & seurats? not here. at the v.f.w. downin straight bourbon bitchin no one knows how to paint a house correctly nowadays. thanks for the help dad-o. howm i supposed to intimidate this bitch when im 16 & cant even piledrive her cuz of this fuckin shriveled thin called my arm? & the bitch is chain-smokin in our kitchen intent on givin me lung cancer along wit my hammered collarbone & moms got the fuckin oven thin on suckin air out the room so i cant breathe. why she accommodatin this bitch? fuck get her a footstool while youre at it. then ol cort-richards at the door leavin wit her son & her hyphen & the bitch winks like were friends from grade school. im in this crammed hot heavy dirty white-gray sling up round my shoulder bound like the fuckin mental health guy in the quiet riot videos & craigs dumb ass sings "cum & feel the noize" every time he comes round me like thats funny. craig goin, "girls fuck your boyz!" & im like "yeah well come over here & ill demonstrate a quiet riot on your ass" & i want to punch him but im a cripple & all i can think bout is how much it hurt when the doc snapped my shoulder back in place. flash to sadistic doc givin the ol one-two-three count & a nice good crrr-ack. & thats my fuckin bone makin that noise. & now here we are wit matt cort walkin out wit his head down. what an actor

when the cortfucks are gone, my mother dearest says, "im sure he did it by mistake." walkin away, under my breath jus loud enough for her to hear i say, "bitch"

i pick up my step for the getaway to my room & catch my foot on the Christmas light cord unpluggin it & all the flashin fake happiness abruptly ends
black

if theres anythin i know in this lifetime, anythin, its matt cort cocked back & nailed me in the shoulder blades for no reason other than his dads an alcoholic scumbag & he cant pass fuckin high school english. either of em. for fucks sake, im takin spanish & still gettin a low c-, which aint a bad grade considerin i cant speak a word of it other than the shit i pick up from cypress hill: "pass the cervesa before i push up on your esa"

thats for my vatos in the quete

gangsta rap is my dad

yesterday ma bought tapes—Straight Outta Compton (which i already own but 2 copies of its okay wit me), Great Adventures of Slick Rick, Ice T's Power, & inspirational moments wit jim neighbors. im like, "whats this last one?" she goes, "it was in the bargain bin." i go, "it should be." she goes, "you shouldnt listen to that violence crap." im like, "what violence crap?" she picks up Slick Rick & reads, " 'Treat Her Like a Prostitute,' 'Lick the Balls.'" hey, she bought em, not me. i go, "thats not violence crap, thats sex shit." mad cuz i swore, she storms out goin, "youre welcome." i struggle unwrappin the clingin plastic. then crank Slick Rick cuz it has the same producers as AmeriKKKa's Most Wanted & cuz ma hates it. these tapesll torment her after all upcomin fights. man, i made out cuz i got these before Christmas. so i can ask for more from santa. ha ha ha! i crank "Children's Story" like 5 times cuz i keep rewindin cuz its the jam. i pump Ren wit "Quiet on tha Set." Rens the best rapper in NWA yet theres no solo Ren like dre & Cube got. no sense. weakass dre blows up & Rens got pure skiiiills & vanishes. ma bought these cuz im on aspirin, bed-moanin. moms like, "what can i do?" thinkin id want water but i want tapes. so i made a death wish list. & all i did is hole up & pump that shit. you cant hear the bass clear & the extras Vietnam Sadler mixes less you got it tenned. wit that volume the rhymes seep. so i promised myself once i could reuse my arm id hit weights wit craig. craig throws up 1000 pound squats. me, i throw up 1000 rhymes. started thinkin in rhyme, bout my arm & doin harm & false alarms. dope shit. even my dreams rhymed. craig neck-flex & kids back the fuk up like garbage trucks. ima do that shit in the rap world. Cubes in my ear & im goin, "scope a moerfuck cuz its time to get real for real." im in bed, cant move. promisin. pump the weights if not tha gat. preppin. mind-preppin. now. its time, now

the tape. The mix tape. time to make Thee mix tape

which is no easy task for me cuz none of my tapes are in the right cases

i hit play/record on a blank tape on my recorder & blast my boom to record straight off it. what to start wit? Lyrical Criminal Ganxsta' R?dd of Boo-Yaa bustin "Psyko Funk." oh yeaaah. R?dd aint even black, he like one of those fatass chinese suomi wrestlers. he say, "psycho alpha doo-doo," if that aint the coolest lyric ever. after that, Ren, Cube, & Eric Eazy Wright bus "Straight Outta Compton Crazy Moerfuck Name Cube." dre aint on that rap so its flawless. then mellow man ace does "if you were mine." jus kiddin. i aint heard a nigga beg for pussy like that since L.L. actually i kicked Kid Frosts "La Raza." real mexican mafioso blue bandana crip shit—the reason i took spanish in the 1st place. to learn how to bus shit like, "im soy antony yo yo soy jefe." get bilingual on a nigga. only 1 come close is Cypress wit how they could jus kill a moerfucker. old school cuz olds cool. then Professor Griff & da Last Asiatic Disciples kick "Pawns in the Game." shits more dope than a new york cannabis bust. most rap wannabes aint never heard "Pawns," fuckin posers. best openin in rap history. gives me chills. that song made me buy the autobiography of Malcolm X titled The Autobiography of Malcolm X written by Malcolm X. wheres X from? Michigan. wheres Magic from? Michigan. where Elijah Muhammed from? Michigan. & where Eazy E from? Compton, Michigan. next i put on Gifted 4s "Sounds of the Mic." moerfucks dont say "party people" like they use to. then the best party jam ever—"Call Me D-Nice." give it up for D. crazy 808. Derrick Jones knows beats. niiiiice. then Def Jef "Black to the Future"—strongest B side opener i know. a Strong positive Black message. then i woulda mixed in me & craig doin "White Boyz in Tha Howse!!," dis solo joint-joint we bus-ed, but i mailed that fuckin tune in the mail yesterday & it was my only copy. on that tune, craigs the beatboxer, im the rapper. we did it on my 1-track recorder in my basement studio in my basement wit all my moms velvet presley shit gawkin down on us haunted house style wit the scary eyes movin & so if you hear craig go "ahthankyouverymuch" at the end all elvis-y, thats why. craig hates that song cuz he says he was doin it to make fun of rap & im takin it too serious but i wanna send it to some execs & did. i mean, on that tape, there are raps i seriously rapped more than fifty fuckin times, no beatbox, take after take, rewindin til i got the shit perfect. we argue cuz im like craig what happens if the execs call & you aint down, what do i tell em? i found an address for the Run-DMC fan club & sent it yesterday marked "confidential" to peek Darryl Macs interest, big breath before i put that shit in the mail, man, fuckin prayed even, which i fuckin save for when the shit in life really matters, like if someones in the hospital who doesnt suck. & i wont be able to mail that shit again cuz it was expensive cuz i put in photos hollow took of me posin wit hand gestures at the town dump & a bunch of paper wit sample raps i wrote out, years of my best shit. "Cold Stealin The Air," "The Criminal Element," "Ripped & Torn/Lyrical Killa," a shit-load more. that last ones fuckin dope though. check this shit:

    the hicks, they cant hang me

    the gangs, they cant bang me

    cuz im livin angry

    & im stuck, between a rock & a hard place

    fuck, my homeys callin me scarface

    or leatherface

    let me explain

    im insane

    yo, im keepin a chain saw

    so, ill be eatin your brain raw

    like cole slaaaaaaaaaaaw

    so fuck the la-la la-la lala la-law!

man, that shit so def moerfucks need a hearin aid. & when i bus it, man, you got no idea. im jus waitin to blow, up. shits in the mail. any second, pho-nell ring, & they gonna be like 'antony seurat there?' i be like, yo moerfuck what? moerfuck be like, 'mc antony x?' i be like, what you want nigga? & then cash, tours, fuckin hos, fuckin dough, fuckin clothes, pose for photos, fuckin the fuckin hos

i rhyme like Darryl. shit like, "wastin like jason & freddy im deadly but ready to rhyme steady." i give a fuckload a rhymes in one installment so moerfucks are like fuck that moerfuck just bus-ed 5 rhymes in 4 seconds & shit. like we read shakespeare for class & that moerfuck was a rhymin moerfuck but i didnt read it cuz that moerfuckd only have like 1 rhyme for 2 lines. he be like

Gloria, thine ears are not melting like the sun that doth shine,

But whence a soldier doth come he will come for quite some time—

like that, like see how theres only 1 rhyme. shit, i jus checked & i got "thine" rhymin wit "shine" & "time." fuck. im so used to those Xtra rhymes i do it even when i try to bus weak ass bill shakespeare bull shit. shakespeare aint nothin but a lil cracker british prison bitch everyone fistfucks on fridays. me? i drown fucks in rhyme. inundate. dictionary skills, bitch. i put the dick in dictionary. me & craig use those big brownnoser words to make fun of moerfucks. we pick words out the dictionary & weave those moerfucks into conversation, craigll say shit like, "that chick is sumptuous." fuckin hilarious when he says it, especially when he does that shit to teachers. latest word is 'inundate.' my new solo joint. mc antony x, Inundatin Moerfucks Wit Rhyme. The IMWR Posse. even if it is jus me. i wish i knew how to beatbox & rap at the same time. i gotta learn that. time for new shit. heres 1:

moerfuck hit me wit a b-a-t

well see who ends up in e-merge-n-c

damn, that shits dope freestyle shit. fuckdamn

i gotta tell you this. serious. wit Licensed i found myself. wit Adrock, you know. i wanted to be him. totally capped his style—hat, hands, postures, photo poses. kick ass shots of me & craig where im album insert material wit crazy gestures, flippin the look. i dream some execll sign me jus from seein a photo of me flippin some crap crip sign. Adrock allowed me to be me. i mean do you know what its like bein a kid wearin a Lions belt (packer fans need to move the fuck to wisconsin), a blue t-shirt & not feel like a person, jus useless, then Adrock comes & youre like you do have to fight for your right to party. in every interview King Ad glows like Christ. & he fucks Molly Ringwald & i mean even craig admits Mollys the fort knocks of hot chicks. sometimes i dream me & Molly are out in hollywood hangin at some fancy nyc diner wit newspaper people clickin pictures & im eatin steak & eggs & her & all this nausea i have from my family is gone jus gone & im happy for fuck sakes once in my life. then i snap outta that & theres hollow leanin on my doorway pantin cuz he jogged over & he probably wants me to walk to mikes party store to play ikari warriors

fuck the whiteboy life

& the original whiteboy is hollow. that moerfuck actually greeted me once wit "howdy"

hollow wants to change my name to antony m. said shit bout how im "contradictory." im like what you talkin bout Willass. hollows called hollow cuz he aint got no brains in his head. the X is for Malcolm but its more than that. it stands for Xcellent & like zeb love X fucks up the program wit his cameo on 3rd Bass "Gas Face" & like i got Xray vision wit my voice, like i flip true skeletal shit

but the true reason, the real reason i chose that name, my name, MC Antony X, & i aint told or showed no one this, is one time i broke out the sketch pad where i jot all my rhymes & one day i was kickin round & wrote my one and only poem, you know, not a rap, some short shit that went like this:

"Most Days This Is How I Feel"

x

yeah im a sensitive-ass moerfucker

Chapter 19: Cräig

Antony needs to tone down the yo yo yo horseshit or he's gonna get his legs broke.

I'm his best friend and even I would like to nail him right between the goddamn head when he starts yo-yoing.

Chapter 20: J

My Dad disappeared.

Again.

He was in the U.P. two months and twelve days, ricocheting around crashing at friends'. I got to see him twice—the day of the tattoo and last night. We stayed up til 4 a.m., telling me stories you wouldn't believe. About being in the Asheville Mountains bushwhack-hiking with Bill when they come by this bluff and hear a scree sound. They look up to find a deer caught in a tree, belly up with its back lodged between a high parting of the trunk, legs kicking in the air. And this other time my Dad was doing ironwork and a guy fell past him. My Dad was hauling a crossbeam and out of the corner of his eye, pheww!, he looks down and there's a mark from a body that just hit the ground from eight floors up. My Dad walked right off the job then and there. He didn't need a book for his stories, no Grimm or Goose, just him, his memories. What a great life.

I guess he went to California. I don't know why there, but he's like that, just catches the south wind and flies. Man, I wish I could be like that. I'm the opposite. The wind blows right past me.

When Dad leaves, it's like I die. It's like my heart becomes a ghost town. All I want is to be alone.

Which is the opposite of what I really want.

I wish he would've said bye.

He never does.

Did you ever notice how most of life is spent missing something? Like little pieces are gone from our hearts. Hollow says that's what his nickname really means.

I wish Dad stayed for Christmas.

He left me an envelope. Under the white plastic tree given to us by Grandma Nancie. "Don't open til you know when."

I opened it. Inside was a twenty-dollar check I'll never cash and a piece of First National Bank of Negaunee stationary folded in half with a short note, "I'll always love you." My eyes got wet, but I laughed before any tears dripped. "See back."

On the back was a phone number, the name "Mindy," and a scribbled smiley face winking. The smile was made from a letter J.

· ·

·

J

And then below the phone number was the words, "Look under your bed."

At first I didn't see anything, except a pillow that had fallen, so I put it back on my bed and looked again. Up by the headboard was a package. My Dad wraps presents in old *Mining Journals*. He's done that all my life—Christmases where you come upstairs and see the news around all your gifts.

The headlines, from a November 1988 issue, Thanksgiving time, read "Students Kill Teacher at Deer Camp" and "Homosexual Slain by Hitchhiker at Isle." I'm sure he did that by mistake. My Dad tends to make a lot of mistakes, especially whenever he's trying not to.

So I unwrap it, not caring what the present is, just happy he thought of me. And it's a Harley cap. His Harley cap. The cap I can't remember him ever not owning. I shake my head and have to really make myself laugh now so I don't cry, but I put it on and go to my mom's bathroom mirror and try to imagine what I'd look like with a ponytail.

Chapter 21: Cräig

Bobbie Bobbie Bobbie Bobbie Boobie Bobbie. I have sex with Bobbie then leave on this camping trip and all I can think about is having sex with Bobbie.

Horny as hell, I hadn't screwed in a week 'cause I went with my parents to Jellystone National Park way down south in Wisconsin. Only my parents would camp in January. They said it's inexpensive that way, no tourists. Good thinking. Dad goes ice shacking while me and my mom huddle in a rent-a-camper fighting off claustrophobia by fighting with each other.

In Jellystone's public bathroom, huge holes are under the stalls. But first lemmy say I refuse to use urinals for one reason alone and that's the splash. Don't tell me you never feel droplets ricochet on your skin. So I piss sitting like a little girlie, giving me time to read. I love to read, the classics—*Circus*, *Hit Parader*, *Black Belt*. They time their articles so one column is a piss and one page equals a shit. It's a good system. I'm in this stall one o'clock in the morn and finally getting to wack, but when I pull my pants down sitting dump-style with legs spread like falcon's wings, this fly comes outta nowhere dive-bombing at my ear bzzzing, going crazy, ruining the mood, the romance, and I didn't have any porn on me anyhow so I was going from memory but the fly wouldn't lemmy concentrate so I was like screw it. Screw it screw it, fly. McFly.

We burnt marshmallows and shared stories about killers with hooks for hands and I crossed my legs to hide my throbbing acre of an acher and found that when I stopped, the urge lessened. By the end, I sorta forgot about that and was a normal kid almost, and kinda was like hey, I can camp and stuff.

I got home with a new New Year's resolution. But an issue of February *Hustler* was waiting even though it was January and I opened it and went to the back where the ads are 'cause that's where the best photos are, and suddenly I went from a new resolution to no resolution.

Damn the glossed up photos of Ginger Lynn and Leeann fingering and some dopey guy with dangling sparkly earrings steps in the picture, blocking the camera with his thumb prick. God, if a male is anywhere on the page, I can't get hard. Even if I think a guy is about to step in the photo, I'm useless. They should have a magazine that's all lesbian. Jesus, I should copyright that idea. I bet those are in heaven. Christ thinks of everything, like mints on your pillow and banning males from porn shoots. I stole the *Hustler*, only the fourth thing I stole since those peashooters with J in sixth grade. And a boom box from K-Mart last month. So this chick, and I don't know who she is, but if she ever reads this, I'd sell my soul for you. She's in an ad about the size of a quarter with all these other ads around her and thank god there's no gay ad 'cause they throw in fag ads and that pisses me off. If you look at the guy, he's lying there smiling with his Gold's Gym abs thrown out like oh look at me, don't you want to do me in the ass? I'm like, "Uh, no." I say this out loud, I look at him, point, and go, "Loser!" I wonder if he knew he'd be in a fag ad with the words, "Ram me HARD" under his name. 'Hard' in capitals, no less. Christ, could you imagine if that was you? His dad must be suicidal. Don't even say he's a straight guy down on his luck down on his stomach, 'cause that's a mofag, and by that I mean mo' fag than anything. Just like Antony's monig.

I key in on my girl's ad for Face Sitting and I guess she's about to sit on someone's face 'cause the photographer got her in that motion, flawless. I could watch her sit all day. Black G-string, long long ink black hair, you only see a bit of her face. God, I want to get her pregnant so she'd never leave. Marry. I'd take her face sitting and all—for better or worse. The phone rings. I jump. Listen. No one's home. More ringing. I'm not getting it. Though I should. The phone ringing, all this oil, reminds me of Bobbie, the first time we met, it was like this, I was home like this and the phone rang . . . Six months ago . . . Six months ago . . . just about to this day, it was . . .

I get it, got it. Greased up. I try to say "Hello" in a regular voice, but end up sounding shaky like a guy caught wacking. It's Hollow. He wants to go to a party. Bored out of his Megadeth skull, he hasn't been to a party in a godless dark eternity, since last dirty black summer. He begs. Oiled up like an Alabama pig, I say no. He says, "This girl's gonna be there. She wants to meet you."

"What's her name?"

"Bobbie."

What a pretty name.

I shower. Nothing is like shouting Ronnie James Dio lyrics with your mouth open under a showerhead. With this great warbling gurgle, it feels like your soul's getting waterlogged.

I scribble a quick REDRUM in the mirror steam and leave to get Hollow.

Schmoozing, Hollow is a jolly green giant click hopper. Before coming, he takes a Michelob can, empties it, and refills it with A & W root beer so he can tell people he's drinking "beer" and not be lying. 6'9", he loves to say, "I'm 6'9, baby."

I hate basketball and I mean hate, but when I got drug to a game where they played the Marquette Redmen and the Redmen are a higher ranked team, bigger school, and lemmy tell you, nobody dunks in UP basketball except the point guard for the Hematites. That's our school mascot, the Hematites. You don't know what that is, do you? Hematite's shit you mine for. Mines are everywhere here. We don't have a mascot 'cause how do you dress up like hematite? Gay. But second half our point guard puts up a shot, it bounces off, and Hollow cocks back, two hands it. On this skinny Redman wimp. Crowd on their feet. His only two points of the game. Only thing that would've been cooler is if the backboard broke and shards of glass went in the neck of the Redmen guy severing his head off with gushing blood and veins dangling. But something close happens. Hollow comes down with his leg twisted. Lands wrong. Bone pops out. In front of, what, four hundred people? I was like damn, *Evil Dead*. He laid there banging his fist on the floor and we waited for an ambulance. In the following weeks, I noticed Hollow became a mild hero, sympathy where the city of Ishpeming was eating out of his hand, sending flowers, cards, recognizing him, saying hi, and I realized that's what war heroes are, little celebrities. They go in and out with a blaze of glory and there's something in that, the meaning of life, in there, buried.

When Hollow's brother, Danny died, everyone felt so damn sorry for Hollow. He started getting invited to keggers. The funny part is a drunk driver killed his brother.

My brother, on the other hand, dies and only eight people are at the funeral.

Last minute, like it skipped his mind, Hollow introduces Bobbie. She's drunk, which is good. I pound 'em, to catch up 'cause I can't talk to chicks at parties. At the gym, yes 'cause I'm buffed up, and in my bedroom, yeah 'cause my bed's there, but at a party, no. So I guzzle. I mix Old Milwaukee and Goebels, a U.P. drink we call a 'Tan and Tan.' Real backwoods hillbilly shit. And some vodka with O.J., which we call a "vodka and orange juice." I'm buzzing 'cause I can't feel my cheeks and that's the test. I poke and can't feel nothing. Bobbie says, "Lemmy do that," and pokes me. I say, "You wanna fuck?" She says, "What?" And I say, "Do you want a drink?" And she says, "No, I'd rather fuck." And that's the coolest thing any chick's ever said. Ever.

We go Al Quaal, a long drive 'cause Hollow's friend lives in the boondocks and I worry her buzz is leaving 'cause mine is, but I drive the posted 25 'cause if cops stop us they'll shine flashlights in my face a good interrogating hour. No one's more dangerous than bored small town cops. We pull up to a Teal Lake overlook where you barely see the lake, and the moon bounces off the ice, increasing my odds of getting some. Nature gets chicks horny. We put the heat on max, go in back, and I'm hard as dried shit, like it hurts, like my heart's inside my dick beating to get out. Struggling, she tugs my pants off and I'm about to bang her but instead I bang my funny bone, ignoring it 'cause any distraction now would be a distraction. Then she sees it. Everything looks good in moonlight, but my dick looks real good. If I could, I'd do myself. Bobbie goes "Oh," which makes me love her, and takes off her top, which makes Tommy love her, and she has outstanding sophomore tits. Those aren't sophomore tits, I say, but to myself, and she gets on top and it's like she's insane 'cause she rides me like a girl that's a woman, like she's dick starved, like she was going Cockrompers' Anonymous and this is a naughty binge she's on. She's on me and I lie there drooling and she rocks and I don't have a condom and she keeps in rhythm and I say grab your tits and she says "my sophomore tits" and I go those senior tits and she looks down on me and it's like I'm screwing Hell itself 'cause she's into it and a bad bad bad girl and I say I don't have a condom and she goes you better come in me so I agree. Cold and sweaty, looking up at her, this vague outline of perfection and a couple pinprick dots of stars outside the foggy window, I thought, I could marry her and be happy forever. And bam I tell her I love her.

Looking in her eyes, I tell her. She asks if I have tissue in the car and some is in the glove compartment but I want to keep it in her. I want to be in her for the next half hour or half year like the longer I keep it in the more likely she'll get pregnant and I wish I could get her a little bit pregnant, just a little bit. And I look up at her breathing with hands on my chest, but it flops out and she reaches up front with her ass in my face. I grab hold and she gives an "Oh" and oh I could marry that "Oh." She cleans up using fifty napkins and we go back.

I kiss her and drop her off at the door, telling her to tell Hollow his leg's healed so he can walk. She says, "I'm not gonna do that." I'm in a real mischievous mood and say, "No, serious, tell him I left and he can walk home. He needs the exercise." She goes, "Don't be a bad boy. Drive him." I say, "Okay," and drive away. Her number's in my pocket written on the edge of a one-dollar bill. The backseat is full of used napkins and I have this evil thought of leaving them there. So I do.

All evil thoughts must be followed.

On the way home, I fast-forward *Reign* until I find "Jesus Saves" and scream along making up my own lyrics for most of the song.

Chapter 22: J

The heater is cranked to get the ice off the windshield and Craig's too impatient and unsafe to wait, so he has the wipers on hoping that will scrape the ice without him having to get out of the car. Of course, this breaks his passenger side wiper so it hangs there at the halfway point immobile like a broken bird wing. He gets out leaving the door open and explodes cursing the almighty in the crisp winter air carrying his words throughout every crevice of the neighborhood block. I press my body parts together to keep warm and my teeth chatter like I have permafrost. We cruise over to get Antony because he has something important to show us.

Teal Lake Ave is icy but the occasional hydroplane is completely ignored by Craig, as if that's the norm. "As long as there are no cars on the road, we can't get in a wreck," Craig says, passing a station wagon.

As always, Craig cranks metal. Heavy metal is such a sad, sad joke. It's the musical equivalent of wrestling, which unsurprisingly Craig does. All his four-hour sauna marathons and one thousand calorie three-day diet plans are going to his head. For three months of football, he's obese; for three months of wrestling, he's bulimic. That can't be good for a body, or a head. To help himself stop thinking, he has on Slayer, always Slayer. He says he listens to other bands, but I've never heard them in his car.

But I'm one of those types that flow with whatever, otherwise you get into pain-in-the-ass arguments and you can't prove heavy metal sucks. You just have to know it.

When Craig plays his music, he doesn't sit idly listening. He thrashes like a doll in a Pine Knob mosh pit. He shouts along, something about ripping a human body to pieces. Typical idiotic metal lyrics. No sense of irony or satire. I want him to calm down because his hands keep coming off the wheel, so I yell over the music, "The lead singer's rapping!" He yells, "Rap sucks!" I yell, "He's rapping!" He yells, "Suck it!" Then before I can speak, he yells, "Nec-ro-phobic!" right with the music, then two seconds of blissful silence until this other pummeling comes on called "Altar of Sacrifice." I know this because he tells me. He has stories about each song, studio anecdotes. He cranks it to head splitting level and I make an oath that the next time he's trapped at my house, he's getting a good hour of my Time Flies . . . But Aeroplanes Crash twelve-inch.

We hit the stoplight by Red Onion Pasties and he thrashes around like we're in a spotlight. A car pulls alongside with a full family of mom, dad, kid, dog, Jesus bumper sticker. Of course they look over at us like we're escapees from the Newberry nut farm, but Craig doesn't even acknowledge them. Instead he whiplashes more. His seat's about to break. Then right when the next "song" kicks in, he looks over at the All-American U.P. Nuclear Family and with a cringing, realistic doom face yells, "Learn the words 'Praise! Hell! Lucifer!'" and makes the universal hand gesture for Ozzy as the light changes. The car in front of us doesn't move. "It's not getting any greener!" Craig yells and rides up on the sidewalk to pass them, then floors it. I shake my head as he yells "Salvation!" cranking it even louder, which I thought wasn't possible, so I scream to turn it off, not down. But he can't hear, so I roll down my window to let some of the sound escape, since I can't, and a shot of cold hits our ears like free Novocain. Craig headbangs in sync with the song's drum and guitar ending and I must admit a cool riff kicks in so just to keep him happy and to keep me warm, I headbang too and this fires Craig up like a double shot of vodka. We cruise down US-41 heading to Negaunee and Teal's to our left and "Jesus Saves" is in our eardrums and ice is below and I keep head-banging and Craig's happy as I've ever seen him. We pull up and already my neck's sore. Rubbing, I say, "I don't know how you do it." I can see my breath, so I close the window. We're at Antony's who lives close to Ishpeming High, which rumor has it is getting torn down soon and Antony's response to this is "good." We pull in and there's Antony. He hops in the car and says, "Just go. Drive." We're like, "Where?" He's like, "Hurry up." So we go to where they love to go—the caving grounds.

Chapter 23: Cräig

It's like a sonic boom.

Nobody's fazed. We're used to it. We're a few miles from Cliffs Iron and it's just after noon, so the daily dynamite blast blasts. Antony says, "The end of the world." No one responds. Antony adds, "You hear Cleveland Cliffs is closing?"

"That rumor's been forever."

"No, it's serious."

"K.I.'s closing. You're mixing the two up."

"No, it's the airport. The airport's getting shut down."

All three—the mine, the air base, the airport—will be gone soon. All that'll move in to replace us is tumbleweeds. Take away Marquette General and the Branch Prison too and there's no employment left in the county, dad says. Luckily the unemployment will keep Marquette General stocked with suicide attempts and Marquette Branch packed with grand theft felons. But if the average yearly income is under $20,000, who cares? Let's get outta here. And that'll soon happen. Ishpeming's population is collapsing like a caving ground mine. The only thing that'll save it is global warming. Turn this place into a New Florida with enough sun cancer for everyone.

Iron ore was first discovered in Negaunee, so it was this massive mining community. Was. Nearby Calumet was supposed to be the capital of Michigan. Now Detroit's the capital. Back in the 1800s Calumet had twelve operating brothels, at least that's what Mr. Pynnonen, the Drafting teacher said, and Pynhead would know. We had a strip club but now it's a pizza place called Palazoni's and the crust gets soggy fast. It's by Negaunee High. The U.P. used to be prosperous. Now all the mines are emptying. What that means is they burrow all over hell underneath the city looking for iron ore so half the city is condemned as caving grounds. All these empty tunnels are underground and over the years, they sometimes collapse. One house over by the Wagon Wheel across from the National Guard Armory just off US-41 had part of their front yard collapse in. This big pipe sticks out the ground nearby to keep people away. That can happen in anyone's front yard here, but especially when you jump the fence where it's condemned. You won't realize you're standing over this mile-long tunnel dug under the earth and suddenly it gives and you plummet into nothingness forever. So of course this is our favorite place to go—the caving grounds, where you can die in a second. A rush. I have to admit, you jump that barbed wire NO TRESPASSING—DANGER fence and your blood pumps 'cause you know you can be dead in a U.P. minute. I mean, what a way to go? Instant, gone. A speck. It's scary back there, with the rubble, the half-buildings, the deserted overgrowth covered cars that make it seem like you're in another world, abandoned. What's even better is when you're hovering at the pit of Hell is if you swallow Mountain Dew mixed with Cat. Cat's the U.P. drug. There's no crack up here, no coke, just lovely low class Cat. Cat tranquilizers. Stolen from veterinarian clinics. Makes you feel invincible, like the evergreens, leaning in, that surround the edge of Hell.

That's our favorite spot. A place we call Hell.

There's also the city Hell, Michigan. I have a cousin down there named Ray, but he's gay, so he never visits. This Hell isn't that Hell.

It's where a cave-in occurred. Me and Hollow were wandering the caving grounds when we discovered Hell. Hollow was like, "What's that?" Up ahead it looked like there was a black hole, a void, missing space, all of a sudden there wasn't any earth to the Earth. We went closer with the quiet of a recording studio. The hole was thirty feet by forty or so. We didn't go any further to the edge 'cause that would be insane, but we were close and it looked like the Abyss, endless. No bottom. These trees were at the edge hanging on for life by their roots, hovering over an eternal fall like god forgot about them. Imagine that. Always waiting to plummet. Down in the hole, it slowly got blacker the deeper you looked, where the sun didn't even try to reach, like it could fall in too. The woods were all quiet, polite, frowning. Wind wasn't even daring to come out. Like the weather was scared. Hollow leaned over whispering, "Hell." And he was right. That's how it got the name. And that's the closest visual I have of hell. That and Slayer album covers. And the time I saw my mom naked.

I've always been infatuated with hell, the concept, the place. My earliest childhood doodles were flames and pitchforks. Red and black scribblings that never got posted on our refrigerator. My mom saved them for drawers and garbage cans.

My original father, not my stepdad, but my original father, was evil. My mom told me. She said he had the devil in his eyes. I never understood why my mom would marry a man like that. Before I was born, they lived down by Detroit, in Garden City, and he used to just jump into that city, she said, into Detroit. That's what she told me. He would jump into the city at night, whatever that meant, and I think it was a bad thing. 'Cause mom said he did bad things and I'll never be in contact with him again and he doesn't want to have contact with us anyhow. I wondered what kind of bad things he did 'cause I mean how much can you do? I have a photo of him I keep hidden 'cause my mom got rid of anything he ever touched when we came up here. All those times are vague, like a huge awful dream. I remember one memory distinctly. We're in Ferndale in the old 1970 Plymouth Ford Fury and all this urban sprawl whizzing by with flower shops and gas stations with different gas prices every block usually more expensive the poorer the area is and in Detroit you can drive straight for the length of time it takes a child to be born without turning once and dad was yelling about how sick he was of silences and mom was cowering in the passenger side corner nervously clicking the door lock like she was toying with the fact that now she was locked in, now she wasn't, now she was trapped again, now almost free, and dad was ranting not like a regular mad hatter but instead with his vicious cigarette waving hand like he could put it out in your eye if he wanted and mom's telling him to stop taking his hands off the wheel so he does it again, and I have other memories too that come in and go but I don't want to deal with them but it's mostly about dad calling my mother a loudmouth whore when the reality is she's antisocial and asexual. We moved to start over 'cause we have cousins up here I could play with, she said, and you should only trust family, mom said, and then I got up here and got older and heavy metal came out and it hit something deep inside my guts.

J played Twisted Sister's *Stay Hungry* and that was that. When I got up here,

I went to my first concert. My mom never lemmy out to do things in Detroit. Huge city and I was trapped in a two-room apartment sharing a bunk bed. I get up here and suddenly, no curfew, no list of rules, no paranoid mom. The concert was at Lakeview Arena. KISS had come through town, but I missed it. But I saw the Ratt/Poison tour. Ratt sucked. The bassist was fat. You can't be in a metal band and OD on Twinkies, only heroin. But Poison came out and they were pure energy. CC Deville ran around bumping into Bret Michaels the whole show and all these women who stood there for Ratt suddenly threw bras onstage and I knew I had just found home. A family of 3,000 black-shirted kids and eight killer amps. I was nothing but metal. Metal and topless girls— the lighting crew was wise enough to put them in the spotlight so they could shine like Virgin Marys. I remember CC's hyperactive adrenaline rush and thinking wow he doesn't even need drugs to be happy, god, I can be like that 'cause that's how I always wanted to act, just like that. When we got out of the concert, these candy corn orange construction cones were alongside Fair Avenue and CC was in me 'cause I hurdled cone after cone knocking them over with my fist and feet and sweat-freezing concertgoers yelled, "Look at the crazy bastard!" and I could've floated into the heavens if it wasn't for gravity and I needed a ride back from Hollow. Hollow and J—Antony refused to come— were like, "What's got into you?" I was like, "CC. CCCP. PCP. PP!" I didn't say that, actually I said something that made even less sense, to them, but it made all the sense in the world to me.

I bought Danzig, Cooper, Maiden, Krokus, W.A.S.P., Accept. I bought Helix, Testament, Scorpions, Sepultura, Death, Pungent Stench. I stoled Vinnie Vincent Invasion, Sex Pistols, Frehley's Comet, King Diamond, Great White, the Crüe. *Frolic Through the Park, Practice What You Preach, World Wide Live, Beneath the Remains, Save Your Prayers, Hell Awaits.* Anything cool, you know, any songs with death or sex in the title, any album with skulls or nipples on the cover. Any tape with "kill" or "Devil" in the songs. Until I ran out of money. Which was quick. So I traded tapes. My Sex Pistols for J's Motörhead.

Up in my room is my best tapes' list. People come over, read it, and argue. It stirs up controversy, to get people thinking about metal and life and that's why I did it, but here's the list and actually it can't be argued.

10)   Metallica – The *$5.98 EP – Garage Days Re-Revisited.* I only like $5.98 and

Kill 'Em All but you gotta respect a band that refuses to make videos and promises fans they'll never record ballads like they said in their Cream interview. That's a true metal band there. Except "Battery" sucks.

9)   Megadeth – *Peace Sells . . . But Who's Buying?* I wish Mustaine was still in Metallica.

8)   Led Zeppelin – *IV.* "The ruin album." Led Zep, come on, that's obvious. If I get a tattoo it'll be "ZOSO" on my scrotum.

7)   Black Sabbath – *The Eternal Idol.* Ozzy's overrated. Any schmuck can bite off a bat head, but it takes a genius like Tony Iommi to lay down that guitar work. I bet Ozzy is forgotten in two years and Tony lives on.

6)   Pantera – *Cowboys from Hell.* "Cemetery Gates" is flawless. Like any good metal tape, it makes me wanna hurt myself.

5)   Tesla – *Mechanical Resonance.* The metal album Elvis wanted to record.

4)   Dokken – *Tooth and Nail.* Screw Clapton, Yngwie, and Vai Halen. Lynch = Jesus.

3)   Fastway – *Trick or Treat Original Motion Picture Soundtrack.* Who is this band? They rule! Most underrated album in the last 666 centuries.

2)   Slayer – *Reign in Blood.* I sent them a letter saying I'd sell my soul to Satan if they sent me autographs. They never did. That's probably good.

Drum solo please . . . by Dave Lombardo . . . on the double bass . . .

1)   Queensrÿche – *Operation: mindcrime.* The penultimate metal album of all time. How's that for a description? And my English teacher gave me a C- last semester. What a dum-ass. If I'm not good at English, then how come I know what a ümlaut is, huh?

Queensrÿche inspired me to change my name from Craig to Cräig.

Queenscräig.

Motorcräig.

Motley Cräig.

I love cover art. I throw the disc on and stare at the cover to figure out what the band is saying 'cause metal bands put a ton into their message. It's not like rap where 2 Live Screw say, "Ladies, on the count of three, bend over." Metal has meaning. Like *Peace Sells.* That's an attack on government, housing projects, urban decay. You get lost in that picture. Megadeth covers are all like that.

Intense. Like Pantera's *Cowboy* cover. Phil flying like a demon. I'm him. I'm Phil. No gravity. I put on "Message in Blood," go to the mirror, take my shirt off and flex, my chest, dink dink, then go back to bed and stare at the cover more. Power. Man, Pantera makes me want to punch someone. If I kill myself, it's going to be to "Primal Concrete Sledge." Except it's a short song, so I'd have to kill myself quick. Luckily from lifting my veins are easy to find. Get this, you know the Pantera tour video where they bet the guy if he can eat the entire cake, well, I'm in it. When you rent it, look for the guy in the Lions' cap way in back, but it flashes by in a sec, so you have to look hard. I rewound four times 'cause Hollow kept blinking. My guitar teacher got me the backstage pass. I took three classes with him and quit. One class for each chord.

The best album cover ever is Sabbath's *Eternal Idol*. That cover says it all. How I feel, have always felt. Study it and you'll know me, inside. How much love I have to give. I'm that guy collapsing into the woman, powerless to her.

And there's Dokken's *Tooth and Nail* with the hands coming from the abyss. Like Beauty and the beast. I'm the beast. I listen to "Alone Again," stare at that hand, and could cry. 'Cause that hand is reaching for someone to hold and no one's there. It's pitch black, dark, like my bedroom or the caving grounds' Hell.

Anyway, we all head to Hell 'cause it's the best meeting point. Antony's in a hurry, "Guys, I gotta get back before my parents get home," but then he goes, "Forget it, there's no way we're gonna make it to Hell. It's March, too much cocksucking snow. Lemmy just show you here." And we had just hopped the fence so we risked our balls on barbwire for nothing.

So Antony pulls it out and it's a gun.

Chapter 24: Cräig

Shit. I had to change the list.

I couldn't sleep.

I put Slayer number one and Queensrÿche second. I just drew an arrow, but I'll rewrite the list neater tomorrow.

I still can't sleep. The snowstorm outside is violent. Tonight it's in the negatives, just brutal, you open up the garage door and get hit with pain, wind that makes you cry, forces you to walk backwards. We'll be holed in our houses this entire weekend, nothing but nothing to do.

You've never heard the wind howl until you've been to Ishpeming. It's like every ghoul ever raised from the grave is pounding at my window to get in. My ears are wide, listening to the dead. Slayer was pissed off so they sent over some banshees to haunt me. Quiet the hell down, demons, I changed the list. Lemmy rest in peace. I put on Sabbath's "Glory Ride" to drown out the moans.

Antony.

All that way for a gun.

He says he's going to start carrying it on him. Where? In his pocket? The kid's gonna shoot his feet off. Antony's a paranoid.

How many guns have I shot in my life? How many squirrel heads have I blown off, collected? Maybe I should take out the shoebox, line them up, count them? I think I will.

Antony said he had something else to tell us, all dramatic, but then the coward never said what it was. I wonder if it was that rap music sucks. I woulda agreed.

Chapter 25: Hollow

Above the finishing chorus of "Unchained Melody" on WJPD, I hear my mother on the phone teaching J's mother how to play cribbage. J's mother taped *The Young and the Restless* so my mother is excited. The two of them went to Ishpeming High together, until J's mother got pregnant and dropped out so my mother would skip classes to go to her house where they would eat oranges and smoke Kents because the two went well together. They came up with disgustingly cute nicknames for each other that they still use, "Lovebug," "Bunny," "Shaggy."

Now they go to Mary Kay parties. Times change.

Overhearing them talk, you would think our families are in perfect harmony, except for a few things . . .

My mother dislikes Antony's mother because Antony's mother did not come to Daniel's funeral.

Antony's mother dislikes Craig's mother because Craig's mother slit Antony's back bike tire when Antony wore muddy shoes in her house.

Craig's mother dislikes J's mother because J's mother said Craig's mother's house "is a den for robbers."

That is the abbreviated reason why none of our families hang out together and why there has never been and never will be a family reunion. An unabbreviated list would include Craig's mother calling our house drunk saying she was glad Daniel was dead because he was a bad influence on Craig's brother, and Antony's father slapping me in the face at a VFW barbecue, and Craig pissing in our garage, and the time I dropped a burning Swisher Sweet on Craig's mother's bed, and . . .

At least J's mother and my mother are friends. I hear my mother's voice, excited, happy, for once, and it is not even about real people, just fake TV people: "Ashley and John did what? Oh, Bunny, I will be over in five minutes! Get the board ready."

If it were not for friendships, we would all self-destruct.

Before leaving, my mother insists I do something with J. "Donna says he has been depressed." Hearing the real names of mothers always catches me off guard.

And J does not get depressed. He gets suicidal. He gets so negative, it is like sleeping in a coffin just to be in his room, and it lasts months.

I like J when he is happy. I like sitting at an A & W picnic table and chitchatting with him. But to go over there and listen to his theories on how worms are drooling waiting for us to get six feet under, I do not need to hear that.

Chapter 26: J

I didn't call the chick on my arm.

On my door was a message with Mindy's phone number. Bill called. I crumpled it up, trash canned it.

I got in another of these states where to put it simply I hate people, all people. Actually it's a permanent state. Where I hole myself up in my room like a bunker. I go straight home from school, shut my door, and it's nothing but "Apathy" and *Dr. No* and "I Don't Wanna Die" and *Moonraker* and "No Feelings" and "It's Gonna Get Worse" and it is.

I didn't want to call up the chick on my arm to have her tell me she has a boyfriend and then give a giggle. And I didn't call up this chick on my arm to have her say, "Where did you get my number?" and have to explain about Bill and have to explain why I called her. And I didn't call up the chick on my arm because there was a good chance she's a lesbian or a perma-virgin or worse. And I didn't call up this chick on my arm because the number's probably cancelled and I didn't want to listen to "We're sorry, the number you have dialed is not in cervix at this time, if you feel you have reached this message in error, dial directory assistance at 8-4040 or take a knife to your throat." And I didn't call the chick on my arm because I have a stupid voice on the phone. I sound like a dying bass. Craig told me. In a silly mood, he said I have a weird phone voice. I asked what he meant and he said I sound like a drowning fish and now I can never call people, because Craig had to be in a good mood and say whatever was on the tip of his Gene Simmons-wannabe tongue. So now I can't call the best looking woman since Wendy O. Williams to tell her I'll move down to live with her because I can't stay here another day or I'm either going to kill myself or get more tattoos or both.

I hate people. There are so many hates for so many people. Seeing Antony in that sling confirmed it. People are pricks and pricks are everywhere. Some asshole could take a bat to someone for no reason . . . I hate people.

Listening to this conversation between mom and Gertie Juorumaki confirmed it. Gertie said, "I was talking with Donnie Pallolozzi and he works in the State Police Building off 41 and yeah he was saying the U.P. has no hate groups. Isn't that wonderful? Yeah and he said only three other states have no hate groups in the entire country and the U.P.'s one of them, yeah." Mom laughed that Gertie was saying the U.P. is a state and she asked which other states don't have hate groups and Gertie answered Wyoming and North Dakota and one other one that sounded like Nevada but there's no way in hell it's Nevada because they have whorehouses and casinos there, so I'm sure they have hate groups too, and it was probably some other state that doesn't have any people living in it like Idaho or Montana, and then my mom asked Gertie if the Lower Peninsula had hate groups and Gertie said, "Oh sure, plenty."

I hate people. Especially Gertie.

This winter has been so boring, there were days I didn't know honestly if I was going to make it. If the boredom would kill me. There are only so many times you can look at your ceiling and still be amused. Craig's Pitfall! and Megamania got old. And going outside for the last month has been nothing but painful. It actually hurts to go outside. Where else in the world do you have to wear four layers of clothing? Three pairs of socks? Two jackets? I mean, where else besides places with igloos?

Chapter 27: Cräig

I hate black people. I know you can't say that 'cause of slavery and everything but lemmy explain, before you go and call me a racist and not want to listen.

'Cause I'm not like Scrabble. That's this loser that's the only KKK person I ever met. There's three K's in KKK and I bet at least one of them stands for Kentucky.

Scrabble was at this bonfire Hollow gave out in the middle of nowhere Palmer in celebration of graduation being under a month away. We're all there, the whole shitty nickname crew. Slosh. Azzy. "Vagina Breath" Thompson. B.C., a friend of U.E. He's called B.C. 'cause he acts like a caveman, hairy and stupid. J's there in his Harley cap which the penishead never takes off nowadays. And Cockschmock Antony. Antony runs around behind people lighting their hair on fire. Swear to god. And I don't swear to god unless I'm serious, swear to god. The ends char and luckily no one's head's igniting. Antony needs a nickname. He tries to make us call him MC Antony P or some shit, but that's retarded. I mean, seriously, come on.

There's not a lot to the nicknames. Hollow's called Hollow 'cause he eats like a racehorse and never gains weight. Poor bastard's dated a Christian Scientist since he was a freshman. Supposedly they're in love. But you have to have screwed at least once in your life to know what love is. If I was dating her, I wouldn't. I'd break up and see what was out there. Which is why Hollow's joining the service. He won't say that, but that's why. Hell, if that was me, I'd have dropped her before the word "commandment" ever came out her mouth. Hollow knows zilch about women. Hell, he can't even decide what to do with his life. How many atheists do you know that date Christian chicks, and how many pacifists join the Marines? That's Hollow.

Man, Hollow's girlfriend hates his nickname, which is why we all use it. She's at the bonfire, so Hollow's acting all polite, which drives me up The Wall. Pink Floyd is cranked on Hollow's car stereo, doors open and headlights pointed at the fire, which is pointless since one thing you can always see is fire. People roam around shivering trying to get near 'cause even in the dead of dead summer, when night comes like god ain't paid his electricity bill, man, it gets frickin' cold. 'Cause we live in the tundra, the permanent Ice Age, the not-so-Great White North. Wouldn't be surprised if the party was interrupted by a flock of woolly mammoths. On weather maps, the U.P. is always coldest, spotless in the rest of the country but splotches of white perched over northern Michigan. We kick Anchorage's ass. We make Maine look like a seaside resort, which it is. Our wind-chills get so bad cows' ears freeze and break off. No shit. Deaf cows. My parents are retards. To live here. Just to work in a Cleveland Cliffs' stockroom. Doesn't dad realize there are stockrooms in Florida? I mean, he could be organizing wrenches in the Bahamas. This meteor-logy geek on TV6 said NMU gets more snowfall than any college in the country. And idiots actually go there, voluntarily. Man, I fricking hate snow. Hate, with a capital 8. I hate snow and I hate cold. And they're tied together like bitching and marriage. If it snowed while it's seventy and sunny out, I wouldn't complain, but that's not the case, now is it? The case is I hate tobogganing and the Winter Olympics and all that Nancy Kerrigan shit.

Everyone's back is to the woods and front to the fire and Antony sneaks in and out like a demon with his Bic burning people he don't like, and some he does. He comes up and says with three beats, "Hair must burn." Wisely he leaves me alone, heading off to some other flammable head. The U.P. is a deadly struggle of nothing to do. After charring Peggy Thompson's ponytail, Antony has to be sneaky 'cause she starts Paul Revere-ing, shooting the evil eye at Antony, who pretty much seems unaffected by her and by life as a whole. Thank god Antony isn't pounding Old Styles or I know he'd pound her and we'd be filling out court order report shit for eons to come. No male messes with Antony whether they smell their hair burning or not 'cause Antony was on the Olympic Teen Boxing Team with this other hardass named T Tack Toe. Toe's real name is Ryan Olutynen, and Ryan and Antony been sparring partners since they were two and didn't even know there was a sport called boxing, just did

117

it naturally, like cobras. Now T Tack Toe is forever punch-drunk and nuts and harelipped and when I say harelipped I mean like someone split his face in half with an ax and when T Tack Toe walks by at the bonfire, he pours beer on his own head like it's refreshing and not in the lower fifties out. He yells, "T Tack Toe! Three in a row! X-X-X in the house, bitch!" then pounds back-to-back-to-back beers. Those two have a license to do anything. That's what craziness gives you—free-dumb. T Tack Toe's been out and in of jail more times than a Monopoly thimble.

Then there's Blind John. Lying in his truck bed, he goes through a six-pack of Jolt his brother brought down from Tech in Hancock. Han-cock. Jesus M. Christ, get a new name for that city. B.J. has the worst eyesight in the solar system and he'll kill you if you call him B.J. 'cause he does Thai kickboxing and that's the hardest core shit of all the martial arts. Makes Tae Kwon Do look like pillow-ballet. Through his Coke bottle glasses, B.J. told me, "You know what the best thing about Thai boxing is? It's I know if I wanted to, I could kill anyone here right now. Including myself." I say, "Except me." 'Cause I'd knock those thick spectacles off his face so quick he wouldn't know what hit him, but I would, hit him that is, and then kill his blind Roy Orbison ass. B.J. will be homecoming king. And he looks like a library geek. A ripped frown-faced flannel geek who showers rarely as head of homecoming court. God, our school's just plain stupid. Last year B.J. suntanned, but took these letters like stencil he cut out saying KILLKILL, so when he got the tan, his chest would read KILLKILL in big letters. It worked splendid and he walked around shirtless as much as he could, advertising his insanity with his chest billboard. And he didn't quit until it was sunburned rash-red 'cause he said it'd be prissy-ass dumb if it was tan. Nothing wrong with that line of thinking.

Then there's Summerteeth. Summerteeth Olutynen. Ryan's brother, older by fourteen years. He's called Summerteeth 'cause summer here and some are there. Most are there. Summerteeth's real name is Bud and when you're named after a beer, you're life is headed for the gutter, or at least to Tino's to get drunk. Summerteeth has one pair of Levis, no friends, and a hat—a Pabst Blue Ribbon cap that's never been washed, just like he's never been sober. One time he broke into an ice cream truck, and this is a true story, he hauled off none of the money but grabbed armloads of ice cream sandwiches. He brought 'em back to his house and the police had a report that he did it 'cause it looks a tad suspicious when you walk down Teal Lake with all the ice cream bars two arms can cradle. Neighbors spot those kind of things. The cops went to his house and knocked and Summerteeth was on his lime green-yellow one-third of a sofa in the middle of Klondyke-Bar-dripping-Heaven and quick thinking he hid it behind his back when he answered the door. The pigs asked if he knew about a break-in by LaCombe and Summerteeth was like oh no I know nothing about that officer sir, and he had strawberry ice cream running down the sides of his mouth like blood staining his already stained shirt and he slams the door in the oinkers' faces. Then there's this Halloween where costumed bunnies and Frankensteins and corpses come up knocking and Summerteeth opens the door and without thinking—which is normal for him—he cocks back and boots the candy out the kids' paws. Their candy-filled plastic pumpkin shoots up in the air like sugar fireworks and Summerteeth closes the door and goes to the fridge for another good Old Milwaukee. He doesn't even bow or acknowledge it or nothing, just sits, head cocked back on the couch, and without missing a beat says, "Hey, I'm helpin' out the friggin' brats, they don't wanna end up wif teeff like dhese, do they?" He spreads his lips apart to show that crater of a Crest-lacking mess he calls a mouth. He was right. They don't want that. No one does.

And that's the U.P. Tah-dah.

That's the dark recesses of the Upper Peninsula with alky forested Finns with high hairdo wives that've left 'em to shit mining jobs that always seem at the brink of layoffs. Hollow's granddad worked in the mines thirty-five years and they had this gigantic machine that squirts oil into other machines and by mistake his grandpa got his hand caught and it inserted into his finger pumping oil straight in his hand, mixing with his veins and cartilage and his finger expanded to the size of three fingers. Filled with oil. It hurt the rest of his life and even at its most healed, it still looked like two fingers in one. He'd vomit out of nowhere. Whenever he'd bump his hand, even softly, you'd hear him curse in Finn: Hevon vittu! People complain that Detroit has rats; but up here, the men are the rats. He breathed in all that dust and ore and copper and dirt and hacked and hacked like a good long lung sufferer. That's what the mine does. And these are our fathers. These underground men. This is the life they've had to live. Dirty hands eating Red Onion Pasties off shovels and coming home and showering and not being able to get that shit off. From a distance, all these husbands look like they have tans, but they're really covered with grime, ore. Then they're called off to trench in the First World War or tunnel rat in 'Nam or cryptanalyze German translations in the bowels of some submarine like Hollow's granddad told us about in WWII. Then they come back to the mines like they didn't miss a beat and don't care if they did miss a beat, and they don't talk about it much.

Then there's us, their kids, at this bonfire, jabbering away, teenage school-children. And this kid walks up, nameless. On his forehead is a jagged swas-tika, tattooed, thin. He says to us, "A nigger's here." Hollow goes, "Who's the asshole?" J whispers, "U.E.'s cousin. He moved here from Idaho." Later we find out he's nicknamed Scrabble 'cause he was playing it with U.E. and T Tack Toe (that's another nickname where I could give you the full story, but it's longer than John Holmes' third arm) but this KKK kid puts down N-I-T-E building off the E in the S-E-X T Tack Toe put down for triple word score. Mind you, T Tack Toe flunked second grade, twice, but still managed to get triple word score with his X and then dickheaded KKK swastika-forehead puts down "nite" like that's how you spell it and he's got this serious look and gets mad when they tell him "good effort but no," but then U.E.'s like, "Ah, let him do it. It's only worth four points and he's losing by 170 anyway," and that's how he got the nickname.

If I told you the T Tack Toe story, it'd take a fricking fortnight.

Scrabble gives this monologue about how he was in the KKK in some French city in Idaho and how they have an impressive following there, but it's under-ground and nothing like in Washington—the state, not the place that's not a state—where the KKK thrives. That's the word he uses, "thrives." Scrabble says they had this guy come in from Tacoma to organize them, but all he did was pass out pamphlets, probably full of misspellings. They're called the KKK 'cause it's the only thing hillbillies can spell.

Scrabble tells us he didn't want to get the swastika tattoo on his forehead 'cause he'd rather have it on his upper arm so he could cover it if he ever wears a suit, the kid says, the KKK kid says this straight faced, like there's a chance in Helsinki he's gonna wear a suit in this lifetime, other than for his court appear-ances. But he wanted to show his commitment to this Washington Aryan repre-sentative and then he goes to get a beer leaving us in breathless anticipation for the end to his story and Hollow says, "What a goddamn loser!" and it's funny when Hollow swears 'cause he basically never does unless we ask him to, but he's all grouchy 'cause it'd be his brother's I guess twenty-second birthday tomorrow, tonight, at midnight. When Hollow swears it's like hearing your mom swear when company's over and she thinks you're asleep in the basement. KKK comes back like we're friends and he's excited telling us how there's a chapter in Michigan if we're interested and Hollow goes, "Jesus Christ," and walks away. J asks where and KKK says, "Caledonia" and we're like, "What's that?" 'Cause it ain't in the U.P. And it's not, thank god. KKK goes into how there's a nigger here and we're like, "What're you talking about?" Scrabble points and there is a black guy at the party, which never happens. It's like suddenly the party is The Morton Downey Jr. Show with people coming out the woodwork, and now all we need is chairs to toss. I squint, and see, it's Charles.

Seeing him in the halls, we call him Prince Charles. He's a janitor at Ish High and has like two jobs where he works all day and night. After games he's gotten me free Pepsis from the Coke machine. We were like, "Man, Prince Charles, you bust ass" and he'd nod. We hardly saw him, just like after football where we'd drive back with our duffel bags after slaying the Kingsford Flivvers and get in around midnight, one. Wearing his beret, Charles would be sweating mopping and we'd be freshly showered and Brut scented and pat him on the back and be like, "Prince Charles is all right."

Charles talks with Bobbie, my Bobbie, so I say, "I'm going over." Bobbie knows him 'cause she's a cheerleader and cheerleaders know everyone. Bobbie's not the cheerleader type, but I'm not the jock type but here I am playing both ways starting cornerback on defense and halfback on offense. I feel jealous but Charles is like forty or fifty and I don't think you have sex when you're that old. Bobbie, the lightweight, is drunk, as usual. One beer and she's ready to take off her top, which is why I love her. I've told her I love her twenty times by now, and she's told me that never. She'll change the topic to Vagina Breath's Alfalfa hairdo or how there's a party at Suicide Bowl or, and I hate this, goddamn quotes from Say Anything. Bobbie has shorts on, so she stays pretty close to the fire and in the firelight her summer tan legs look like two gold statues from Greeceland. She's hot as hell just like the fire. And she can do the splits. I've seen her. I'd ask her to do it in the bedroom but we haven't dated long enough, yet. Her back's to the fire and I see her behind smooth, real tight Levi jean cutoffs driving me wild wild wild we'll get wild wild wild til dawn and I think I could marry her. I snake up and pat Charles on the neck. He acts startled like you're supposed to and we talk about how boring the U.P. is in the spring and in the winter and in the fall. I tell him to go to July Fourth Pioneer Days in Negaunee 'cause if you're lucky the wind blows the fireworks in the crowd and you haven't lived until you see a family fleeing for their life with blankets in hand. Also there are free trips to visit the B-52s at K.I. and Palmer has raffles where you can win free money from dollar scratch-offs. Charles says he sticks to Marquette. His family's from Detroit and I ask where and he says downtown. I tell him we lived in Detroit and he asks where and I say Ferndale and Rochester Hills and a bit in Garden City but I was too young to remember it although that's a lie. I tell him to take care and I ask Bobbie who she came with and she says Peggy and I say, "Didjou drive?" She says no Peggy did and I say, "Didn't she leave awhile ago?" but Bobbie blows me off. Finally I just go "oh burn in hell" but not out loud, mostly to myself. I go to give a kiss but she pulls away so I whisper, "What's wrong?" Looking mad, she goes, "Not in public," but gives a wink just to confuse me and rip my heart and get me excited and it's like she has a chain around me and can tug at will like she's Pinhead and I'm a *Hellraiser* cenobite. Then I leave her with Charles.

J talks with the KKK bastard and I can't believe J's talking with the KKK bastard, but J's like that. He likes convicts and losers and mutes. He reminds me of Christ. J talks with this drunk that hangs out in front of Citgo and he acts like he's their buddy, but when he walks away, J goes, "You see him? I'll never be like that." But that doesn't remind me of Christ. They're nice to J 'cause, you know, I don't know if I told you, but J's got . . . not multiple personalities, but, what is it? It's like multiple scoliosis. Multiple some shit. His back's messed up and he walks bad, but J's cool. He's one of those guys that, even if it's his last pinch of Skoal, he'll give you half. Nobody's cooler. Except maybe Hollow. And my cousin Roy in Hell, and "Vagina Breath" Thompson. J's a regular goddamn Lloyd Dobler. Christ, I hate when Bobbie squawks about John Cusack's heart shaped fricking face. If I could, I'd rake it with a tractor and see how many lead roles he could play other than starring with Cher in Elephant Man II.

One time I called J a cripple. I was young, like fourteen, and he, umm, he kicked my ass. I wasn't as big then 'cause I'd pulverize him now so hard he'd really have something to stutter about. I'm thinking about steroids too. 'Cause I'm not insane enough, like these other U.P. guys, and that'll even things out. Like Danzig's a midget, but he's on steroids so that makes him a huge midget. And what's another drug to Glenn? He tosses it in the morning cocaine pile. Plus he sold his soul to Satan and that helps you win fights, and get groupies.

I go back and Scrabble won't look at me 'cause I talked to the black guy so we wander away from each other which is good 'cause I'm about to unleash the wrath on that KKK kocksucker. From the other side of the fire, I hear J laugh with KKK, probably exchanging tips on forehead tattooing, and I see Charles' arm around Bobbie and he gives her a two finger neck massage like her neck's a clitoris so I chug Miller High Life so I can feel some of that high life and U.E.'s friend Matt Cort shows up and there's about enough tension here now to explode half the goddamn world in two. Antony was winding down from being a hair arsonist, but he got his second wind hopping around like a rabbit on speed and that's the only way to describe it. You can tell he wishes the sling was off, which I thought it was but I guess not, so he could throw blows and Cort goes over to Bobbie, my Bobbie, and Bobbie's still laughing, playing into this, like she wants me to fight, begging me to kill. Although it hasn't happened in a long time, like since Jack the Ripper and stuff, but people freak when they report news about serial killer sprees, when I'm surprised it doesn't happen daily.

Since I'm not pounding faces, I pound beers. Which isn't smart. The smart thing would be to sober up, get ready to brawl. Seventy-two percent of fights are won by the person most sober. But I want to kill it, every brain cell. 'Cause when I hate life, I drink. I don't know what the rest of the world does. Then I puke. It's quick, unexpected, and Hollow's like, "Cräig, that was hilarious." Now I have to pound the brews to make up for wasting good buzz juice and 'cause it's getting late. They want to put out the fire—before I've lost consciousness, and I'm not going to allow that to happen, so I punch a hole in the side of a Bud with a car key and put the hole to my mouth and squeeze. That's a U.P. martini. Some people drink in gulps, but if you learn to open your throat, you can down a beer in eight seconds flat. I learned that from our nose guard. All the guys start pissing on the bonfire, and I don't think there's been a more impressive painting drawn and hung up in the Kremlin than that sight of ten cocks pointed at those rising red-yellow flames. God knows, every one of us Red, White, and Blue bastards have streams coming out of us like human fire hoses. But it's not working 'cause the fire is gaining and has worked itself up all night and therefore and hence and whatnot and Vagina Breath kicks one of the logs. Taking a leap, he boots it and jumps back out of the fire and this gets a nice crowd response, especially with the flames kicking up, crackling, reaching for him. I think to myself in my drunkenness that Bobbie blows me off 'cause I'm not psycho enough so I jump in the fire too. As Metallica says, "Jump in the fi-yah!" I take my time jumping back out and this gets hoots and hollers out of everyone except Cort and they yell "Cräig." So I yell, "We shall die!" Then I go to Hollow, "Man, that's hot," and notice one of my shoes smoldering so I kick it in the dirt 'cause there's no need to stop, drop, and roll when Hollow can step right on my foot to help snuff it and with all the piss and turning over of the logs allowing air in to let it breathe and grow the bonfire's getting bigger with burning ashes floating in the air like fireflies landing in Peggy's hair, which serves her right since she wouldn't let Antony light it. Or is that Peggy? I can't tell. Faces blur and I can't think but Antony comes up and I think it's him 'cause he found gas and throws it on quick, on the fire not Peggy, 'cause if he pours it on slow, the gas'll ignite go straight up in the tank and explode in his hands mutilating him for life not just the summer and he won't be able to get laid again 'cause women are only attracted to men who can haul shit, so he jerks the gas on and it poofs and Vagina Breath finds an aerosol can and throws it on and says it will blow up if we all wait, which is what we do, leaning in, nice and close and stupid, and I decide while waiting I might as well walk on fire so I say to Antony, "Watch this," and for no reason he gives me a dirty look but I ignore him and cruise across the fire like Jesus in hell and take my shirt off and flex on the other end and some girl says, "Careful," and she has a great tender voice like a child actress and I want to screw her and I want to screw her voice and I want to put my dick in her hair and I'm about to look for her to tell her this in detail but some idiot yells, "Search and destroy!" 'cause it's the end of the night and I wish it was the end of the world so something could happen, give this dead night energy, but the idiot doesn't know Metallica 'cause it's "Seek and Destroy" and this gets me angry so I flex again, yell out, I yell,

124

scream, "Seeeek and destroooy!" I can't find Bobbie and this is what you drink for, so your mind and life can come unhinged and happen and everyone was standing around bored all night waiting and talking and this is the end of the night where it all starts to break apart and it feels nice so I jump in the middle of the burning bonfire again and I'm numb, always numb. I'm always numb. I'm always numb.

Chapter 28: Hollow

Despite it all, despite the vicious-minded American Legion bully pinning me to the La Combe outfield warning track to see how close he can spit near my cheek. Despite the makeup caked pompon socialites who go to the airport drive-in to exchange saliva with that same ignorant jockstrap. Despite the summer days where a five-mile hike through the backwoods to the Ishpeming Cemetery is the only cure for the monotony of the day. Despite it all, I love waking up, a second time, this time at noon, on the last Monday morning school snow day of the year to look out my bedroom window and see the soft way a light snow attaches to a birch, hearing the Rice Krispie crackling of a new log added by my mother to an upstairs chimney fire, and knowing high school is about to end, infinitely, forever and ever, amen.

Despite it all, there are those brief times when you can forget everything, and it feels good.

Chapter 29: Hollow

I wish you could do that with people. I wish when you see something beautiful, when you notice the rare something wonderful, those brief seconds, in life
. . . a window framed snow scene . . . It is like witnessing a flicker of God . . .
Like the Miners' Shack tennis court ice rink reflecting the low sunlight while
nearby the Calvary Baptist Church bells ring . . . I wish you could run home
and talk about it.

I did not realize that until Daniel died. I am trying not to talk about it anymore, him anymore, although I never got to talk about it with anyone.

I wish my parents would go back to normal. I prayed for that last night. And,
like a blessing, God gave me a snow day.

On snow days, my parents shop, go to the Marquette Mall, for hours of sales.
They know not to wake me.

Like them, I vow to spend the day outside of the house. Because in the summer when the house is empty with only me, I hear creaks and birds' wings
flapping in the walls and the bats in our garage rafters, so I turn on the TV to
drown out the sound and get sucked into hours of sitcom laugh track couch sitting. But in the winter, when it is even quieter, no birds, no bats, no creaks, the
TV cannot get loud enough to drown out the silence. So today, I promised—no
Alan Alda womanizing with nurses in Korea, no Tom Hanks walking through
sprinklers while Billy Joel plays, no Martha Quinn interviewing Billy Idol.

No staring into mother's sewing room.

Just enjoy the day.

With the goal of catching the sun setting, I hike toward Negaunee Township,
alone, on the railroad tracks. The tracks are elevated, made for sightseeing. I
know nicks and crannies of these woods that are so stunning photographers

should pay me to escort them. One spot in particular, I love. This bridge that I found. Below, through the railroad pylon cracks, you see the gradual drop-off. At the midpoint it is a straight football field length drop down.

By the time I get there, the sun has set. The woods lean in, around the tracks, like they want to whisper, while my eyes adjust to a world of two colors, the water-like blue hue of the sky and the great black mass of the woods. The tracks are slippery, so I walk alongside in the snow and my feet become painfully cold. Like whistling in a graveyard, I jiggle the change in my pocket to remind myself I could duck out of the woods, find a gas station, make a phone call, get a ride, if needed.

Getting out to the center of the bridge is easy. The night's oncoming air is cool, a slight wind, bringing any sound for miles (the crack of a branch, a whisper), so an oncoming train could be heard from a vast distance. With no sunset to admire, no stars to break my neck to enjoy, just blackened sky, reaching the bridge's midpoint, I look down.

And down.

And down.

To the river below, white, jagged, frozen, its waterfall a series of icicle stalactites, and I envision myself falling, attempting to create that troubled sense of aliveness that is vertigo. It hits my toes.

Nearby is a plank, a carelessly tacked on arrangement of cheap boards added as a safety measure, the only available means of temporary escape if a train comes, catching the person at a point where they couldn't run back safely to either side. So, I step out on it. One foot, then the other, and hear a creak. A lot came to mind—Craig, the front of our house in fall, the Negaunee water tank, my father in a hallway with arms folded, the whitened bottom of the drop, the widening woods all around me somehow at once majestic and demonic. I take another step forward, slow, cautious, like stepping in Lake Superior water, testing, ready to pull back, foot down, another, and another, until I stand, no net, at the boards' edge. My breath picks up and I see its puffs of clouds of life, exhaling cigarette fog, butterfly's wings, a train's exhaust, and I imagine again falling. This time, it hits my entire body, like a high.

I enjoy that, that feeling, a minute, two, three, at the edge of the world.

Then I walk home.

Chapter 30: antony

lately im actually forgettin my arm. like the shit dont hurt. almost. i mean its fragile but i can tie my shoes at least. & i can sleep now cuz i can lie on my side & so i aint thinkin bout killin a cortfuck cuz i can do shit other than obsess bout killin a cortfuck

like i can play galaga at bucks wit hollow now

& go marquette mall where theres this machine you stick your finger in & it predicts your future. i aint lyin, craig stuck his prick in there. put in a quarter & his prick. his fortune was somethin bout "you are a good friend who can be counted upon"

funny ass shit. & thats what i need so i dont keep picturin stabbin a cortfuck in my mind & write rhymes like

> mc antony x, my turn to hold da bat
> bustin out bitches that sit on my lap
> 1 time a motherfucka interrupted my rap
> i say yo, shut your fuckin trap, bitch,
> he did cuz he knew i woulda blew his ass sky high
> coulda put his head between his knees & kissed his ass bye-bye
> cuz when your fuckin wit me, then you fuckin die

yeah, not writin rhymes like that now. calmin the fuck down. lettin bygones be

maybe

i mean, i been carryin a gun. & how forgivin are you when youre carryin a fuckin gun? but one thin ill tell you bout havin that bulge in your jacket—man, you dont pick fights wit no one. shit dont bug you, cuz you jus think, man, i could blow your fuckin head off right now if i wanted to & suddenly the little shit dont matter.

Chapter 31: Cräig

A fun game to play is while watching Oprah, every time someone cries, you and your friends have to take a hit of acid.

But there's no acid up here. I miss Detroit. Where there's so much acid, it's in the rain.

We're left with the number one U.P. drug. Liquor.

Liqueur. Lick-whore. Licker, lick her. Liquor liqourliquor.

Drinking alone is for pussies, and George Thoroughgood. So I grab Antony. He's always in a shitty enough mood to coax into getting blind piss drunk.

And nothing makes you drink harder than having someone to catch up to.

And nothing makes you drink harder than being told not to drink, which my mom said as I walked out the door. Carrying two bottles of J.D. no less.

Before that, earlier, and this is what triggered making sure I got drunk today—Mom comes in. My room.

My low ceiling room.

My room where Hollow walks hunchback.

My room where my mom's hair touches the ceiling.

She says she's concerned.

Christ.

She's concerned twenty-four hours an hour.

I'm so sick of concern.

My dad comes up for parole. My old dad. My birth dad. Comes up for parole. She knows the month, the day, the hour of every hearing. Says she "knows he's getting out this time." Do you have any idea how many times I've heard this?

Well, it's official.

Auntie Susie called from Boulder.

Auntie Susie is the family parasite, a one hundred percent Death Valley of gossip. Auntie Susie knows more about you than you know about you.

And so my mom comes in the room. This is what she says, "He's out." She spits this at me, no warning, nothing. I'm folding warm laundry she poured on my bed and, as if to punish me for finally doing something saintly in this lifetime, to ensure I'll never do another chore again, she follows with, "Did your father ever touch you?"

I stop folding a pair of wrinkled gray-pink underwear. My underwear. My mom washed them with a red shirt, says I did it, but it was her. I'm hard-faced, straight-frowned, cold and distant as hell's South Pole.

"You'd tell me if he ever did," she says, asks. My room is tucked in the basement, a far corner, with a prison cell window—small tight rectangular thick glass much nearer to the ceiling than the floor. My room gets no sunlight. So I set up an old nicked full length mirror, angled it near the cellar sink's larger window, so that sunlight could reflect off it at the only time it makes it into the basement, 5 p.m., when the sun is at its weakest, scraping treetops, to give my room some faint light. And that light is dead on my mother's hair, making it look not like she has a halo, but more like her head is about to burst into flame.

I speak. I say, "No."

Chapter 32: antony

pops has guns. a few guns

    like sadler, pops was in vietnam. he calls it vietnam, hates when fucks call it 'nam' cuz its not called nam. thats people actin cool. pops said vietnam was easy. he said "a piece a cake." he said people who sob bout it are babies who should shut the fuck up. that people need to die. its called honor. pops is a tough fuck. he dont talk wit me bout nothin. jus grunts, in empty rooms, the basement, the pantry, the sauna. so when he does talk, i listen like a tape recorder. pops has a rock face, like from mount rushmore. chiseled. he does 1000 situps every mornin & craig slept over one night & woke to gruntin & got in this annoyin giggle mood cuz situps sound like sex

    pops is laid back & angry at the same time if you know what i mean. when hes in a good mood, like after a piston win & some straight scotch, he messes up my hair & i push him away

    downstairs, boxes overflow wit stuff like his badges wit 88th on em. that numbers on everythin. vietnam dusty ribbons rainbowed up wit cheap tiny stars. i found his letters to ma. so faded you cant hardly read em. i snuck down there to figure out what goes on in pops head but his head is full of weather. in his letters he talks about rice swamp rain drizzle mud humid heat sweat more mud rain missin ma & cats & dogs. vietnam was weather and food—chocolate chip cookies & canteens of kool-aid are in bout all his letters. no 'sincerely' or 'love' at the bottom. jus every once in awhile a 'be home soon.' on mistake i ripped a letter so i put it back bein all museum piece careful & found a photo. pops face back then was like a tan kid. he smiled, in vietnam. hes here & dont smile, but back there, where life was easy, a piece a cake, he smiled like someone jus told a great dirty joke

pops has guns

guns are a michigan thin. detroit or u.p., everyone got em. we even get off school for the openin of deer season. playin war as a kid in my backyard, id hear gunshots, real ones, & never think nothin of it, jus hunters, & go back to usin my finger as a gun. you dont hear bout breakin & enterin up here cuz to break in someones house you gotta be suicidal

pops got one in the basement locked up. sometime, when hes nervous, when my sisters are gone to their pussy lingerie sleepover cuddle parties, he puts one under the couch in the rec room, almost like hes hintin for me to take it, so i did. & since ive had it, its been easier to take shit from my sisters, pattin that thin in my pocket

tanya & tracy

i woulda told you bout em already but theres nada to tell. ma lovingly calls em t.n.t. & i lovingly call em "tweedle-dum & tweedle-cunthead." i stay out their way & they stay the fuck out mine. tanya wants to be a lawyer & tracy wants to be a dentist—two lousiest professions on the fuckin face of the earth. they spend years of their life in the bathroom takin sissy dumps & teasin their hair like valley pinup girl fuckups. at the dinner table they say, "antony, what you want to be when you grow up?" while stuffin burnt hash browns down their throat & i say, "a nigger," & they make this ugly "tch" sound wit their bitch tongues & ma drops her fork on the table & my sisters drop their hair curlers on the table & all of em shoot me a dirty tilt-head-to-side look shakin their chick heads & i bus a quick rap: "whos pooh? i dunno bro yo tiggas a nigga clock money like honeys my pocket get bigga now what da fuck do you figga?" they dont even know what that shit mean. all ma says is, "watch the language, watch the language." thats what i do. i watch the language! clock it mock it like hancock i rock it so don't knock it. bitches dont understand—im a lyrical gangsta. moerfucks dont know talent. moerfucks talk bout cloooooothes & shit. colors they like & shit. catalogues that came in & shit. blouses, outfits, holly hobbie lunch boxes, goddamn care bear pillow cases. cute shooooes, & all that painful strawberry shortcake shit. dont even listen, when i drop knowledge wit a capital K. i said i wanna be a nigger cuz i do. shits true. more i listen to Cube, more i live life, more i want to be Black

Am Black

fu-uck bein white—watchin confusin skate-in-every-direction hockey, get-tin hand cramps from playin ikari warriors at bucks party store, eatin beef-n-cheddar sandwiches at beef-a-roo (barf-n-chew). sittin aroun all day doin jack. man, fuck that. fuck that. fuck that, fuck that. like fresh prince said—moer-fucks jus dont understand

i love black women wit a passion. the ones in the heavy d & rakim videos, those are women. no heehaw square dance straw mouth horseshit. they move. aint talkin weird freak shit craigs into cuz he got problems. he pissed at my house & the door was cracked & i glimpsed him wipin his dick like most folk wipe their ass, gonorrhea drip shit nasty. nigga got porn mags drawer hidden & i mean this is one woodshop moerfuck cuz he got the dopest secret passage shit ever & i aint into porn cuz the porn i seen is white chicks lookin like sluts, in a bad way, like sick sluts, pneumonia drippin out their noses & aids infested arms & shit. i look at porn mags & im like fuckin aids, man, drippin off the page, ya know, they all got fuckin aids & they wanna give it to you bad cuz they hate men, man, & they give you aids & fuck that shit

craig tells me to dial this porn number. he was like, "its free. totally." he was gettin sex-ual-ly agit-a-ted so i was like calm the fuck down man cuz its like you tryin to fag me & shit, cuz im the only nigga in this room & shit & he was like, "youre white." i was like let me see this shit & yanked the shit out his hand & he was like "be careful," like it was a Bible or some shit. i look round & saw this 900-TEEN shit & was like, "craig, pleeease dont tell me youre a pedophile cuz i will report your ass. serious. they arrest you for life & kill you in prison." he was like no & said that shits wack so i was like thank God cuz thats sick ass 80-year-old-in-toys-r-us shit & he showed me this photo of this perfect chick to him & perfection to him is a 35-year-old wit small tits so i was like good cuz i was glad the slut was older than 16. then there was more of this sick shit wit a girl probably 17 wit TEEN PUSSY written cross her chest in sloppy paint & legs spread & smilin! i was like, "how much cocaine does it take to get a bitch to do that?" & for the first time in my life i worried bout my sisters, who i usu-ally give a fuck less bout, but let me tell you if this shit ever happens to them ill hunt down the camerafuck & slit his throat from neck to bellybutton. ill jump rope wit his intestines. eat his eyes. then i started worryin bout craig. & all this worrying was new to me cuz normally i dont worry bout no one but me. but craig had granny porn & i was set to power barf & punt that mag cuz 3 old dykes were dykin it dutch-style all complicated & i mean they were old like king cole, but then i saw 'Hot Black Sluts' & was like, "dial this." i was like, "i aint into that slut part, but dial that." craigs like, "you like black pussy?" i was like, "black women are beautiful." he laughed, sayin "grace slick." i was like, "you dont know what youre talkin bout, man, you never seen the 'nuttin but love' video." he was like, "what?" & im like, "heavy d." he goes, "the fat guy? aint he fat?" im like, "no, he got these chicks who are not fat, jus dial the fuckin number," cuz im like "i aint dialin shit." so he does. 800-666-4188. craigs got it pressed to his ear & mouth a bit too hard, like he tryin to shove the phone in his face holes & im like "nigga, gimme the fuckin phone." he does & this chick comes on & talks in this fake exaggeration of bein black & i think it was a white chick actin black if that aint a fuckin crock & tribal drums were in the background & everythings a big minstrel show offensive wack weak hoax horseshit. im thinkin, "& fags jack to this?" i throw the phone at craig & he listens & then its done & borin so i get up antsy, grab his dirty packer football & throw it off the wall & hes callin more numbers. im like, "lets do somethin" but he goes "lets make stuff up" & dials 800-OLD-FUCK & 800-DOG-COCK & hes laughin cuz it ends up bein lawyer offices in chicago & real estate offices in zilwaukee & hes like "dont these people know they have 800-HOT-PONY as their office number?" hes so into it, i toss the ball hard gainst the wall & its a football not a baseball so it ricochets in crazy ass directions & thats the fun part, knockin shit over. he dont care cuz hes into his porn phone so i wind up & let the football fly knockin over a pile of stacked tapes & its all metal crap wit group names like death & leprosy & im not makin this shit up. im like, "does a nigger really wanna listen to the sounds of leprosy for a fuckin hour?" craigs not listenin cuz hes faggin out & he got this other band named helloween & im laughin like, "people buy this shit? helloween? thats pathetic." he gets pissed yellin not to touch his tapes if i dont like em & jams the phone back in his ear hole. then his pops thankgodfully rolls up the driveway & craig slams down the phone all rushed like we were plottin to pipe bomb australia or some shit. craig whispers "you know 800-CUNTS-4-U is columbia pictures in hollywood?" im like "man, who are these chicks?" cuz im holdin his poison look what the cat dragged in tape & im like, "man, the cat dragged in some ugly fuckin bitches"

& he snatches it out of my hand goin, "thats the band" & i go "they transves-tites?" cuz i want to push him farther cuz im bored & cuz craigs easy to push over the edge & cuz his shit sucks worse than new kids on the block & he needs to know it. this is a good education for him, better than ishpeming high school anyway. under his breath craig goes, "better than that nigger shit" but he dont say it loud enough for me to bother acknowledgin but im surprised cuz he never uses the n- word, not round me, & then to piss me off he puts in the fuckin poi-son tape like i want to listen to that fingernail chalkboard shit & the songs called "cry tough." if that aint the worst song title in the history of music includin the seventies then i dont know what the fuck is. he cranks it. "cry tough" cranked. unnecessary. i go "why you listen to this shit?" he goes "cuz listen to this gui-tar part." im like it sounds like hes tweedlin. im listenin & craigs on his bed in the buddha position lookin like this is impressive music & he looks pathetic & goes, "they actually play their instruments." i go, "why you listen to this shit?" & he blows up, "cuz it fuckin rocks, jonestown!" im like, " fuck that, that shits shit." he goes, "so is your mom." i act cool, right? like aint no problem, but he knows i hate that mom shit. he knows this, so i nice & spastic throw the foot-ball gainst the wall & it bounces off bout every fuckin possession in the room, knockin over a lamp & hittin his boom box so the song cuts off, like i broke it, but the song kicks in again & real comical he pops up pissed bout to hit me, fist clenched leanin in. even injured i would murder his slow weightliftin fatass & he knows we cant come down to fisticuffs. thats craigs favorite word—fist-icuffs. & the dickhead tackles me. i bang my spine gainst his dresser, ricochet into the wall nailin my shoulder snap into the lightswitch & its like a bolt of lightnin—what did you say?—a bolt of lightnin & i know this is bad bad bad, but bite my lip so i dont show it. dickheads head is in my gut grunt-laughin. my body goes limp & he steps back, & his pops comes in. his pops is like "ya, eh, boys? whats wit da noise, eh?" & craigs like, "nothin," real punk-like, like his dads a asshole which hes not. his pops bout the coolest pops on the penin-sula. his dad goes, "duzn antony have the, uh, arm there? huh? jus out da cast there, eh?" & craigs like, "yeah," & his dad goes, "well, then no rough-housin wit da boy in da howse, eh. dis aint the bowery boys." craigs pops dont make sense. he uses terms like "shucks," words that died years ago. or worse, finn slang craig has to translate for me. i cradle my arm so his pops goes, "hows dee ol arm there, poika?" 'poika' is finnish for boy. & i wanna laugh in the old mans face cuz hes this old finn from like the 1840s & shit & he got a chew in & he got the old milwaukee gut & hobbles wit a bum knee from when the car jack fell out from his friends van & he wasnt even workin on it, jus close by & the van didnt fall on him, jus sideswiped his knee good & vicious & he still limps to this day & like craig says you go down to new mexico & theres a lot of people wit birth defects like six fingers & missin teeth cuz thats where they drop the bombs & you come up to the UP & thats where everybody limps cuz thats where they drop the vans. half this citys old people hobble like movie zombies on a brain hunt

but craigs old man got this cheery old demeanor & skoal lip bulge & deep set eyes like a mongoloid who could really actually give a fuck bout me & my shoulder & plus his whole body is mangled so you feel sorry for him & under-stand why he feels sorry for me. all i say is "it was my shoulder, mr. koskey," cuz his pops goes by mister. no bob shit wit him. its all mister & miss wit that old fucktooth finn so i give him what he wants. i still trip he dont have the same last name as craig, but that how that stepdad shit works. craig wants to change his name but hes lazy & dont want to deal wit the paperwork. his real pops a loser but i wouldnt say that to craig. his good old finn pops spits in a mountain dew can in his hand & leaves wit a grunt & a nod of the head. wit his dad gone i finally allow pain to come on my face but try not to give out enough for craig to see cuz that fuckhead likes it when people hurt & plus im sick of lettin dis-comfort get to me. but all im thinkin is this thin is never gonna fuckin heal, not wit idiots like criag & cortfuck round, so to move my mind off the subject, i go, "your old mans a trip." craig clenches his teeth cuz he hates that conversa-tion. "a fuckin trip," i say & its like i went too far cuz he goes, "hes a good guy" & im like, "i know hes a good guy, craig, thats what im sayin" & craig goes, "lets get outta here" & we do & thats good cuz he turns off poison which is the perfect name for that band. in fact the only more fittin name for em would be Four Gays Wit Three Chords. the song he cuts off is this horrible other ballad & im like, "thats not even heavy metal." craig goes "they do ballads too" & says it real proud like this shows the group is multi-talented & i let it go cuz theres such thin as bein too easy a target. we leave & his dads feet up sprawled out on his la-z-boy wit the tv6 news on & that carl pellonpaa freak dronin bout a dc-10 crash on full blast like his dads half-deaf which is a possibility from the mines but if i remember he dont work in the mines & his reclinin pop gives another "eagh" & a head nod & snuff spit stains dot his shirt & then were gone

theres only one thin to do now, to feel better. get the real aspirin—beer. n theres only one place to get it—jacks

we had 2 buyers. summerteeth was 1. summerteeth was the man cuz he lives by citgo & its like stop by & 3 minutes & 5 seconds later you got a 40 of pabst blue. we timed that shit. we were like, summer, if i got a p.b.r. 40 in my hand within 5 minutes, well get you a 12er of anythin you want. moerfuck bought beast. milwaukees finest urine. piss ass sludge. hell, ol boy did it in just over 3. we woulda bought him expensive belgian swill but the dumbass dont know shit bout beer. or life. jus guzzles the shit like its fuckin syrup on a cannuck pancake. one time u.e. & Tack Toe wanted ta get lickwhored up so they go to summertees but summer jus got a d.u.i. he got like 3 already, ridiculous amount, & this bonehead has so much community service he dont have time for a regular job so this rockheads stealing food & shit & gettin into petty thief shit & theyre catchin him cuz this is a small town wit cops wit nothin to do but theyre lettin him go wit these heavy warnings cuz the guys got like food stuffed down his pants from the i.g.a. & they tell him theyll give him free canned food from the salvation army box if the cocksmoker wont steal so hes like ok, cuz summer aint a bad guy, jus dumb, jus a hard core finn alky which is really the same word—finn, alky, alky, finn. what the fuck ever. so u.e. & Toe go to his house & summers like he cant do it, but they aint gonna hear that & theyre pissed & Toe's got pure anger streaks in his ass cuz his pops beat him daily since he was a zygote. no exaggeration

craig witnessed the beatings firsthand, how T Tack Toe would walk in & his pops would attack his ass, cuff him wit a love tap from his fist & the moerfuck got hard but that shit work cuz old boy went from lowlife camp palmer shit-for-future to u.s. flag-wavin Olympic boxin hero pimp boy in no time flat. only 2 whiteboyz on the whole fuckin team—me & Toe. all these dope thick ass niggaz trained from D-town who are pure gangland chicago west side born kedzie housin project straight up moerfuckin brawlers, then Toe comes bouncin in. Tack's a trip cuz, man, when we was trainin at n.m.u.s Olympic Center & all them niggas was like, "T Tack Toe's the man," you know, like he was fuckin david letterman & famous & heroic & shit. like me, motherfucker

but T Tack Toe wasnt hearin "no beer" from summertee so he went off like his pops & punched summerteeth in the fuckin teeth. & summers old, man, his teeth are old, you know, got rings like tree trunks, & hes weak like a fuckin pothead, empty lung-ed & no fight in his bones & goes down. now T Tack Toe has no control of his mind or body or nothin so he kicks summer in the chin & rumors that thats what did it. that summertee coulda understood a punch to the gut, but kickin a man, a fuckin buyer, when hes down, & in the teeth, when his teeth are jus waitin patiently to fall the fuck out, that shit aint cool. so blood-mouthed summerteeth vowed hed never buy again & half the city, everyone under 21, was pissed at T Tack Toe. see, thing is, summerteeths an alky & hes hardcore nothin but Unemployment Checks For Life, but that moerfuck keep a promise. cuz he wont buy shit for no one now. & i mean no one

now its all on jack

i mean moerfucks all got their own buyers they had to find outta the wood-work, like j has his dad when hes in town & hollow got his baseball coach for us, mr. lehtinen. & craig got jack

jack got 6 brats, sometimes 7 or 8 when his sister throws her kids his way & he takes em like a u.p. orphanage. they all got different moms & dads. its con-fusin calculus complicated shit to figure out who the fuck is whose pops at that house. the youngest, toivo (which is a finn name that means "anus"), is from jack & his first ex-wife who we call "sludgefest," for obvious reasons, i mean jus look at her. the next youngest, swee pea, is a urinatin bitch & shes from jack & his current wife whose real cool so we call her "cool-ass sludgefest." the next kid is from some cat drug dealer (the dad robs vet clinics) & jacks current wife. i told you shits complicated. then the oldest is from jack & some chick he banged named denise. jacks 24. but he looks 42. he was gettin scouted by the spartans for noseguard in high school, but then started fuckin. didnt realize condoms are Gods gift to man. jack loves to fuck. & eat. fuck & eat. eatin fuck. him & his wife are in a competition to see who can weigh 400 pounds first. its a close race. combined they weigh over 500. throw in the kids & you got 1000 pounds of family. jacks real name is amos, but he hates amos cuz it rhymes wit too many swear words, so we call him jack, cuz were like, man why dont you jus jack instead of pumpin out the kids? its like he wants to ensure a life of poverty. hes succeedin like a motherfuck

craig says he has the plan how we escape jacks life. craig says hes gettin a filthy rich chick pregnant. right. he jus gonna fuck someone filthy. & for two, craig says hes gonna make it so that his t.v. is hooked to a conveyer belt & for his wife to watch as the world explodes soap bullshit, shes gonna have to get her heart rate up to 360

we go over jacks. the door is off the door & on the ground. craig bends over & knocks on the floor. no answer so we step over the door & walk in, past the kitchen. flies rub their greedy hands together on the counter & a dog roams round. jack dont even have a dog, jus kids, which is enough, & the dog goes down a hallway tail waggin. out comes tony, one of the jack army. he crawls out the woodwork & there he is quiet as a pissed off mime wit his pre-school head & pint size hockey player face, & were like "wheres jack? wheres your pops?" the tike dont say a thin & were like, "he gonna be in soon?" tony shakes his minia- ture jack head 'yup' so we sit on the couch & a squeak-toy squeaks. craig pulls it out his ass & throws it in an empty broken crib that was built round the time betsy ross was drawing flags & its propped gainst the wall next to a fan thats slowly goin back & forth & back like the most borin appliance ever invented & tony—whose not named after me but after jacks grandpa who was u.p. famous for his fifth of vodka breakfasts—stands there toothless from a recent accident, which i think means hell always be missin those teeth, but hes still chipper from the mishap called life. fuckin kid knocks out teeth quicker than they grow, a regular midget version of summerteeth makin me wonder if jacks truly the father. craigs nerfs still in hand so i go, "hey tony" cuz he looks like he wants to play & im good wit kids so i throw it. the ball bounces off tonys head. craig laughs & tony giggles like a freak & this makes craig laugh louder. the football rolls over by craigs foot so he goes, "hey" & throws it at tonys head before he even has a chance to turn & it ricochets into a corner. i look at craig to get up but his lazy ass aint goin nowhere, so craig looks at the ball, then at me & says "get it" & im like fuck that & fuck you. then jus like tennis, tony becomes our ball boy. he gets the football & places it in my hand. tony goes back to the cen- ter of the room wit his hands at his sides, all straight, waitin for us to throw it at him again, eyes closed. so wit my girlie left hand i underhand it. hits him in the shoulder & bounces back, so i do it again. tony giggles but not as loud as the 1st time & gives it to craig. craig cocks back & rifles it causin tonys head to snap & the kid bawls like he jus found out that pain exists in the world & that theres no santa which theres not. im like, "fuckface, what you do that for?" craig gets up sayin, "it was gettin old." he goes to the cabinets & i go to the freezer to grab a chunk of ice to put on my shoulder. "whatre you doin?" craig asks in the biggest i-dont-give-a-fuck way imaginable. "hey!" he says spottin the jack daniels that was a Christmas present to jack cuz jack loves jack but thats not how he got his nickname & its only ¼ drank so craig grabs it so i get the cue & go to the fridge & one-handed grab all the anheuser i can grinch & walk out wit the kid wailin & craig says all friendly, "tell your pops we borrowed some stuff." i add, "well return the returnables"

we drive home

i put a cold beer on my shoulder, wincin, figurin im gonna have to go back to the fuckin doc. craig goes, "X, man, if i hurt your arm at the house or some-thin . . ." & then jack passes in his chevy wit the keyed sides & fender barely hangin on & to top things off, his car dont lock anymore so he drilled a hole in the car door & put a bike padlock through. we flip him off drivin by & he rec-ognizes the finger but not the face

ha!

we get to craigs house, a real slapped together worn wood gray chipped paint two story that got so many slivers stickin out it youd think it was designed to keep the tweezer industry in business. we go in but craigs parents are full plate-toss ragin. i mean craigs mom knows how to hate like no other. she got this face wit wrinkles so sharp its like she has the expression on her face that shes had most of her life permanently ingrained there & the world can see her main emotion has been one of worry & shes in the middle of wide-mouthed bitch-fumin. its all onesided in that hellhouse of a hell of a house. its the mother that wears the pants & the shirts & socks & shoes & the frowns in that fam-ily. craigs pops has bout as much fight in him as a nap-addicted senior citizen so we expect him to jus be takin the abuse, quiet as a titmouse. if it was me, id kill the bitch. we round the corner expectin him to be couch-slouched cowerin but the house is empty as ishpeming high at midnight except for craigs moer-fuckin psycho bitch ma ravin in her alcoholic voice to thin air. its funny but you can tell someones a recoverin alky jus from their voice alone. sometimes you need the extra clue of lookin at their face too, but normally all you need is the voice and youre like, "yup that's one a.a. bitch."

"you know the rules!" shes howlin & shes got a saw in her hands, a fuckin saw. like the type youd see a hillbilly play in some shitass heehaw jugs band. but more an instrument of death than a instrument of country music cuz the fuckin things got teeth, no joke, dagger sharp, & why the fuck this is in her hands i have no idea. now recoverin alkie freaks have jittery hands & virginia slims always jammed between their gums & craigs ma is no exception to this rule, hands jitterin like they should be in an earthquake museum. good God, put down the saw!

every once in awhile she cracks down on "no beer in the house," usually when shes mad bout somethin else. earlier craig asked her to buy & she said no. actually she said a lot more than no but long story short, craig told her wed get our own buyer. no harm done

then craigs pops comes home, all work drained, unsuspectin, wantin to put his feet up, rest his tootsies, get a bud out the fridge & football it up on c.b.s. craigs ma sees the beer & the rest is domestic disturbance history. she chased him out and now hes at the congress downin beer after beer after beer after beer jus to show her he can do what he wants

craig motions with his head to the door like, "lets go." but, corner of her eye, the old bat sees us. & worse, sees us haulin Jack Dee under our arms. she gets all hysterical, "you see what youre doing! your son is bringin beer in the house!" & we run. like benny hill. hootin & hollerin, "wa-hooooooo!" craig unleashes a yell of "Jackie Deeeee! & his ee turns into an arrrghh! & were back in the car, laughin, squealin out, on the run, fists bangin on the dash in glee, outlaw gangsta fugitive dork homeboy bad-ass mad-ass cuntheads & best friends & fuck off world & fuck the world & "world, fuck off"

we get to my house

my house is a pink shuttered nightmare

my house is a raggedy ann & andy invasion

my house is decorated, redecorated, & re-redecorated by my ma & my sisters like its one big doll house but with the added shit bonus that i gotta live in the fucker

& my house is the same as craigs. parents in the middle of world war four over a fuckin snow blower or some shit

the snow blowers broken

some shit

its my pops fault

some shit like that

stupid ass shit

Marriage Is Hell

Hell Is Marriage

but my parents dont have the guts to scream in each others face, tell each other to fuck off. instead they get silent. they vanish to attics & basements & suddenly have projects & skip meals & play mind games & act like librarians with mental problems, real elementary school retard behavior that i hate & ignore & jus step right the fuck over wit frowns & no eye contact

we get in & stillness reigns like evil owns the house. a clock ticks. thats it. this clock. like a bomb beggin to go off. like the clock speaks, "ticked-off ticked-off ticked-off." we go straight to my room, spy-carryin the liquor shoved underarm, get to my room & each of us has a fifth to swig but we open jus one & share, buddy style. one gulp two gulp three gulp four. back & forth. i wanna put on "If It Aint Ruff It Aint Me" cuz itd fit the mood perfect but itd ruin the mood cuz craigd bitch like his ma so i jus keep it silent. craig goes to my window, tugs a couple times til it opens & a harsh cold bolts in. "what you doin, man?"

he dont answer, jus puts his hand on the ledge right in the snow. "hit my thumb. when we were runnin."

"on what?"

he dont answer. theres no clock in my room. i take a swig, pass it, & he swigs, lookin out the window. & if we didnt let the silence in, nothin would matter, but now we hear it, the silence, & were both thinkin & thats not good, cuz its sad thoughts, cancer thoughts, prison scarecrow razor thoughts, so i cover by spewin out whatevers in my head before my room turns into some kind of weepy sorrow feeling bad about our lives horse pussy shit & i didnt even know it was in my head but it was. i say, "we gotta do somethin. to cort." i wonder where the 'we' came from but its there and its waitin

craig says yeah, quick, real quick, too quick, yeah, but he looks at me & hes buzzin i can tell, but hes serious which goes hand in hand wit drunk for him which is a reason i dont drink wit him a lot, cuz he gets too serious. but he follows wit, "we should do somethin. big."

craig finishes another long swig, the first time one of us has taken two in a row, & he broke the pattern, & his eyebrows are low & corrupt & his eyes are all red & screamin & he says yeah, he says hellfuck yeah

he puts down the bottle & without saying bye, leaves

he does that all the time drinkin, jus leaves, jus gets in his own bizarre head & wanders off, usually to puke. hell be back. he always is. probably wit his gut nice & empty, fresh puke-breath, ready to drink more. i hear the front door close

the window is open. i feel the cold on my feet. a breeze, frigid, creeps along the floor, sneakin in the room. i go to my bed, lie down, waitin for craig to return & in the meantime i let the chill come

Chapter 33: Hollow

This is how life works. You are bored, exhausted, thinking nothing is going to happen. And then, it does. It is quick, but it does.

Craig should tell this story, but he never would—unless he was drunk. And then, he would slur half his words. Trust me, it is better if I tell it.

I did not do anything all night except watch *Saturday Night Live*. I guess Gilda Radner died, because Steve Martin was near tears during his monologue and they played a clip with her and him not being funny. And, you have to work hard to make Steve Martin unfunny. The women on that show never make me laugh. I said that and Shelley punched me in the thigh. I said, "What? Victoria Jackson? Come on!" Shelley's head was in my lap, the faint sweet smell of shampoo. I kept staring at her hair, each follicle turning from blonde to black the closer it ran to the roots, tracing with my eyes, and feeling a sorrow, a hollow sick vacant rip, but not in my soul, in my heart, but not in my heart, somewhere. She caught me in the reflection of the TV. "What are you looking at?" She rolled over, looked into me. You never have to ask a woman if she is in love with you. You can see it in her eyes.

She is.

Shelley is.

I felt nothing. I should have told her from the beginning, but how would you word that. My parents needed me to have a girlfriend. We needed another person in the house, a fourth body.

While Gilda danced, Shelley cuddled deeper.

Shelley's grandmother died last June, old age. We bonded off that when I first met her, parallel deaths, compatible feelings. Shelley melded in, with my house, the still stillness, like we lived in Koskey Funeral Home. Shelley is so gentle she could fit in anywhere, even at a funeral home, even here. And, here we are, the volume low, the whole continual feel in the house of whispered eulogies—even when watching comedy.

Hans and Frans reminded me of Craig. After the first hour, which happens every week, the show stops making sense, gets artsy, so I shut my eyes. Shelley tiptoed out, driving home, down the coldest streets in America, past houses of hibernating children, fathers drinking, mothers dying inside. And then, the show went from the SNL cast waving and showing their latest shirt slogans to the waving US flag Pledge of Allegiance lullaby. The station turned to snow echoing the world outside. Early May in the U.P., the last hanging remnants of winter.

The static put me to sleep. It was a good sleep too—a good summer sleep where you do not remember a single dream and the air is not too humid or bitter, just cool with my window cracked, a rarity in the Upper Peninsula at night, but our wood fire was blaring. I could hear its pipes along with the Koiranen's dog barking next-door. I had the floating sensation right before you nod off where you feel bigger than your body. And, lastly, deep deep sleep . . . Ruined by a tapping on glass and muffled voice.

I thought it was Gilda Radner at the window.

"Hollow," whispers a voice, "Hollow."

I pretend to be asleep. The knocks on the window become heavier. I have the feeling the glass will break. My squinting eyes see Craig. In all honesty, I am one of the only strong points in his life—one of the few solid figures. I roll over. He breaks the screen. I flick on the light. "Craig, what are you doing?"

"Sorry, sorry," he repeats. Seeing my pillow hairdo, he laughs.

I shush him. He tears off the remaining screen. Pushing his face, I tell him to "go around front." Saliva is on my hand. The last screen is dangling, mangled. My dad will kill if he sees this. I look at Craig as seriously as I can, deadly serious, begging, "please."

"I can take it off carefully," he says. It falls into his hands like a woman would. He tosses it to the side and climbs into the room. Upstairs, a toilet flushes. Both of us freeze. This is my father's way of letting me know he has heard us. Craig has this blank look—eerie in the light. A cool, steady air streams over my arms. On Craig's arms, blood. He has blood smeared over his shirt and his chin. I tell him and he says he knows. He looks down and says it looks cool.

"Does it hurt?" He looks around my room as if he has never been here before, which is not the case at all. I say, "You need to wash?"

He has a coughing fit. Through the hacking, he tells his story: Apparently he was at Antony's drinking, left Antony's to bring his parents' car home, walked a good half hour back to Antony's, then they went to Hickey's through the back door; they knew the bartender. Matt Cort is off in a corner table facing the bar. Cort talks loudly, trying to draw a crowd, but it is not working. Except with Craig who cannot keep his eyes off him. Nathan Holmberg wobbles up. Nathan is a jerk, but he is Antony's neighbor, so Antony talks with him. Craig cannot hear a word. Nathan is one of those types who never knows what is going on; he tried killing himself years ago by jumping off the bluff near the water tower, but he did not jump from high enough and landed in ferns. He only bruised his tailbone and in class he would have to sit gently as helium. Nathan has crutches under his arms, probably from another suicide attempt. He tells Antony to go over to his table. And who is Nathan there with? Matt Cort. Antony still says, "Sure." Like he was looking for a fight, even with his sling still on. They follow behind Nathan who is drunk on crutches and bumping into people to ensure everyone in the town will hate him more than anyone, even Cort. U.E. sits to Cort's left. They both see Craig and Antony walk up. The beer-soaked wooden table is the only thing stopping fists from flying.

Craig tells me this jittery voiced and every once in awhile looks out the window, scanning the night. Without saying anything to Craig, I kill the light. "Good idea," Craig says and adds, "I am in trouble, man oh man I am in trouble."

I say, "Why?"

"I pulled it out," Craig says.

"What?"

"I whipped it down, my zipper. And pulled it out, you know, it."

Craig is getting blood on my bed. I keep worrying about Craig getting blood on my bed.

He continues, "Cort and U.E. put their hands over their eyes, you know, not realizing I have a bit of stage fright. I didn't pull it out to be a perv. I pulled it out to piss all over Matt Cort's face." Craig laughs, coughs, and stands to act out what happened. Pretending it is in his hand he waves back and forth like he is putting out a fire. "It just streamed. A stream. Carp River. All this beer I downed on the drive over because who can afford Hickey's prices? Then it went nuts." Craig fills in the details with gasps of information. When he gets involved in the story, it feels like he is sober, a real storyteller, but he catches himself and purposefully acts more drunk, to lessen culpability.

The photo-like images give me an idea of the night's events—an arc of urine landing on the table and Cort ducking under the table, U.E. pushing Antony into a pile of pool cues, Antony knocking Nathan over on his crutches, U.E. kicking Antony, Craig trying to piss on U.E. but running low, Cort coming up from under the table, Craig pissing in his pants as the two turn a good fight into a bad wrestling match, clawing faces, gauging eyes. Antony grabs a cue, takes a swing, misses U.E., hits Nathan in the leg. The bartenders swoop in, become bouncers. Then the run-for-your-life of all involved.

If I could use one word to sum up Craig, it would be "running." His nose running or running from the police and even running in his dreams. There are dreams he has told me when drunk, of him running, endlessly, through parking lots and down alleys and in and out of forests, the forests of Ishpeming, with stake, pitchfork, and torch carrying townspeople hunting him down until dawn, until he awakes feeling unrested, agitated, unready to face another day of actual running.

"We split in different directions," Craig says. Antony dodges down Tino's alley, but the cops pull up on Craig bleeding from a sharp piece of wood from the bar's dartboard. They corner Craig and take him in under suspicion, drunk and disorderly. "I let them arrest me," Craig says. On the way to the station, Officer Ramess Stegnowicz says he knows Craig's old man and cannot wait to inform him about his son's behavior. Taunting Craig is never a good idea. Craig tells me as soon as they took the cuffs off he wrestled to escape. With two cops on him in the late night Negaunee cop station, underneath the city post office and public library, Craig put up the fight of his year, a fight the sleepy-eyed graveyard shift cops were not prepared for. Craig told me he was squatting seven hundred easy now and had done nine hundred pound calf raises for thirty reps last Monday. All-State his sophomore year, he is a three-year wrestling letter winner at 184 pounds, although he had problems keeping weight and

struggled in heavier weight classes and has been kicked off the team twice for
chewing. Stegnowicz is a lightweight micro-cop, Gepetto's evil twin; he should
have retired or died last year. Craig dropped to the floor for leverage and kicked
out cop feet like it was a videogame. Craig knocked the wind and the forecast
for the next three days out of Stegner's partner, even punched him in the ear.
Then, he kicked in the trophy case where they had their softball "2nd Place –
U.P. Finals – N.P.D.," broke free, and ran.

Craig stops the story, looks me in the eye and I see a wolf-like intensity there
lit by the moon. I am glad we are related, otherwise I would be afraid of him.
He says he jogged through the woods, the back paths, to get here, listening for
noise. If he heard anything, he dove in the bushes, quieting his breath. Michigan night's woods are known for their noises. But lying there, he could only
hear his breathing, letting dirt go in his mouth and in his wounds. It made him
want to be a Seal. He always thought of the military. "Craig, you are going in
the Marines, right?" Actually I was meeting with the Navy recruiter, and only
meeting with him so not exactly 'in.' He said if I went, he would join too, but
Craig is all talk. Except when he is angry; then, he is all fists. Craig's breathing
was heavy, his eyes darting, like he was still in the woods. Then, he got teary
eyed, which let me know he was still drunk. In between heaves, he said he was
afraid and screwed and sick.

"Again. I am getting arrested, Hollow. Again."

"Maybe."

"That is two now. One more and I am . . ." A toilet flushes again. "Stegner
knows that, he wants me."

"So just be good."

Craig says under his breath, "Ramess is the Devil."

Then Craig said I was his best friend and was always there for him and asked,
"There beer upstairs?" Before I could respond, he asked where the bathroom is,
as if he had never been here before. I pointed, but he kept talking, telling me he
needed to talk tonight, more, to get it out, like Craig was not Craig. Grabbing
me by the jaws, he said, "I love you." He grabbed so it hurt, as if he could only
reveal love if he gave out an equal supply of pain, hovering like he was considering bashing in my face. I did a move I learned in Tae Kwon Do years ago to get out
of a chokehold and Craig collapsed toward me. I pulled away, rubbed my neck.

"I have to tell you everything, man. Everything." Eerie, deranged, beyond the boredom. He held his crotch like he had to pee, but kept talking, "Do you remember when I told you about my dad?"

"Bob?"

"No, my old dad," he goes, "The asshole." Craig walks away, down the hall, to the bathroom.

"Do not flush," I say to an empty room.

Craig told me about his father before, twice. Once, we were in the woods behind my house. We like to walk around until we are lost, buried deep, and try to find our way back. It gives us time to think, see hawks, find unknown rivers. He just opened up, said, "I miss him. I really do." That was all he ever said about it. Until the other time, he was drunk. That time he just gushed, details about his father giving him a tab of LSD with Batman on it when his mother was out of the house, telling Craig, "Time to quit being a kid," and about the two of them going to a Tiger game where Jack Morris pitched a three-hitter but still lost one-to-nothing, even with Willie Hernandez finishing. Craig only tells me about his life when he is drunk. He uses drinking as this allowance to be honest, and insane. Except last time at Thompson's, he did drink eleven beers and he was rolling around in their upstairs bathroom crying and yanking down the Thompson's curtain rods. But there have been times at Miners' when I have caught him pouring out beer. I ask, "Why did you do that?" and he lies, "I saw cops."

I never drink.

In the spring of '79, my brother got in a head-on. The car accordioned.

My brother owned a pick from B.B. King. He bought a feathered hat like Stevie Ray Vaughn, only wore it in the house. He was losing his acne. He was learning harmonica, played "Jingle Bells" and three chord blues. He spun donuts on ice in the Westwood parking lot. He owed me eight bucks.

My father used to take daytime walks with my mother along Teal Lake; they stopped. My father started going on walks at night by himself, trudging through snow with no boots.

My mother had blinds installed, black, thick so no light could touch her. My father told me not to turn on their bedroom light. My mother slept curled up, entire days. Opening the bedroom door as slightly as possible, my father would bring her bowls of chicken soup, split pea with ham, IGA Mackinaw Island Fudge ice cream, no solid food, like the tonsils of her soul had been yanked out.

But the darkest room in the house was the room next to mine. My father turned Daniel's bedroom into the sewing room mom always wanted, but she has not sewn a thing since. I avoid the bathroom at night, because I have to walk back and look in there, at this brand new sewing machine reflecting the hall light. It is dark as cancer in that room's corners, and if I ever stop and see the dim shaded view from the hall's night-light, I can see my brother standing with his back against the wall in a frayed Levi jean jacket, staring, haunting me.

Nights, I lock myself in my room.

My father used to be explosive. No more. We screamed arguments. Now he is a monotone. My older brother drank, like both my father's parents. My father's mother, Grandma Marle, got put in a mental institution in Covington, because she drank so much she could not think straight. When we visited her, she gave me a rusty screwdriver she found on the railroad tracks. No tracks are by the place they kept her, but I believed her. Later my father took the screwdriver from me and said, "She just found that dirty thing on the road," and threw it away. That was the only memento I had of her.

Once every three or four years, we visited her. She was passed out in her room, so I studied her face while she slept, her skin all ridged and jaundiced. My father whispered, "That is what alcohol does." He did not cry, because my father never cries, except when Daniel died. Even then he went off, locked the door, but I heard, sobs. Teary, but not crying, dad said, "See." It just got it in me, inside, deeper than any Nancy Reagan campaign could ever reach. I have never drunk once. Could you imagine if my parents smelled alcohol on my breath? I would have to join A.A. But I have smoked with J. We were watching a Dungeons & Dragons cartoon and my sight got more 3-D. J said pot does not kill your mind like alcohol.

Alcohol kills more than your mind; it kills families.

Craig comes back, his face damp. I am sure blood is in the sink, a white towel now turned wet pink. He asks if I remember what he said about his dad. I do. He is sober now, and strangely I feel as if I have to be even more careful. What I remember is that when Craig was three years old at home in his room the cops came and arrested his real dad. His old dad has kids all over the U.S. One of his daughters in Colorado, near Fort Collins, but not Fort Collins, some city with under three hundred people in it, and this girl, his daughter, filed charges against him with her mom, rape charges. Raiding the house, the cops found padlocked crates of pornography. Craig said neighbors were huddled on their lawns watching police haul boxes of porn from his house. Craig said this was one of his earliest memories, when he and his mom lived in Grand Junction. His mom moved back to Detroit to get as far away as possible from Colorado, although strangely Detroit is where Craig's real dad was born and raised.

Craig said he missed the Christmases where they would drive to see his grandpa in New Mexico. He could remember candles put in the road, hundreds of luminous candles. They do that in the Southwest and he said it was "beautiful" and Craig never uses that word, ever. Craig has not seen his grandfather since. Then he said, maudlin, "My dad has been coming back in dreams." He said he does not want to become his father and there was this loss of control I could feel, like his father was in the room next to us, waiting to come in, a very real shadow, just beyond your vision. I had an urge to turn on the light, but resisted. Craig went on that his dad was in a nightmare of a house with endless rooms, countless doors, his father in the hallways and Craig going mad: deja-vu. "I see his face. Perfectly," Craig says, hushed tone. He sees his father's sky-high forehead, the cauliflower ears, the neck rash, the razor-sharp pointed nose, the fingernails bitten down to nervous bled nubs. "You do that, you know, when you have not seen your father in years, eleven years, once in eleven years, you memorize him. Which I should not have done, because now he is in here." Craig beats on the side of his head with his finger harshly, then rubs the spot.

Craig keeps on, "He talked about the law. I drive over there, I find out he lives in—" Craig is lost in some thought, then continues, "He called me. He called me." Craig sobers with every word. "Man, I beat the shit out of my phone, the receiver, it is gone, man, shattered. After he hung up, I battered the hell out of it. Why call me? Now? He just got out. Southern Nevada Corrections. I told him . . . What?"

"Nothing. Just."

"What?"

"I think about my brother. Sometimes when you talk."

152

Craig is annoyed I interrupted. He looks at the blood on my bed, continues as if I had never spoken, "He was in Briggs. In Detroit. Briggs neighborhood. Bragging it is by Tiger Stadium, north. Have I ever been to Tiger Stadium? I should come by. A white neighborhood, he said. Like he was bragging about living in a white neighborhood. Briggs is the poorest neighborhood in Detroit. I go over there. He missed some court appointment that morning, overslept, and that is all he talked about the entire time I was there. That. The law. The law is evil. Pigs run the city. The whole conversation, F- the law. Drinking, he tells me this. Scotch. I never been so afraid of someone. He had a limp. My dad. He had scabs on his knuckles. Picking at one. It was bleeding. Shaking." Craig clears his throat. "I was shaking, Hollow, shaking."

It is quiet, in the house, my house.

Craig clears his throat. "When he got up, I saw he had a limp. From playing baseball, he said. Playing ball. In prison. They have teams. One guy, my dad slid into second, and one guy, another prisoner, spiked him. They actually let the prisoners wear spikes. And he came down on my dad's ankle. He said it never healed correct."

Craig peers straight through the wall, into my brother's room on the other side, like he can see through it, me. I rub my arms. Craig blows on his hands, to keep warm. I close the window and it gets quieter in the room. Craig continues, "He turned. On the heat. Killed him to do it. Turned it off the second I left. I bet. But he did turn it on. Then. There was a humming in his house. My father's house. Like the humming of the world. Like tinnitus. Like you just got out of a metal concert. What it was like in his house. Probably always like that. Like a radiator about to explode." He stops. "Your parents got beer upstairs?" Craig stands up. "I can get something. Upstairs."

"No."

"I can just get water."

"No."

Craig walks up our stairs, tiptoeing near the wall where the steps creak the least. He turns on every light, leaving a bright trail behind. I follow and as soon as he turns on a light, turn it off behind him. He gets to the kitchen and grabs a green and yellow NMU coffee mug. At the sink, he pours a half glass of water, drinks it. "Ice?" I nod. He motions to the freezer, opens it, breaks some loudly.

I take the tray away, turn it upside down carefully, and put some in his mug. A cube slips from my hand, falls on the floor.

"More," Craig says.

I open the freezer and when I do, he goes straight for the cabinets.

"What you doing?" I whisper-yell.

"I need a drink."

"No."

"A small drink."

"No!"

Craig goes in the dining room, where my mother has an oak cabinet, from her childhood. He opens its doors and there it is, a row of booze, which I did not even know existed. He bends down, searches, and extracts some vodka.

I grab Craig's arm. He pushes me off, laughing. Spilling, he fills his glass. I struggle with him, but lose, trying to be quiet.

A throat clears behind us. It is my father, black-robed, stern, foreboding, large, a piece of ice by his foot, his slipper. My father does not go into any spiel, no talk, just a flat, "Craig, you can leave now."

Craig does not say a word, just motions a thumbs-up, a grin okay, and heads for the nearby door, shutting it behind him, quiet. My father locks it, says, "Two in the morning. Get to bed. Your mother works tomorrow."

My father walks by me, to the bedroom, disappears in its darkness. Bending to one knee, I pick up the watery ice cube, stand back up, and black out.

Even with eyes open, all I see is black with waves of red wires, like the inside of a toaster. My forehead is hot, and with my cheek to the cold tile, I wait until clarity returns, the sight of my parents' narrow hallway, and at the end of it, by their door, my father's feet again, pointed at me, his arms crossed, and seeing me blinking, he turns back into the room, closes the door, leaves me.

I go downstairs. Craig is in my room. Mug in hand, he snuck in through the window, again. Closing the door, I say, "Any loudness, I go upstairs and wake him myself."

Craig grunts.

"Trust me, you do not want him to come down here." Craig downs the rest, tapping the glass upside down. "Craig. Trust me." Craig and I play a game of stare-down. He loses. Suddenly I sound and look like my father—the same tone, definitive, incontestable, hard—which I hate. But it is that hate that Craig relates to, understands.

I stare at him. He stares at navy-blue carpet. A sadness belongs to Craig's face that you cannot find except on the news—escaped prisoner mug shot expressions, exhausted old-timer weatherman faces, footage from countries with extreme poverty, Bangladeshi food shortage children. The irony is Craig has it all—as many groceries as he can eat, a strong body, athleticism, and women who fawn over him. And yet his face is like a legless refugee's, lines of remorse that should not be forming at his age. Yet he laughs more than anyone I know. Cruel laughter, mocking every person's most minor mistakes. But it is funny. Even I laugh, sometimes.

"Bobbie." That is all he says.

I never liked her. The only time I met her she was talking about Anton La Vey like he was a human and not "a bald Hitler schmuck" as Antony calls him. She said the Satanic Bible is not what you would expect and it is all about "self-sufficiency, like Ayn Rand," whatever that means. I have to live with the fact that I introduced Craig to Bobbie.

Craig says all this got triggered by her and how he loves her and he says her eyelids are flower petals and he can see his face all distorted in her pupils, but I think he means irises, and she does this thing where they sleep together and she makes him turn away from her and she holds him and no woman has done that before, and he said he never felt anything like that, protected. It is called 'spooning' he says, but then Craig got tense and, while holding him like that, Bobbie said, "I have to tell you something" and Craig was like, "What?" and she goes, "I love you" and it is the first time she ever said that to him.

Craig looks at me and says, "I need to get married. This is the one." He says it all deep and alcoholic and all dark in the night under the moon in my room on my Tiger bed sheets and my parents sleeping upstairs with the cocker spaniel hiding under their bed with its own fur paws for pillows and Craig goes on that she made him look at her

Chapter 34: Cräig

And she says to me, "I want this to go further." I say I do too 'cause I do and she says she has to tell me something and I look at her and think, "God, I love you" and she says, "I slept with Charles" and it shoots through me, lightning, flash, right through.

"Charles? Charles who?" I'm thinking freshman. "Charles Riekkola? The dweeb? He doesn't even play football. He's on the High School Bowl team."

"He works at the school."

"A teacher?"

"No."

"The cockdamn principal? Who?"

"A janitor."

Those words scrape down my throat, rip my lungs, and I pop out of bed. I pause, pace. She says to come to bed. I say, "You screwed . . . Prince Charles? The nigger janitor." I can't believe I just said this. I cringe when Antony says it. I've got in arguments with Antony about that word. All these feelings come up like vomit. I don't know any blacks, just one. The only black person I've ever spent any time with, really talked to, ever, in my life. "He's like fricking forty," I say.

She holds her legs in a ball in a corner of my room on my bed and my parents aren't home and the windows are open, so I close them and go to the door and close it, then lock it and say, "Did, he rape . . . 'Cause if he fu- . . ."

She cries now.

I'm like, "That motherfff . . . If he . . ." and I can't say the word. It's becoming this actual word, this real word, and I can't believe I'm about to use it in my life, with my girlfriend, who I love, and I say it, "raped you." I kick my generic garbage can over and punch the wall so hard my fist kills, the side of my hand throbs, knuckles broken, sprained, and I hold my wrist saying, "Goddamn. Damnit, damn damn damnit." I'm too consumed with hurt to think about pain, so I forget my hand, saying, "I knew this'd happen." She cries louder, trying to drown my voice. I go over and with my injured hand, which I hold carefully, I push her chin up. She has motherly eyes, a math perfect face, this incredible pouty aura. She's Aquarius. She told me a million times. So she has "complex feelings." She's even more attractive when she's tear-streaked. I want to hit her. I want to save her. Looking in her eyes, I say, gentle, controlled, "Did he . . . do it? Force you?"

"No."

"He did," I say, "Tell me if he did."

She lets loose, says, "It was the . . . at the party. The bonfire."

"The one I was at?" I say, an aside that no one, including myself, hears. I stand over her, making a face like I can't solve a math problem.

"We went down toward one of the camps and, we did it."

"What?"

She tucks her head in her hands.

"Did what?"

"Had sex."

"What did he do?"

"We had sex." Her demeanor tells me she wasn't, more than wasn't, possibly enjoyed, it.

"You mean he didn't . . ."

"No."

"You wanted to . . . With him?"

"I guess."

"Did you have a condom?"

She doesn't respond.

"Of course not." My brain is lost. "What did he do to you?"

"I told you it wasn't rape!" she says, wiping tears away. Psychotic. Like mom when she loses it, mad, shouting, wild. I don't like it, this, now, life. I look out the window to make sure no neighbors are in their yards raking to eavesdrop. Luckily a lawnmower runs a few houses away, grinding in the air.

157

"So you screwed this nigger, at someone's camp." I say, "Whose camp?"

"We weren't going to a camp. And don't—"

"You screwed him outside?"

She looks up, says, "We did it in the road." She says this so disgustingly, so devilishly, so womanly, so hate-filled. It's like she set me up, like she's so evil she'd wait for someone to fall in love with her and then go screw a black janitor on a camp road in the middle of goddamn Suomi and then scream it at him in his own bedroom.

"Get out," I try to say.

She doesn't move. She stares me down, like she's the strong one, tears rolled off her face to stain my sheets, my bed, my life, not hers. Exhausted eyes, nothing is left but her revealed self, the bitch.

I see the scene in my mind singeing like a metal shop soldering iron—Charles on top thrusting away. I'm ashamed I told her anything, about my dad, my life. If I wouldn't have done that, if I'd kept her as a . . . fuck, from now on, I don't say shit.

Charles saw her as she is, knew it, how easy it was, she was, and did it. Right under my eyes in front of me. He must have loved that. Look at the Emilio Estevez jock, real winner, class B champ, can't even keep his girlfriend.

That seals it. I'm taking steroids. I'm not strong enough as is. I don't care if I die, veins collapse. I understand what women want. Charles knows, her legs spread, her saying, "Do me, hard, harder hard-er," like I thought she'd only done with me. What a laugh. Really into it, her, and he hits her, in the face, a good slap, hair tug, her back pushed in the road, jabbing rock. I look at her face and want to kill. Her. I want to punch everything so punch nothing, instead I just boil. I run out the room, trip, slam the door open, swing at the hallway air, jump the basement stairs, bang my head on the low ceiling, stumble, rub my forehead, and rummage around until I find dad's rifle.

Actually my rifle.

When we hunt, this is the one I use.

Seven-hundred ADL bolt action.

Thirty eyed goddamn six.

American walnut.

Kick ass sight helped me get a buck a year for the last three and that's when

I started going.

Monte Carlo stock with cut checkering.

That's my gun.

I jog back, bolt into the bedroom, and her head is down. I say, "He ever comes here, you tell him this is for him. This."

She looks up. The gun is in my good hand, held high by the barrel, pointed at the ceiling. She sees it and freaks, gets up. Mad, that's the only emotion I see now, anger. She goes, "Point a gun at me!"

I don't even have it pointed at her. It's pointing at the ceiling. I wouldn't shoot her, only Charles. Or myself. She storms by and I go after, but the rifle slows me down, so I put it on the hallway floor and take off. She's already upstairs, out the screen door, in the front yard, having closed it behind her but I don't notice 'cause it's invisible and I run smack into it, knocking the screen off its hinge. I try to open it, but it's stuck, so I yank, breaking it more, and pull the whole door off the hinge, then spring after her, grabbing her arm. She turns to me, fierce, like a mom at a misbehaving brat. She says, "You. Let. Go." And I do what I have to.

Falling to my knees, I say, "I love you." I grab a pant leg, pouring everything into this, sniffling, groveling, a Christian at the foot of Christ, "I love you I love you Iloveyou Iloveyou." A kid from down the street rides by on his bike, circles back, one foot dragging, one on a pedal, and I don't want the neighbors to see but I do this, I say, "I need you." I grasp her leg, tight, and bawl like a kindergartner. "Or I'll kill myself."

Then it happens. She says, "Don't say that." Her hand comes down, soothing, goes through my hair, calming, so good, goose pimples on my arms. "Let's go in," she says, "And talk."

I need Kleenex. We go in. I blow my nose and say how much she hurts me and ask if I can go down on her. Please. I actually say "please." I kiss her cheek and she kisses back, moves to my lips, quick, smooth. Tears blend on our tongues, and it tastes better than sex. She pulls away, looks into me, smiles. Nothing is more lovely, more graceful, sweet than a girl crying, especially topless. I assist with her shirt. She says, "We shouldn't," undoes her bra. She might think we shouldn't, but we should, we really should. Life becomes bra, its pop—pleasure. Her breasts peak, hard. Her nips are three times the size of any girl's. Massive long red bizarre wide enchanting saucers, and I'm not much for this 'cause of the scent, the sight, the smell, but I go down. I want her to, you know, I know Charles didn't make her and I want at least that, this. She's Scotland wet.

"Why so moist?"

"All the excitement," she says, "Don't talk." Okay.

My tongue hasn't worked this much since mom shoved a stack of Xmas card envelopes in front of me last Xcember, but this is something I do for girlfriends and it's official now, but to make sure I go, "You're my girlfriend?"

She breathes, "Yes," and it's sealed. I left off at lick number 199 figuring she wasn't seeing 200 if she said no. Antony played me his Kinison tape where Sam says you should spell the alphabet on women, and luckily I remember my ABCs 'cause instead of the straight up and down, we get some nice curves and swerves. She loves Ss and Qs, so I repeat them a good eight or ten times, spelling SQSQSQQQ. Like a Baptist speed freak, she's into it. Running out of alphabet, I go back to counting, spelling the number with my tongue and she loves it, O-N-E, T-W-O. I lose count so go back to numbers as numbers, 1, 2, when lockjaw sets in like a mouthful of lemon drops. She encourages me to keep on keeping on by pinching her nipples and rubbing her abdomen, actually more for her than me. My neck hurts 'cause I saw Megadeth at Pine Knob two weeks ago and whiplash headbanged with moshing of teeth so now my spine hurts like a garbageman's but I lick away. She tells me put a finger in, so I decide which and figure the middle one makes sense. I'm glad to rest my neck, but she commands, "Lick too, lick too." She moans and it pops in my skull that Antony recorded a chick once and it was the best tape ever since Warrant. And he was dry humping, so this would be a thousand times better, lip smacking Dolby, so I look around but there's no blank cassettes. At 400, she epileptics, orders, "Lighter. Flick it. With your tongue," and I wonder how many guys she's done but I lick and flick like a flame snake fire serpent. She convulses, Helen Keller. Her hand shoves my forehead, and she takes over, rubbing with real nymph ferocity, erupting gasps, eyes pinched. She bucks and there's no room for me down there, so I enjoy the view, hard as hematite, slipping off my pants. She itches that scratch with the fastest strokes, real gymnasty. It's Niagara Falls, a goddamn dam breaking. My face is covered with her. She tells me to wipe off, so I run to the bathroom naked, window dodging, praying mom doesn't come home. Returning with enough spare Kleenex to wipe a nuclear spill, I clean my face, chin, neck, chest. At the end of her Richter scale, calmed, she pants, "Now." Christ, I want to wed this beast. I slide it in smooth as bubble bath. "Hard," she insists. Okay. She spasms, gyrates, looks dead on, wonderful evil changing color eyes. She goes, "Is anyone home?" "No." Gritting, she yells, "Do meeeee!" Real comical, but you can't laugh. I say, "I'm gonna!" She goes, "Do it." This is what sex is like with Bobbie, over the top, on top, real emotional psycho good. She looks in my eyes, locked, grabs her neck, pinches her throat, and goes, "Am I a slut." I don't know how to respond and she repeats, "Am I a slut!" and it's not even a question, now is it? I come. In. My face is Spanky, a little rascal. A bad bad boy in the grand style of U.P. chalk-boy goof-ass hard-prick high-school dumb-jock bastards. I collapse like my testes are wrecking balls and she's the building. I breathe like a fat man on an escalator and all that matters is Bobbie's happy and glowing and pleased and content and and and. She uses heaps of Kleenex like a Valdez oil spill spilled, which it has, wipes outside, inside, nooks, crannies, elbows, and puts the stack to the bedside. "I'm gonna have to wash sheets," I say. She laughs, but I don't 'cause I hate laundry and I definitely can't leave those stains for mom the my-dear-Watson detective and there's a pause and christ there's a lot of pauses in this lifetime and a spider is on the ceiling, sitting there, the little perv. God-like, I let it live. I say, "I bet Charles didn't make you feel like that" and it's the wrong thing to say. She doesn't say a word, no rescue. Suddenly he's in my head, Charles, is back, strong as ever, and I think, "I came in her." I say, "You on the pill?" She says, "Fuck off," which means no. She looks me square in the forehead and I say, "Did he make you come?" I say it mean. She gets up and dresses faster than her clothes came off. It's all going to hell faster than Bon Scott did. Faster than Cliff Burton did. I say, "'Cause I know he didn't lick like that." I say it so pathetic I feel tears form, again, damnit!, males are allowed one cry every eight years or else you're a fag crying wolf. As dad said, cry when someone's dead. So I suck it up. I want to grab her, but she'd kick me. In seconds, it's shit. At the door, she turns, says, "You raped me more than he ever will." I follow her. She steps over the gun and humphs. I make a mental note to put the gun back sometime in the near future. She's out the door. I stand there, the screen off the hinge and punch myself in the head. It feels good. I want her to see, so I yell, "Bobbie!" She turns and glances with a huff so I punch myself in the nose. It hurts like a son of a cunt, my eyes watering like mom is onion-chopping, but Bobbie doesn't see so I yell loud enough so she'll hear but not the neighbors, "You whore!" Turning away, I look at the blank house with carrots sitting on the counter when they should be in the fridge and the cluttered Sears & Roebucks in the corner I've masturbated to seven octillion times and I start swinging, unleashing full tilt on myself 'cause there's no one else. Christ, I wish Matt Cort was in front of me right now. Or Charles. Or dad. Or Sugar Ray Leonard. Or god. Anyone. But there's just me. I give one-two-three shots to the cheek, skull, chin, then slam my good hand, loosening a wooden cabinet, and I open its door at head level smashing it in my face, and I feel so sick, such pain, my skull hurts. It's quiet, like no one would care if I blendered my hand in the disposal. Nothing. No lawn mower. No refrigerator humming. Just death's silence. Left to think.

Charles is on me.

In the opened cupboard, I see a holder of knives. I search for the largest, a thick-bladed black-handled brute with a mirror of light reflecting in my eyes.

Charles is in me. In my mind, my mouth, on my cock. I'm deranged with Charles, like I'm gay, feel gay, used, like he screwed me. I drop the knife and run not knowing where to go so I open the back door and everything is encaged. Walls.

Our neighbors who attend the loony church on Teal Lake Ave have the snoopiest kids ever hatched who play war in their backyard 'til midnight even on school nights. They're unidentical twins, which makes them even more frightening, especially considering I can't tell what sex they are. They love to spy on my mom when she gardens, so they ruined the protected, secluded feel you usually hope for in a backyard. So dad hammered up a fence. The asshole neighbors retaliated by putting up a massive jungle gym so when mom sun-tanned and dad was lawn chairing with his Michelob their kids could climb up and sit there gawking like Mata Hari Krishnas. So dad built the fence even higher, so now it's ridiculous. It's this immense suburban highway partition, a joke of a wall, a barricade eyesore that continually has to be explained.

And I was there with this backyard hiding me from being discovered by the world and suddenly in the house I could hear the soft persistent ring of a phone, like the world was letting me know it was there, waiting, hunting me down, no escape. An old toy whiffleball bat was by a plant, so I picked it up and gave the plant a thorough beating, onetwothreefour, a bludgeoning I'm sure it'll never forget, and then the nausea magnified in the sun's air hobbling me over in pain, like my insides were infected and I puked on the grass, throwing up everything I ate that day and it was white vomit, alien vomit, marshmallows I'd raided, fettuccini alfredo, milk, all puke, white white white.

Chapter 35: antony

i dont like it when people call the police "pigs." cuz pigs are cute & there is nothin cute bout a fuckin cop

the n.p.d. calls. the negaunee po-lice

FUCK the npd

ramass stegnowits. anyone wit a name like 'ramass' would have ta end up a cop. & if your last name is stegnowits, its sealed. id know that old geezer voice anywhere: "can i speak with antony seurat?"

"no"

pronouncin my name "sewer rat." fuck you, copper. man, if this aint the copper country, what the fuck is?

ignore ramess, thats what i say. i hang up. whos that, pops asks, comin in fannin himself wit the days mail

"nobody"

again the phone rings. i snatch the receiver before pops can. im slow cuz the brace is back on my shoulder, sloppy. i dont know how to put that fuckin crisscrossin brace back on properly, like a doc would, if i could see one! pops said since i reinjured it fuckin round wit craig, craig can pay for it which is not gonna happen. this fuckin arm is never gonna heal, its like people go outta their way to wail on it. so the pains back & wit the pain, the agony of my arm, the hate is back. hate of cort, of cops, of this town. hate hate hate hate hate-hatehatehatehate

pops tosses a package on the counter while geezer voice squawks at the other end of the line. i dont wanna deal wit some pig interrogatin questions bout their shattered trophy case which i know nothin bout except that its shattered & its funny. so wit the phone half-ass at my ear, i talk, pretendin its a friend, to put my pops off on the old wrong track so he dont know cops are wantin antony x, "oh hey how you doin, frank." (i dont even know a frank.) i laugh loud in the earpiece, at nothin in particular other than i feel like laughin. cop voice continues squawkin, 100% stegnowits, official & cunty. so i laugh louder. unsuspectin, pops exits, rippin into some envelope & from the other room i hear him bitch bout the police. last week he got a speedin ticket—goin 70 in a 50—he musta jus unwrapped paperwork, fines, dollar signs. which is beautiful timin on his part. the bitchin is pops way of sayin he has no money. i already know, fuckrock

my way of sayin i dont wanna talk to no cop is to hang the fuck up, again. & ill keep hangin up from now til doomsday. see, cops dont know that we dont care jus as much as they dont

i grab the package & see its from Run DMC. my fuckin heart jumps, skyrockets, fuckin hopes. til i notice its the package i sent except wit the added bonuses of havin "return to sender" stamped the fuck all over & the package is nice & properly mangled like serial killers were usin it as a punchin fag. what the fuck? i open it & out comes a picture of me at the dump. the tape is broken, unraveled

i squeeze the bulge in my jacket & count to ten. twice

then i figure fuck it & unplug the phone line wit a swift cord yank that has a piece of the wall accompanyin the plug. i want to scream a word, 1 word, & that word is fuck so i do

fuck

fuck it

fuck rap

fuck him

fuck pigs

fuck fuck

fuck cops

fuck pops

fuck the 5-0

fuck run dmc

fuckin wit me cuz im a teenage-whore

fuck the police comin straight from the upper peninsula

fuck them speedin ticket jaywalk ticket parkin ticket badge-in-your-face fucks speedin round town when they aint got nowhere to go, jus showin off they can speed & we cant

    always agitatin. fuckin wit ya. pushin ya. jus kids, out drinkin. not causin no harm. kids, out shootin hoops at miners after dark, no harm. but they gotta come, siren it up, searchlight blind ya, ask for i.d. im 16, what the fuck would i have i.d. for? they piss ya off, push push push, out cruisin all day all night, doin their best to turn people to crime

    speedin tickets are meant so people late for work end up so broke they cant afford for their kids to see a doctor. so their son gets mad & that night finds some long neon light bulbs stickin out a dumpster & hauls em to lakeview elementary to throw em off the school wall, glass burstin in air. the son dont get caught but if he did hed be in marquette county jail. in juvie, learnin to hot wire cars, do phone scams, all the heavier shit. cops love that, their whole system of makin criminals better criminals to ensure they get to bash heads the next million years. nothin makes a cop happier than another criminal. thats why they put everythin they got into petty shit & let rapists go free

    you bored ass pigs want somethin to do, ill give you somethin to do, you fucks

Chapter 36: Cräig

I was backyard puking when my mom came home. Seeing the gun, she thought I was dead. No wall of blood, no floor of corpse, but still she assumes this. She actually talks to herself saying she never should have let my father "buy those Ozzy records," which is funny 'cause she's the one that bought 'em, and she's going around the house yelling my name—bedroom, basement, kitchen—you can tell from the different echoes. I hear her all right when she gets to the back door and opens it and there I am puking on her azaleas. I stayed there trying to think of a good lie. She goes, "Are you okay? Did you shoot yourself?" She actually sounds concerned. I go, really mean, "No, mom," like she's an idiot, which she kind of in a way is. She goes, "You been drinking?" I go, "No," like I'm all cool. I try to stand and act like I was doing anything other than puking even though there's vomit covering her magnolias and weeds and I know that's got to piss her off. I go right by her, straight to my room, and close the door. She opens it. I put on *Reign* and the bitch comes in, standing there in Wonder Woman pose, and goes, "You're going to a counselor!" I head-bang and Billy Idol sneer and she continues to give me a blahblah bath about "wait 'til your father gets home blah" and she leaves and comes back with the gun and mouths, "What is this?" She goes over to my stereo and tries to turn it off. Tries, but gets frustrated 'cause it has more than two buttons and she ends up turning my treble all the way off so I hear nothing but Tom Araya's bass on "Criminally Insane" and it sounds pretty cool. But I take the headset off 'cause after all my crazy mom's standing there with a goddamn gun and she doesn't even know what a safety is. I go, "What?" in this Vinnie Barbarino way and she says, "What is this gun doing in the middle of my floor?" I'm like, damn, why didn't she say, "What is this?" one more time 'cause I wanted to say, "A gun," but instead I have to think of some other snotty reply so I say, "I dunno." That's the best I can come up with. Mom goes, "We don't know. Well, your father will like to hear this" and this really sucks 'cause she's talking like some sixties mom and 'cause me and dad were finally getting along for the first time in months after our last blood-bath of a feud about not drinking directly out the milk carton and 'cause some time in March we had been eating dinner and he kept saying how easy math is and I kept saying how hard it is and he was saying it's easy and I say maybe it's easy for you and he says it's easy for anyone that listens, math is listening, and I say, well, then I guess I don't fucking listen very well do I? and he erupts like Mount St. Helens, lava spewing out of his trap, a real nutcase, which is rare for him 'cause usually he's all happy-go-Gandhi too goddamn tired to speak from doing inventory all night in the stockroom at the mine, counting ham-mers and contracting contractors and all that sleepy shit. But nothing triggers the old man's rage like a well-placed f-word. He goes off yelling and I bolted manic-style out the door and jumped the low point of our back fence 'cause he was gonna give me a good old session of hair tugging and it would have come down to a royal fisticuffs. Even if he does have thick forty-year-old veiny bis, I'd still pound that midgety cockhole into the ground and Awfulsir Stegner'd be at our doorstep in a microsecond. So I got outta Dodge and ran to this chick Amy's who's this hot smart glasses chick who helps me with my un-Advanced Algebra and I tried to bang her but she kept moving away and you have to be able to touch to bang, unless of course you have a good imagination like me, and I wasn't gonna force her 'cause you only force stupid wood shop straggling chicks and plus she's gotta be a virgin and I don't want to screw a virgin 'cause most times they fall in love and that becomes this huge hassle, a big old minus that you don't need, and anyway now I was sitting in my room waiting for dad to come home so he could kill me, so I decided there's no better way to wait than with a little music. I mean, isn't that the slogan of every elevator and phone company from here to goddamn Iowa? So I listened to "Reborn," "Epidemic," "Postmodern," and "Raining Blood" off *Reign in Blood*—I hate when people confuse the song with the album—and, right after the rain finished falling on the last track, both me and the side started to flip over, but I heard a noise that sounded dad-like, a gloomy noon door slam, and working the shit shift I was assured he'd be crabby as a corpse, so I go out to inspect, to get to him before ma fills him full of the bullshit truth, but it's just mom in the kitchen with a familiar mangled plant in her hands so I have to play her like a stick of dynamite, and unwisely try to explain before she can even begin the third degree—if I was smart, I'd still be headphoned in the cocoon of my room. I say I was showing Bobbie the gun and I got sick and had to puke and put the gun down quick to run to the backyard so I wouldn't do it in the house 'cause I know mom just cleaned. My mom's doing dishes 'cause she does chores when she's mad. It's this ritual where if the house is dirty, one of us fights with her and the house'll be spic and span within the hour. She scrubs so hard, her hands bleed. Not looking at me, she fills the sink, asking why Bobbie would just leave me sick like that and I say Bobbie was feeling sick too and mom looks into me like I'm the biggest liar on the face of the earth, which I am, and she glares like a *Clash of the Titans'* Medusa, looking for any sign I'm making this shit up so she could turn me to stone. So I had to really believe it myself and then she sees something and I'm like oh what now 'cause all Sherlock needed last week was for the couch to be an inch out of place to figure out I played football indoors while she was out JC Pennying, but she says tender for her, "What's wrong with your face?" I say, "Nothin', what?" Touching my cheek, with added emphasis, she goes, "Did Bobbie hit you?" I have her on my side now, for a second, so I cover quick and go, "No, mom, Bobbie got sick so I told her to go home and take care of herself." Mom kept staring, so I went on, "'Cause you know how if you see someone puke, it makes you want to puke too" and mom's face changes. She goes, "Don't use that kind of language in the house," and now she's back to scrubbing dishes, which is good 'cause without the eye contact I can lie better and I'm like, "What language?" She goes, "Puke!" I'm like what, is it a four-letter word? But she's being a nutcase and goes, "Vomit. Say 'vomit.'" I guess 'cause that's a five letter word.

So, so badly I want to say, "I vomited all over the motherfucking place, mom," but instead I go, "I vomited, mom, and it was good she wasn't there 'cause remember that time when I was young and Hollow came over and I was sick and we were in the bathtub together and I vomited in the tub and he was in the bathtub and it made him so sick smelling it and stuff he vomited too and then there was his vomit and my vomit in the tub so it made me vomit again and we were stuck in the tub of vomit not wanting to stand up 'cause then it would cling to our chest so we couldn't get out and we both were crying and I was going, 'Hollow, I think I might vomit again' . . ."

"All right, enough. That's enough. With the vomit already."

But I am messing with her good now, so I continue, "And then you washed us off. That's all I was gonna say. With the hose. Backyard."

She goes, "I had a real hard day, so please take that into your kind consideration." I can see she is about to spaz, like an alien's about to leap out her throat and maul me, and I'm afraid of all that E.T. shit so now I'm graveyard cautious. Sure, ghosts are B.S., but who the hell knows what's up there passed where god lives. I don't know what's wrong with me, what sort of internal unknown shit is going on in my insides, but some part of me wants to still push her, to push her right off the bluff edge of sanity. To get her so mad she'll grab a fork from the wobbly kitchen drawer and stab me in the face repeatedly until I'm disfigured as a China man. But some other good conniving part of me insists I calm her down, so I go, "Look, mom, me and Bobbie were arguing a bit, okay." She turns to me and goes, "I knew it!" like she just figured out some big Angela Lansberry mystery and I go, "But I was just showing her the gun, that's all. Promise." I go on, "But listen, I'll go to a counselor. okay, I'd like to talk about stuff, and stuff."

And boom, five days later I'm listening to Bananarama's "Venus" over muffled loudspeakers in a rectangular glass waiting room in the Marquette Medical Clinic where all the bedwetters go, but I don't care 'cause I avoided a good clubbing from dad.

But lemmy back up.

At the dinner table, mom tattles, "Today Cräig was showing Bobbie one of your guns," and dad just butters his peas and ham and, well, hell, he even butters his butter, and is all caught up in his sports trivia thoughts between occasional commands of "pass the frickin' yams." Unaffected. And why? Why does he not care that the screen door is no longer a screen door? 'Cause my mom told the old man I was going to counseling and he was like, "Well, thank goddamn god 'cause it's about time." Funny thing is when mom asks him to go, he calls it a bunch of hospital hocus-pocus. But if it's suggested that I should, suddenly it's authentic therapeutic shit.

At the psychologist's, I am one nervous bastard 'cause I flunked every science mankind ever invented—and if they give me a quiz, it'll be further proof that by society's standards I'm a retard. I took an IQ test once and scored seventy-eight, which isn't bad for not studying, but that score triggered holding me back in seventh grade, and they kept thinking I was dyslexic, but they couldn't prove it 'cause I'm not, but staying back a grade was no problem 'cause then I got bigger for football. Truth is when it comes to tests, I like to blow them. I'm good at it. I'm good at knowing which is the wrong answer, like a talent. It makes me feel good to put the wrong answer down even if I know the right one, like a grand F-U to principals and cops and fathers worldwide. This psychology shit's just another test where they judge you so they don't have to focus on themselves. The psychiatrist room has art in it, but it's art like from senior citizens' housing, stuff you put in a garage sale labeled "5 cents or best offer" and still won't sell. It smells like science in the building, like rotting science, but rotting science mixed with friendly photos and shitty magazines. What sort of asshole reads Time? This guy in a frock or smock or whatever it's called smiles at me like he is one necrophilia bastard and tells me it'll be just a bit and a woman comes over and for someone who works in the health system, the young heifer sure hasn't heard of the word exercise which makes me wonder how many patients they've lost based solely on first sightings of her. I note fire exits. She gives me a fat pen and makes me fill out five sheets of paper, which is the one thing I hate more than anything. Whoever invented paper should be shot. I think it was the Egyptians. They invented everything. And they should be shot. Them, the Greeks, and Chrissy Columbus. All shot. They should have put more time into inventing Atari.

Five pages.

Five pages of fill-in-the-blank, multiple choice, and short essay. Even at doctor's offices I fill in goddamn circles. One thing I learned in school is how to color in a circle. Quick swirls of the pen leave my paperwork showing I have a heart condition, chronic back pain, and am a forty-year-old recovering alcoholic divorcee. I hand the form to another chick in a frock smock who is hotter than any thermometer can handle. She asks me to follow her and I'm like, "Cool," so I think about positions and how awesome it'd be to do it on one of those patient tables with the sterile pillows and I remember movies where patients screw their psychologists and it's always good sex, all vicious throwing each other around the room, knocking over plants, and let's get it on! We go in a room and it's empty as Antony's head. White paint, a dull table, and that's it. Psychiatrists are cheap. She lets go with questions, real cop-like shit, and now I wish she was a guy 'cause guys know not to do that and also 'cause then I wouldn't be all attracted and distracted and horny, so relaxing isn't a possibility even if it's what she tells me to do. I keep thinking of boning her, hard, right up the old smock, and upon close examination she's not even hot. She's just the most normal looking chick in the building. It's her or the cow. She asks what would make me comfortable and I blurt, "To be over there." I don' t know where that came from, but I point at this kid's room next-door, a playroom, and I'm like, "Christ, she'll never do me now." She goes, "Then let's go over there." I get hard and cover it on the walk by un-tucking my shirt, pretending to look for a stain, and she smiles so professional I wonder if her face is gonna explode Scanner-like. I wait at the door so she'll walk in front so I can check her out, but she makes me go first 'cause she's catching on that I'm not the usual psycho patient, but then I wonder if she's checking me out. We go in this room and it has everything, well, that's an exaggeration, it's got some toys, some cool ones. She goes, "Go ahead, touch anything you want." Anything? She's real encouraging and suddenly dumbed down, treating me younger than I am. I don't know what to do so I sit in a chair and she goes, "Also you don't have to. If you want to just talk," and I sure as hell don't. Christ, psychologists should give you a drink, a couple beers, loosen you up. I go over to this game that has these insanely colorful numbered blocks you place in this tube and it makes no sense. I wonder if it's supposed to make no sense, like they want to see if it frustrates you and I don't want to get into any mind games and have to talk about "Did that game frustrate you?" So I go to a dollhouse and it's almost instinctual, but I pick up a hard plastic doll, some Barbie wannabe, and I'm like, "Christ, what am I doing?" Every second I get further away from making love to my sweet sweet psychiatrist. From the corner of my eye I look over 'cause I don't want her to notice and I want to see if she's checking me out, you know. But she looks at her clipboard, and that's all I need is for her notes to get into the hands of someone at school, be mocked for life. And there's her, so goddamn expert, like she's better than me. How she's situated, she can look at me with little movement, so I grab two dolls, one in each hand and figure forget it, I'm mad at being there and my mom's in the waiting room and I figure I'll mess with this psychologist chick and one of the dolls becomes a husband and the other's the wife. The wife goes up to the husband and hugs him and I look over at the psychologist and she looks at me but doesn't move or anything, just invisible almost, and I smile back like one of them Martians from *Killer Klowns from Outer Space*. I have the dolls walk around, "La-la-lala-la," and the wife trips down the stairs and the man runs down and says, "Oh, can I help you?" and this is me speaking, I'm saying this, sucked into this mini-life and it's like the psychiatrist is hypnotizing me to do this. The wife gets up and I've moved my body so the psycholo-chick is permanently in my sights and can't suddenly stab me or anything and I hate being here. And the man, the husband, kicks the wife in the ass with his stubby doll leg. I'm like, forget this fake stuck-up chick earning her paychecks by toying with me. I have the wife doll bitch-slap the man doll and he gets pissed and I pull off his shirt. At first it doesn't want to come off, but I force it 'cause I'm a lot bigger than any frickin' doll, and he flexes, the guy doll flexes and goes, "Check out my abs, woman" and he's cut and tan 'cause dolls don't have anything to do in their spare time, so they do crunches and hit the tanning beds. There's another doll about six times bigger than both of the others combined, so I put down the wife doll and grab this other one with its mammoth head that doesn't even look human compared to the Barbie and Ken-like dolls and this new doll comes in and it's got no neck muscles 'cause its head flops around like its on drugs big time and I make it head-bang and laugh 'cause the head jerks like mad so I make it head-bang again and this cracks me up. I have it act like Godzilla and destroy the house, throwing chairs and cars out the windows, couches and teacups down the stairs and on the floor, not the dollhouse floor but the actual floor. And every time I have it do some form of mass destruction, the gigantic flopping head does a head-bang and I make a guitar riff sound with my teeth clenched and lips pursed and I have quite a variety of riffs to choose from but I start with "Killing is my Business and Business is Good" and I go back to dollhouse thrashing and smacking mom and dad and then Godzilla tosses the couple out their own front door booting them in the ass on the way out with a couple nice added Mr. Bill sound effects and then I have rock-n-roll Godzilla say, "It sure gets lonely when everybody's dead." The psychiatrist looks at me and I have this big doll sitting in this empty house it just ripped through and it's sad and bored and I'm boring and I look at the sad psychologist and her smile is gone and I bet she doesn't want to screw me at all now, and I'm thinking, "You're a psychiatrist, you're not supposed to have feelings."

She takes me to the waiting room, calling my mother over. I grab a seat. Godzilla's clenched in hand and the psychologist talks so I can hear. "We can only help if he's interested in being helped. Right now he shows no concern about getting help of any sort. In fact, he prefers it. If he ever changes that view though, we'd love to have him back. Until then, we'd be wasting his time, yours, and ours."

Nice speech. Suddenly I want her again.

On the way home I talk with mom 'cause she wants to know what happened back there. She talks about how she went to a counselor after we moved to Michigan, about how she was so depressed she couldn't leave the house, about how it helped to make an appointment and talk with a counselor. And she was actually nice about it. I knew she wasn't in a bad mood 'cause she lets me put on Q107, which I don't like but it beats oldies. She says the psychiatrist had her do something symbolic that would help her life and the symbolic thing she chose was she took every possession that had any connection with my old father and burned them. Including board games I played as a kid and books I loved to read like Mother Goose and Dr. Seuss' *Thidwick, the Big-Hearted Moose* and my old clothes that were still good at the time. She bought us new, well, not new, but stuff from the 7 Mile Road St. Vinnie's and that's how we started over, out of the ashes.

And with this whole Bobbie thing, I wanted to do something symbolic, something crazy. In my room the next day, Antony came over and mentioned how he wanted to kill Matt Cort and I thought it'd be symbolic if we did and Antony agreed it would be.

Chapter 37: antony

goin craigs is like playin russian roulette. you pray to God his ma aint home. for one thin, shes fat in that way thats scary. when she holds up her arms fat swings in the breeze drippin off her arm like butter. she sweats gravy. but a more important reason to avoid her like The Fat Plague is when shes there, its nonstop bitchfest. nonstop

before goin over, i take off my nasty ass brace, washed but the sweat dont come out. i gotta be careful now cuz numbnut craigll horseplay again, forgetful ass moerfuck, & permanently frankenstein my ass. but the brace aint goin back on, im sick of the comments, & if i wore it over there craigs ma would have a field day

i get to his house, if you can call it that, & knock, wait, ring the doorbell, wait. knock, wait. wait, wait. wait fuckin wait wait wait

my luck is shit cuz the door opens & theres hagface in a bright yellow sweater lookin like a fuckin negaunee miner/green bay packwhore fan. she jus stands there, says nothin. i go, "craig home?"

"no bandage i see," she says. the smell of tuna salad hits my nose like a left hook

"no. is craig home?" i ignore, or attempt to. my eyes blinkin

"no shoes in the house," she says & walks to the kitchen table two feet from the door where a muffin sits half gnawed next to a fifth of somethin a.a. dont allow her to drink

holy mother of pain, how many times have i heard that statement? 'no shoes in the house.' it plays in my sleep. im gonna start goin over their barefeet

i put my adidas next to a sand dune size pile of dog toys. i never seen a dog at that house but craig insists they got one. its probably chewin a babys arm

175

off as we dont speak

im bout to make my exit to craigs room without any harassment when she catches me wit, "so anthony, your dad found work yet?"

"no." i bout run away from her. give that hag a minute to ask a few simple questions & shell have you wishin you were dead in no time, which i do

"no noise!" she spits as one final bitch. in hand, i have my tape recorder, which she mustve noticed. i know, i know know know shes gonna be waitin at that table for when i come back for my shoes, & thats gonna give her a hour to think of evil shit to ask me. fuck, i shoulda brought my shoes down to the basement so i coulda snuck out the backdoor

craigs room is in the basement, a fuckin dungeon torture chamber. you descend an empire state building of stairs & find yourself in a world of pipes. its like mildew & rat turd mixed wit the smell of burnt laundry down there

craigs on the cement floor doin crunches, ruinin his spine. his room is like a garage sale exploded. orange caps & hunter vests & piles of tapes & a old mark gastineau poster littered wit holes from ninja throwin stars & magazines wit chicks in bikinis lyin on camaros. on his window sill is a row of jolt cans filled wit tobacco spit. red-faced, he touches elbows to his knees like i aint in the room

i sit on the bed & am like fuck it & go to plug in the tape recorder when craig says, "what you doin?"

"well," i say & explain how run dmc aided by the u.s. postal servass destroyed my, well, our tape, & if he wants we can recut the album

"what album?" craig lies on the floor, eyes on the ceilin

"you know. White Boys in the House"

craig laughs. i dont. craig gets up, puts his shirt round his neck but not through the arms, goes to a mirror & checks out his abs, flexes his biceps. i look at the ground, at a pair of levis thatve been stepped on so many times their wrinkles are flat to the floor

"you wanna go lift?" he asks

"no, i wanna fuckin do the tape, do this tape"

craig yawns. "im gonna lift"

"i cant do this without you, craig"

"well, you will"

176

"i cant!"

craig looks at me for the first time since i got in the damn room, whispers, "man, shut the fuck up." he looks at the ceilin again, & i know hes really lookin up at where his ma, God, is probably seated, ready to charge down at the sign of a peep. we couldnt do the tape even if he wanted to, cuz she wouldnt let us

"jus go to my house," i plead

craig gets dressed, throws random clothes off the floor into a duffel bag

"the cops called me," i say

"so"

"i didnt say anythin"

"bout what?"

"bout you fuckin up their trophy case, kickin one of the cops"

"man, youre a dick." craig sighs, shakes his head, walks out the room

i unplug the recorder quick, run after him. hes at the basement door

"craig, you said, man, remember, you said you wanted to do somethin." i lower my voice, "somethin big." he jus stares, like he doesnt know what to do wit me, but i have him listenin. the only problem is i dont know what to say. "lets, you know . . ."

"antony, nothin is ever gonna happen"

what does that even mean? nothin is ever gonna happen?

craigs basement reminds me of the u.p. dust bunnies like tumbleweeds. ghosts wouldnt even bother to haunt this place. my hand goes loose, the tape recorder cord falls to the floor. i eject the tape. nearby the dryer is a tiny dirty white garbage bin, a bucket, heaped wit years of laundry lint, never thrown out once. i toss the blank tape into it

craigs expression dont change, jus hard, dead, weightlifter dull, like nothin affects him

"let me grab my shoes," i say

i run up, grab the shoes, & my face is so sour craigs ma actually leaves me alone

at craigs feet, i tie up a sneaker, sayin, "hear bout bobbie?" i look up & his expressions changed. i look back down, pull the strings tight. "rumor shes wit cort now."

i tie the other shoe without lookin up at craig

"bullshit"

"thats the rumor," i get up, dust off my pants, "matt cort"

"i hate that fucker," craig says

"we all do"

craig stands there, eyein me, flexin his frown muscles. a good 10 seconds pass. i wait. when craigs thinkin, ive learned to wait. finally he says, "what were you gonna say?"

"bout what?"

"you said somethin bout we could do somethin"

"i wanted to record those songs, those raps"

"no, somethin big. you said. somethin big"

"well, i thought wit the raps . . ."

"thats not big. thats small, antony, thats not big. you wanna do somethin big . . ."

while craig talks, i pick up a yarned kitty cat craigs ma tried (& failed) to make in some city art class. the heap of string is a mess of colors. you can make out its a cat, but a cat thats sufferin in a stranglin puke of colors, wit an innocent cat-face stickin out of that yarn pile. i hold it up to show craig & he cocks back & punches it out of my hands, real comic & hard, three stooges meets moshpit

laughin, craig nods to his room & we go back over. i give the cat a good boot on the way over. we get to his bed & sit

"you still got that?" craig asks, "the gun?"

"no," i say, "yeah. not on me, but. well. yeah"

& craig tells me. tells me bout hate & how nothin ever happens up here & bout bobbie & how sick he is of his fuckin ma & bout doin somethin. big. he says maybe we should jus pound corts face in, double-team him for a beat-down. but then says he feels like he could jus fuckin kill him. & says that thats crazy though & i say its not that crazy & he says if you were gonna kill some-one what would be the best way to do it, like my favorite way. & i say i always wanted to do a driveby & an evil evil anger you wouldnt think could come up comes up. in me

but i dont think bout that. i think bout craigs ma, listenin. she always listens in, through the vent. quotes our conversations weeks later. & i like the nervous-ness of wonderin if she can hear us

we keep whisperin
bout shit you wouldnt believe
plans
that im not sure are real, but, God, i think they are

Chapter 38: J

People suck. All people. Suck. Nuns. Suck. Politicians. Of course, suck. Smiley wives. Suck. Math teachers. Suck. English teachers. Suck. Principals. Suck. Gym teachers. Really suck. Dentists. Really, really suck. Porn stars. Suck, because they get to screw all day and I don't. The chicks in my school. Suck suck suck. And often from what I hear. Dumb wenches think because I have cerebral palsy, my dick don't work. It works. Trust me, it's fully functional. Too much so, in fact. And you suck! Healthy people. Suck. Joggers. Suck. Football players. Especially suck. Potheads. Suck. Alligator preppies. Suck. U.P. valley girls. I don't even have to say it. Teachers. Suck. My aunt from the Sault who works as a flower clerk every summer at the Grand Hotel on Mackinac. Sucks. Women. Don't even get me started. Men. Beyond suck. Everyone. Sucks. Everyone in my hometown. Sucks like a vacuum. Everyone in my high school. Sucks like a black hole. People who think just because I have cerebral palsy that I can't control my arms or my voice or my thinking—suck. People say, "What's up, J?" and I swear I'll answer, "Fuck off" and they laugh, like I'm a comic, but they only laugh when I'm a sarcastic, pessimistic asshole, like that's my natural position in the school and in life and they're comfortable when I'm that and only that. I don't know what it is, why I have them charmed, or if they're just afraid since I'm the only punker in the entire county. Except for Davey Wrzesinski. And he's not really punk, just sexually confused. But all of them, including Davey, suck. And animals . . . fucking cats and gerbils and caterpillars and squirrels fucking squirrels and grasshoppers chirping all damn dusk and spiders that I have to squish and throw in the toilet or pound them with a shoe. Suck. And let me just expound upon an example of how people suck. When I kill a spider, I hold the door open first to see if they choose to walk out, but generally they won't, which means I have to pummel them mercilessly with my size 11s, and well, for me to work up the courage to kill, I have to lose it. I have to put on "Holidays in the Sun," which is saved solely for spider murder. But fuck Brit punk. Ever since Sid died, those posers suck. I'll never forgive him. Ypsilanti is punk's cradle. All hail James Jewell Osterberg. He'll live forever. And die for longer. Just watch. Drum sticks stabbing flesh, body bent in half, microphone mashing teeth, walking on hands like water, that whole peanut butter world. Then, psyched off "Holidays," and "Penetration," I pound shoe to brain of daddy long legs—the spider on every U.P. summer lawn, a plague of legs. But first time I did this, mom comes in and I explained and she thought it was so cute. That's why mom. Sucks. I kill kill kill with body splattered blood and it's "cute."

Death. Sucks.

Killing. Sucks. Craig's tendency to wear bandanas. Sucks. Cousin Hollow's eternal flood pants. Suck. Anthrax fan club members. Suck. Bands that open for Anthrax. Suck. Rap groups that collaborate with Anthrax. Suck. Circle jerks. Suck. The Circle Jerks. Suck. I can't believe I bought Wild in the Streets. Worst album since Kajagoogoo's White Feathers. The Jerks' backwards E. Sucks. D.R.I.'s album cover. Sucks. Do we really need another skeleton mascot?

You may be asking, J, but J, what does not suck? All right. Traci Lords' Ex-Lovers' lyrics to "Just Another Scum Rock Band" on the N.Y. Scum Rock: Live at CBGB tape I hefted from the Wonderland Music bargain bin doesn't suck, but the fact that I sent the only fan letter I've ever written to them care of the lead singer at P.O. Box 100270, Brooklyn NY 11210 and they never wrote back to me does fucking suck. And you know what else sucks the biggest cock ever? School. School sucks. Every moment spent in that school. Sucks. Its bricks. Suck. Its lonely long halls. Suck. Sitting in Trig holding a fart. Sucks. Tripping on the way to your locker and having to play it off like nothing happened. Sucks. Waiting for the bus in the rain. Sucks. Waiting for the bus in the sun. Sucks. Waiting for the bus in the snow. Sucks. Eating another slice of cardboard fucking school pizza. Sucks. Homework sucks. Pretending you care about school sucks. Pretending you care about life sucks. Having people ask what you want to do after graduating sucks. And the fact that I don't give a fuck and do all my homework in study hall and never bring it home ever and I am still in the top ten percent of my class sucks. And our grad ceremony being in less than a week. Sucks. And the fact that we're graduating three weeks after every other school in the area because we have the stupid rule that we have to make up snow days—sucks! And the school counselor who has a man's haircut and comes up to me saying we need to talk and I smile back fake, but she doesn't even notice, and then go in her office with the fading motivational mountain peak poster and the fucking bubbling clock fish tank or fish tank clock and she says I should apply for scholarships to N.M.U. and I do it, in study hall, of course—that really sucks. Not U of M. Not State. She says Northern Michigan University. The idea of me not having committed suicide yet sucks. Living passed the age of twenty is stupid and I know I'm gonna surpass it.

No one's died younger than Sid. Not even Buddy Holly. Name one person that died under twenty-one that's famous.

See. You can't name one. Other than Sid.

Sid's the fastest comet the world's ever seen.

A saint.

A fuckin' nasty little bastard Saint.

My tattoo already sucks. I hate it. What was I thinking?

Craig and Cousin Antony catch me looking at it in the mirror, because I didn't hear mom let them in, if she let them in at all, due to my having *The Day The Country Died* on and now they're interrupting my listening when I'm in the middle of concentrating on the storyline, trying to tie it all together, and right when I was about to toke up and I hate people when I smoke, especially just before I smoke. I want to be alone and think and rot and sit and stare out the window at the whitened evergreens at the cocained horizon at the chalky sky and my snowy bedroom walls and just think and not think and here come these two bouncing fuckers acting like they're a combined age of eleven and I'm trying to get into "New Age" but have to turn it down, then off, for them to tell me the big news and they say it's important and "psycho" and I gotta do this and don't tell anyone. Let me just say I never hang out with these two. I never invite them over, I never call them, I never go to their houses, and apparently they can't take a hint because they have stopped over here consistently unannounced for the majority of my life. And here they are again, going on and on and I'm like, whatever, I'll do it, look, don't tell me and then when I have to do it, we'll do it. Because I ask if we're going to do "it" right now and they say "no" in unison like twin imbeciles. They say we're gonna do it soon enough and I ask what. They're acting like foolgirls, like lostboys, like the CIA tapped my room and they want to know if anyone's home. Mom is, but after an hour of Subhumans she's probably deaf and they sit down, these clods, these fucking UP idiots and finally they tell me what it is, what this gigantic adventurous news is.

My cousin says they want to do a driveby.

Like this is Detroit.

Like we're not lousy Yoopers.

There are reasons why I hate people. A variety of reasons. Reasons like sheer, raw, innate stupidity. And in the UP, they breed it. They inbreed it.

Chapter 39: Cräig

Oh my god. Or lack of one.

We go over J's and get in the biggest fight. I don't get why J always and I mean always has to be glum down and rainy day acting. I'm the one at night creeping in the woods behind Bobbie's house to catch a glimpse in her window, my heart aching like it's goddamn missing. I'm the one who had Stegner call and tell dad there's a warrant for my arrest. They passed it down to the Marquette County Sheriff's Department, which makes no sense, other than they want me to drive fifteen miles out my way for their stupid questioning and speeches of 'one more strike and I'm out.' Dad says I'm waiving any rights to a lawyer (he insists on this like eight times—I heard you already!) and says I'm going down there first thing in the morning, which I have no problem with 'cause I get to skip both Biology—which I am flunking at a level that'll have teachers lounge-talking for years—and Metal Shop and I already finished my projects in there, so all me and Belten do is go around and help others or make shanks in our free time. Belten says he's practicing for prison. What a idiot. Probably true though. Out of place Kraut bastard.

And with all these cop hassles, am I depressed? No! But look at J. He looks like he just got out of Auschwitz. The meaning of pain. Cheer the damn hell up! Depressed as death—and he doesn't even like the Cure. Thank god, otherwise I'd never hang around that dickface. Only chicks can be Goth. With guys, it's just gay.

J drowns his sorrows in shit music. Turn that crap off and he'd feel better. Some cricket-head Brit shrieks, "Oi oi oi I was allah tha bly!" I'm like, "What in god's hell's this shit?" 'Cause it's shit. A three mile field of manure on the ride to Palmer shit. J mumbles a response—the "music" is effecting his speech, like osmosis. (Take that Mrs. Kukkanen, you Biology teaching cunt.) Antony drools, "Look who's talking none ah ya know shit 'bout music." J goes, "What?" I jump on Antony literally and go, "Man, saying bitch fifty times does not a lyric make." Antony shoves me off, but not before I knock the cap off his bald head, then kick it when he reaches for it. J tells Antony to name one good rap lyric, one that isn't laughable. J goes, give us the best lyric in rap, the very best. And we all decide to make a bet to come up with some metal lyrics and J's got to come up with punk lyrics and Antony's gotta come up with some crap lyrics and we'll see who has the best, and it won't be Antony. So Antony thinks with the cogs in his head churning and then says this rap about abortion, real sick, he goes, "Okay yo yo yo I'm not worryin' 'bout money 'cause I'm gonna straight kick the bitch in the stomach." Doesn't even rhyme! Me and J moan and Antony's like, "What?" We're like, "That's weak." Antony's like, "That ain't wack, that's Ice Cube." J goes, "Exactly." I go, "Not wack. Weak." J goes, "Ice T sucks." We're tag-teaming Antony. I go, "Yeah sorry, but you ain't gonna win with your Vanilla Ice nursery rhyme. Go sit on a goddamn tuffet." Antony gets mad, which is cool, so I go, "Yeah, you know, you don't be needing to talk about women like that." J jumps in and goes, "Be respectful, eh? Mom's in the other room. She can hear." And J's serious and I'm not. Antony tells J to suck his dick and flicks the bill of J's cap so it falls on the floor and I wanna kick that one too but hold back. J doesn't move, keeps his hands on his knees, biting down on his teeth, and stares at Antony. In a bedhead mohawk and skull earrings, J isn't someone to mess with. I get kind of excited inside hoping they'll fight, so I'm silent because silence encourages brawling, but Antony picks up the cap, punches it gently a couple times from inside, and extends his arm out waiting for J to take it. J doesn't move, so Antony places the cap on the bed beside him. And J, all smooth, recites his lyrics like the incident never happened.

For J's turn, he gives weird quoted shit about his mom dying of cancer when he was five. Antony's like, "J, your ma's in the other room." What a idiot. It's lyrics, not facts. Except it did have something in there about Jesus not existing. And Antony's Lutheran, I guess, 'cause that's the only religion up here, no other choice. I mean, what the hell would a Buddhist do up in the U.P.? But Antony doesn't go church and never wants to discuss it 'cause he doesn't know anything about it, just had enough lectures seep in so he's brainwashed enough to be scared of god. Hell, don't he know nothing's sacred. If you don't know that, you're lost. One time I asked him who the Luther was in Lutheranism and he said, "I dunno, Lex Luther. Hell, if you're so interested, you go church." I have a one word response to that—"No." And another—Jonestown. 'Jonestown' is a word I save for Antony any time I want to get under his skin, like a scalpel. At my house, I offer him Kool-Aid and give it to him with an evil grin. But Antony goes to J, "Don't talk about Jesus. That's not cool." And he's serious. Bizarre.

So they go to me and I'm thinking about my lyrics the whole time, so I have the advantage, so I let them have some Pantera:

"Through these complex years I been alone, but you, uh. Shit." I had to think. I was nervous. "I. Don't look around, or, make this world my, uh, own. I cried when she left, but . . . damn, the flight was in my life, uh. You left me, completely. You went, uh, the men are here. Believe me, words unlock my doors, and cemetery's gates."

Reciting it, eyes closed, I shook. It's so close to me. I shouldn't have done that. You should never open yourself up like that. But I had to. My brain started throbbing, a migraine, which I never have, but in the last few days, it's like the front of my head is on fire with pressure, on pressure with fire. When I got done, Antony rolled his eyes and I almost smashed him one in the face. Something stopped me though and that something was I was sober, but man if I'd had even one Miller in me, I'da killed him.

But they both admitted mine was the best. And it was.

Actually they bitched about mine too, but you have to admit, mine was the best.

Without asking, I got three Tylenol from J's bathroom 'cause the bottle said not to exceed the recommended dosage, and the Tylenol company can go bite me, so I swallowed it pretending it was cyanide, and then we talked about what we really went there to talk about. To tell J we're getting a little vengeance.

Charles.

Bronson.

Chapter 40: antony

today i was hummin "fuck tha police" round the house. thats how happy i was

    my arm felt so good that for the first time in a long time i could actually give a nice long whirlwind of a middle finger, jus throw that shit dan quisenberry style

    im bout ready

    you can backstab me. but when my back stops bleedin, you better be bulletproof

    im ready

    gettin ready

    some people obsess

    im one of those fuckin people

    but for today, today im happy

    zippidydoodah-zippidy-yay, blast o gunshots is comin corts way

Chapter 41: J

This is what I do every second week, although sometimes I miss an appointment and then it turns out to be only once a month. I go to the clinic and a young nurse named Shelley Lehtinen or else an older nurse named Patty Zinetti comes into a room where I'm dressed in my regular clothes. They used to have me do the hospital gown get-up, but I've been doing this for years now.

Quick note. If a name in the U.P. ends with –ski, it's Polish. If it ends with –etti, they're Italian. If it ends with –inen, it's Finn. I guess it probably translates to "-son" in each language. I don't know. But you can figure out the nationality of anybody's name in the U.P. if you know this rule. You hear roll call in school and it's, "Bonetti. Zanetti. Lehtinen. Wrzesinski. Pynnonen. Frachetti. Suku-puolinen. Louinski. Kauppinen. Hytonnen. Thomson." Nobody has a one syllable last name around here. Nobody in the U.P. is named Smith. It's funny in a way, but most saps don't even recognize this shit.

This Finn and this Italian, they walk in and they twist my legs until I grit my teeth in pain. This was three times a week for a horrible forever, but in the last few years it's been this every second week schedule, which according to Doc Sanguinetti, a real upbeat Sicilian, is going to continue to be my schedule 'til death. And when even the eternal optimists are pessimistic, you're fucked.

I could do this at home, but when I was unsupervised I stopped altogether, so mom makes me come here because it motivates me to really do the stretches. It's not that sophisticated. They do my heel cords. Stuff like standing on the edge of a step, you know, like standing backwards on a diving board. I sit Indian style, for my hamstrings. Bend over, touch your toes. That kind of thing. I told you I could just do this at home. They check to see if I'm getting any worse or better. There's never any change. No matter how hard I work. They check to see if my spinal column's curving. Nope. Always the same. That's cerebral palsy. Be like this and just like this forever. They make strides in every other field but mine. Cure cancer in another fifty years, but never this. Be nice if we had a fucking telethon. No joke. Have you ever heard of a cerebral palsy telethon? That's because there isn't one. And if you're thinking of one, you're thinking of muscular dystrophy and muscular dystrophy is not fucking cerebral palsy.

Only change that'll happen is when I get older, real older, things'll get bad. Much worse. That's a real treat to think about. So I don't. Like I've said before though, it's not that bad. Things are only bad when you think about them. Otherwise it's just not. I mean, yeah, I get sharp cramps sometimes in the middle of the night, because they tighten up, whatever, you gotta live with it, be strong, no big deal. Keep stretching, keep salt in your diet, if you bite your lower lip it's an acupuncture point that eases cramping—does it work? I dunno, I still do it, did it last night. Every bit helps. Every bite helps. That's why I'm punk. Punk's about coping, seeing, knowing how massive the swindle is. Like working at the great American wrench factory and tossing one in the machinery at the end of your shift. Fuck it. Punk just speaks to me. About pain and life and shit and suffering and humor, dark humor, making fun of society, people, people's stupidity, people's cruelty.

I listen to it all day. Subhumans, The Damned, Black Flag, Dead Kennedys and Milkmen, Hammerbrain, the Pistols, Stooges, solo Ig, Lou, Dave. I only own about twelve albums. Sometimes it's eleven, sometimes thirteen, depending on if I lost one or lent one or broke one or whatever. Records I don't listen to, I give away. Friends'll be like, "Are you serious? I can just have it? You're not suicidal, are you?" But what's the sense of keeping something you don't need? Why be owned by what you own? I own the only albums worth having anyway, although the Circle Jerks are the worst, but I'm saving it for a bonfire or an M-90 or something, a rainy piss day. Like the time I bought a Suzanne Vega album on sale, *Solitude Standing*, and me and my cousin Antony and this other cousin of mine from Des Moines all drew swastikas on it, gave Suzanne a goatee, drew a balloon coming out of her mouth saying, I fucked Luka.

I fucked him on the second floor.

The swastika isn't Nazi crap. Nazi crap is for idiots. The swastika was originally a Finn pagan symbol and one-testicle-having Hitler warped it and ruined

Finland. So I have a swastika key chain and people ask why. I tell them it's Finn and give them a big fuck Hitler speech and they love it a bit too much, but fuck Hitler. I have cerebral palsy; do you know what Hitler would have done with me? He'd Zyklon-B my ass. Fuck him. Fuck Hitler and fuck Germany and fuck the Northern Hemisphere.

I like to relax. Me time. I don't like no heads coming over talking kindergarten philosophy, giggling like Lars Ulrich, and saying, "dude." I like my room to myself with my posters of Cheryl Tiegs and Sid and Samantha Fox and Ig. I don't like one crevice of wall to show. Just all them faces looking down on me. But I don't listen to punk when I'm high because you don't need punk when you're high. You need Ian Fleming.

All I read is Ian Fleming. I have all the books and I reread all the books and when I'm done with one book, I start up another and forget everything from the last one. While reading, I listen to this album I have that's all of the James Bond themes reproduced on synthesizer. The best track is "Live and Let Die." They really break down that song at the end. I can almost cry. "Your heart is an open book," you know, and it is, and because it's instrumental, you sing the song in your head or softly out loud, remembering the lyrics, and the whole story, his whole life, James Bond's, all comes running up on you, this spy, you know, all this stuff that's going on with him, he's perfect and really gives it to the women and touches them, you know, he really gives them bliss and they're thankful for that and saves his country and all that, but James Bond's also kind of lonely, because he can't let people in. He never had parents and has to serve England and all. That's tough. Even if it is England, which is like smaller than Rhode Island. So fuck England. After Sid, fuck England. After 1979, fuck England.

I pretend I'm James Bond, but in America, in Michigan. James Bond in Flint.

The reason I'm telling you this is because when I'm going through torture with Patty and Shelley, I go into this fantasy where I'm Bond, James Bond, and it's like a real long movie I'm laying out in my mind, intricate. It'd really impress you if you could watch it. Better than anything Hollywood. I've got all these characters, hundreds of them, like a Bible movie, and these villains, I've got villains, and they are trying to set up this nuclear Holocaust that will only attack people that are in the North, so that only the South can live. Militant Confederates, bearded Ayatollah clones in John Deere caps. Despite their beer bellies, they're really tough and scum and quick and they killed my dad by injecting a cold virus in him. I'm out to get them no matter what. And they have evil annoying Southern accents. I end up getting trapped down in Dallas and all of Texas is anti-North. Not only do I have to escape, but I have to find their headquarters, infiltrate, and destroy it and then give this big Abe Lincoln speech where I convert everyone into Northerners. I never give that speech though, because I'm continually escaping, so that's when Patty's making me stretch my quads and I squeeze the guardrails 'til my knuckles are hot white, because she makes me work, overwork. I tune out, run for my life in a Texas desert with helicopters chopping the air and I'm in camo with my quads bleeding in pain. I want to quit, but I have to keep going. Have to.

What Shelley lets me do is she plays the James Bond Film Themes for me. I bought it on tape just for the office. It took awhile before I could ask her to do that. Because that's my thing. Mom doesn't even know, because I only play it on my Walkman in bed. I fell asleep so many times with that on. Rolled over on two Walkmans already, breaking the headsets. Mom's like, "You go through Walkmans like you go through shoes," but in a nice way, kidding. So only Shelley does that. But listen to this: She was playing it for me one session, humming along so soft you have to listen close to hear her, and she says "Nobody Does It Better" is real romantic. Afterwards she gives me massages, because I get tense and can flex up and not stop and it hurts worse than any stretch, like my muscles are lifting a half ton, but she won't let that happen, so she gives me these pro rubdowns. We were on the second time through listening and "Nobody" comes on and she just got real into the massage. It was kind of sexual and medical and emotional and I know she did it on purpose. I was so aroused I had to shift my body, real gradually. Goose pimples ran up my arms, but I didn't say a word, because saying a word ruins everything. Silence is wisest. And she didn't say a word either. She just kept kneading, my back, my arms, my legs, really concentrating on my legs. I was so peaceful happy. Because no women ever touch my legs, ever. They are careful not to even bump them, like in the cafeteria or on the bleachers, and it would be so nice if a girl'd just put their hand on my knee one time, once, so I could feel they knew it was nothing, my cerebral palsy, you know, it's just a leg, it's fine, I'm fine. So anyway she's massaging

191

my thighs and calves and I'm buried in the white paper covering and I have this smile like the chubbiest kid in the world after he just got his first kiss.

Another time we were listening to the tape when it got bunched in the machine. She tried taking it out and rolling it back, but it sounded like bugs. I said, "Guess no more double oh, eh?" And the next time I went in, she had bought two copies! One for the office and one for me at home. I think I love Shelley in a way, but that sounds weirder than it's supposed to be. It's not that Patty's mean to me or anything. Not at all. I mean, she does a good job on my legs too, but Patty's young, in her twenties, and I just don't like or trust young women. You can't trust makeup. Old women rule, like Shelley. They have wrinkles and they care and you can just close your eyes and listen to an old woman, one that you know has lived her whole life and you can hear some magical shit in their voice, some real learning and some . . . just life.

Everybody else can burn in the depths of hell, but old women they go to heaven.

Chapter 42: Hollow

My decision to join the Navy is sudden.

My father was talking about how I need a job and I knew this but there was nothing I wanted to do. I applied at the mall music store, but they were not hiring. I looked through the phone book, from A to Y, and read every job from Abortion Alternatives to Youth Organizations and I could not find a single job that interested me.

In the Mining Journal, I found a cold study that looked interesting. They give you either the flu or a fake shot that is not really the flu and then they do tests on you. My father said, "You are not doing that. You do not even know what they are giving you. They did tests like that when I was young and they gave you LSD and the kids went mad, diving through windows to their deaths, lifelong depressions, jail."

I was like, "Cool, dad. Calm down."

I go to the recruiter's office and tell him I am ready. He shows a list of "rates," but the jobs look the same. MP interests me, but it is full. The recruiter talks me into going "un-dez" ("undesignated"), saying if I am lucky I could end up with the most adventurous job in the Navy—Boatswain's Mate. Like he knows my dreams, he says the U.S. has been in peacetime for years and you get to lie out on deck and look out at an ocean of stillness.

At home, after signing, I lie in bed and wonder. I try listening to the radio, but every station in the U.P. suffers from exhaustion. There is a rock, a classical, a pop, and two country stations. I listen to the pop one sometimes, but if you listen all day, you hear Paula Abdul sixty times before bedtime. Q107 drives you crazy. My room is silent a lot.

So, all I do for three hours is throw a basketball at my ceiling one handed.

This helps with my shot release. And, it helps me daydream, about left-hand lay-up drills after lights-out at Miners' because I could not see in the dark to shoot free throws. And, shooting threes in the snow at the bent-rim netless court at the bottom of our hill, wearing gloves, balancing on ice, the ball so cold it would not dribble. And, shooting up onto my roof, pretending there was an invisible rim up there. And, balling up my T-shirt and dunking with that when Charles Asgard took his ball home. And, losing the first game of the playoffs to the Fliv-vers, a team with twice as many regular season losses as us, getting back to the locker room, Eric Korinen crying, and it hits the entire team, tears, and I would not have cried, but I kept thinking about Hank Gathers, Loyola, funerals, left-handed free throws, March sadness.

Basketball, the only sport worth living. And, it was over.

J and me graduated. J skipped the ceremony and I skipped the ceremony men-tally, walking across the stage like a ghost, silence when they called my name, the biggest graduation insult—silence. How quickly I will be forgotten in this city. One day you are a name on an attendance list, the next a memory.

At the class all-night party, Antony forges J's name to enter the four of us in the lip-synch contest. Doing "Fight For Your Right To Party," we tear down the hanging decorations, banners and posters with IHS CLASS OF '90 in rain-bow spray paint cheerleader graffiti. The principal stops the music, banning us from the competition. Antony and Craig were happier with that than if we had won. The fifty dollar grand prize went to five straight A, straight hair, straight-laced girls with braces who did "Walk Like An Egyptian" in sign language. Our argument: there was no lip-synching involved.

Antony is my invitee. After begging my girlfriend, she invited J. Steve Thomp-son is here with Craig. Every senior is allowed one guest, so all of us hang out. Craig says how lucky I am to be going in the military and that he is going to kill himself before he does another year at Ish. High, how he does not want to do two-a-days with Coach Puletti when the end of the summer rolls around, how he does not want to take wood shop or study hall or anything for that matter. "Ishpeming Homo-tites," he keeps repeating loud enough for the principal to hear. I go to the bathroom, because I do not want hard feelings between Prin-cipal Antonetti and me. He is losing his hair, is getting divorced, and lives by Antony, so he does not need any more hassles. All night Antony keeps impersonating Rick Dees' impersonating Donald Duck. He does it pretty good, but it becomes relentless so I go to the bathroom again. At seven am, right before finding out the class bully won the grand prize brand new used 1987 fire red Ford Escort, Shelley talks to me about how if we have kids, three, they can never go to the hospital. I say, "Why are you telling me this, here?"

She leans into me, squeezes my arm weakly.

I ask, "What if they have the flu?"

She says, "They will never get the flu."

I say, "What if they do?"

She says, "Then we pray."

One of the Bangle sign language quintuplets unsuccessfully jumps to grab the string of a balloon clinging to the township hall ceiling, the balloon looking for an escape hatch up there that does not exist.

I say, "Can they dance?"

She asks, "Who?"

"Our kids."

"You said 'our kids.'"

"Yes, well, can they?

"Why are you being ridiculous?" Shelley says.

I ask, "Does that mean yes or no?"

"Of course they can." She kisses me on the cheek. She notices Craig and moves the kiss to my mouth. Finishing kissing, she clenches my hand, webbing our fingers, and says, "But I want home schooling."

The next day, today, fully under the effects of sleep deprivation, I visit the recruiter, and finalize all the papers, dozens of signatures that get sloppier with each new sheet. In two weeks, I leave.

At home, my mother sits upstairs scissoring off her split ends, peeking out the window at the deadest neighborhood around—what is she looking at? The little cemeteries of the night that are our neighbors' empty porches? She is always sitting, thinking, remembering, something. I ask what she is doing and she says, "Nothing." I hug her, go downstairs, and stare out my bedroom window, thinking of her, my mother. She wears polar bear pajamas and old gray sweats daily. She hides bags of Milk Duds on the top shelf above the washing machine. She never reads now, never listens to the radio, nightly watches the

TV6 news, leaves the room to prepare for bed while sportscaster Mike Gleason does high school scores. She blows her nose so hard she gets nose bleeds. She is worried I am going to leave. I am. I have to. She is not ready for this, but my parents need to be alone in this house and they need to either break apart forever or bond. After I leave. After the house gets as quiet as it can get. After I go overseas, volunteer, do something heroic, so they can be proud, happy, for the first time in eighteen months. If I do not leave, I am going to die.

The way I see it, the only way of getting out, and getting out now, is joining the military.

On the phone, Craig sounds excited. As a going away present, he says he is going to give me his poster of some New York Jets player I never heard of and that I could never take with me to boot camp anyway. He also says Antony wants to shave my head before I go, but there is no way Antony is getting near me with a razor blade.

Lastly, he says we have to hurry, because there is something we are all going to do—J, him, Antony, and me—before I leave. He refuses to tell me what, because he says if I know I will not do it. So I tell him I am not doing it no matter what then. He says, "Yeah, yeah" and says he is swinging by Antony's to see what he is up to. And, Antony is always up to something.

Chapter 43: antony

a guns on the bed

smack dab in the middle

pacin, im thinkin, in my room, in my underwear, in my bathrobe, hood up, one sock on, one off, pacin, pacin, wit a pillow, my pillow, in my hands, over my head, over my ears, mufflin, so i can think. if this is the right thing to do. shit, i mean i have to, i mean shit

but moerfucks dont know!

moerfucks live with blinders on!

moerfucks act tough 'n' shit!

fuck that

moerfuck that

ima be tough & shit

no more candyass life. no more "oh im a punk ass bitch, take me out with a fuckin louisville slugger, i wont do shit, im afraid, wont retaliate, ill fuckin suck my own cock all day in a corner." fuck that. fuck that, fuck that fuckthat. driveby on a bitch. drivemoerfuckinby. the D, the R, the I, the V, the E, the B, the Y

moerfucks dont know

moerfucks wit blinders on

moerfucks act like detroit aint pumpin in the blood of the u.p.

michigan is michigan. bitch

michigan is Michigan

this the shit you live to tell yo grandkids bout. this the real shit. grab the bozack, punk

guess ma knocks on my door, but i dont hear. its unlocked & corner of my eye i see it openin, slowly. without lookin, i drop the pillow on the bed, where i split second estimate the gun should be

"can i come in?" ma says, standin in the door, mousy voiced

"no"

we stare

we stare at each other, my robe open, a look on my face of what has to be a cross of racin heart terror & little boy stillness. i stare in silence, at my mothers wounded face, like she knows, when she dont, but she could have, if shed barged into my life, years ago

& not til the door closes as gently as it opened, do i look, see the pillow, coverin the gun, the pillow luckily, or unluckily placed, really, by the hand of God

Chapter 44: J

The letter says I won a scholarship to Northern Michigan University. A Recognition Award. I knew I was getting in, but this scholarship has been a long wait. I get $200 a semester. That's it. $400 a year. I wait months, sitting, hoping, praying, months, and they tell me, "Congrats, you have won a scholarship." There's no way I can afford school, so I'm excited, right? I'm going to college. Nobody in my family has ever gone. Ever. Ever. I mean, it's not like I can wait tables. I can't stand for more than fifteen minutes without having to take a serious break. It's not like they'll hire me at the mine. It's not like they'll hire me for anything in this fucking town. But with a degree, I could use my mind. But how do you get the degree? With a fifty-dollar a month scholarship?

I tell this to Bill. I'm back at his place with Hollow. He drove. We talked on the way and the conversation for the entire fifty-minute trip to Rock, MI was about leaving, out of here. Hollow surprises me and tells me he leaves in a few days. A few days and he's free. Everything is making me want to run, like Hollow is proving to me that you can escape. I told him I'd join the Marines if they'd let me, but they won't. Hollow tells me that wherever he ends up stationed, I should go. I'm not gonna do that. This whole ride over, I've been thinking, about all this, what my life is here, and let me tell you what my life is here, because this is what my life is here.

Craig got me pumped to play football. Craig told me how there were positions for me. I could hold the ball for the punter. I'm strong, he tells me, tough, and I am, in different ways than football players, better ways, and he begged me to come out for the team, said he'd block for me, if anyone tried to tackle me, he'd knock them on their ass. It was a feeling like flying, or better, like attempting to fly. Anytime you tap into that, that feeling that you can do what others do—like when I couldn't ride Big Wheels. Everybody on my block rode one, and I couldn't. But I could ride a Green Machine. It's like a Big Wheel, but better. They fit my legs, not all compact like a Big Wheel. I could stretch out, relax, and actually ride something for once. Whoever designed those—thank you. Well, thinking about playing high school football with the team gave me a feeling like that, like riding down West Barnum with the trees bent blocking out a picturesque about-to-rain sky and you're doing joke birdcalls with your kicking cycling buddies zooming on each side of you, free. Like that. An "I can do anything." So. I go up to the coach. Coach, who never acknowledges me in the halls. Coach, who teaches Civics. Coach Puletti. Mr. Puletti. Rodney Puletti. Rod. The end of a school day and he's in the hall and I'm at my locker psyching myself up. I slam it and take a long intake of breath. He goes past, but I run after, "Mr. Puletti. Mr. Puletti." He stops. I step up, another breath, deep, brave: "I want to play."

I'm expecting him to say that's great. Instead I get, "You want to, what, be an equipment manager?" I explain, let it out, how I can do it, beaming, talking loud, I want the junior girls nearby to hear, I want any jock walking by to know, you know, that I can do this too, even with cerebral palsy, I can tackle as well as the next guy, block, cheer, memorize plays, encourage, get my face in the mud, it all. Puletti tells me he will do everything in his power to make me quit. This man has a college education, mind you, and this man looks at me with his curved posture where he's always showing off his chest like we're all operating at the level of peacocks and I want to rip his mustache off. He says what would happen if I get hit in the leg and my leg withers and shrivels to the bone. I can't believe people can actually think like this.

And let me tell you what else life is here. Life is going through high school and not having one date. Never. Prom. I went. With Hollow and Shelley. I danced with Shelley. She asked me and she was so elegant, feather-light. Head near chest, she leaned into me and I wanted to kiss her so bad; you have no idea. There's a smell to girls that you don't get, realize, fully, until they're right next to you, and then it makes you shake. A slow song came on and she danced with Hollow and I watched, looked around at all these perfect-legged couples, and a tear came, but I swallowed it, hard. You can swallow tears. I know how: you scream.

So I did.

A banshee. A real Rotten yell. From me. At the prom.

Of course, that drew looks from the Negaunee High student body. They had to stop their perfect lives for three seconds. But the funny part is when they saw it was the punk kid that did it, they went right back to slow dancing, empty circles. Anyone else and it would have struck something. They would have called the cops or an ambulance or at least rushed to my side. But from me . . . in the middle of a live version of Steven Tyler wailing "Dream On" . . . it's somehow expected. Ignored.

Who wants to date the crippled kid? Nobody even asks about my legs. Not one girl ever even asked. They're all quiet. Or worse, smile, flat polite mouths. Even the girls that were my friends never asked. They were afraid. What's to be afraid of? Don't these people understand something that's actually frequent in society? I mean, three other people in this city have cerebral palsy. John Woods, who's like forty and works at Bunny Bread has it. And James Raddomyselskiy who was a freshman last year and whose sister has the law firm that does social security disability, Raddomyselskiy & Morgan. And Eddy Makinen. And people have the nerve to ask me if they're my brothers. They'll say, "Is John your brother?" And I'll say, "John Woods?" And they'll be like, "Yeah, is he?" And I'm like you fucking idiot. You know my last name isn't Woods. And it sure the hell isn't Raddomyselskiy.

Idiots.

And here's what else life is in this town. It's having an old codger drive up when you're walking along Iroquois and he rolls down his window to ask where Iroquois Drive is, but that's not the problem. It's that he's asking you this question like you're mentally retarded. He talks slow, speaking like you're a foreigner. "I'm not retarded," I say. He looks embarrassed, but then asks again and he's still talking as if I am retarded! I tell him he's driving on Iroquois, but I answer exaggeratedly slow, "Yerr ahhhhhn Ir-ahhh-quois." He gives me a funny look.

He gives me a funny look.

And here's what else. It's like growing up in an uninformed hick town where a January wind-chill of negative ten is no surprise.

It's trying to blend in.

And failing.

It's feeling self-conscious, so you let your mother buy you a preppy shirt and you comb out the Mohawk and go to school and do your best to be pleasant and say hi to cheerleaders, but they don't buy it. Neither do you. They actually treat you more rude when you do this, so you go home and put on a Reverb Motherfuckers T-shirt that you made up with black block letters at Go! Go! Tees! in the Marquette Mall for $12.79 and you mousse back up the 'hawk to its highest heights and on the way to the TV you walk by your parents' bedroom mirror over the table where your mom keeps her microscopic earrings and blow dryer gun and Dixie cup of barrettes and in the reflection you see how you walk, the lumbering, how you walk like no one else and how helpful it would be to walk exactly like other people, that same boring fluidity. But you go over to the mirror and say this word clearly to yourself, you say it, "Cripple." That word hangs in the air, reverberates. You look in your eyes, actually one eye, one hazel eye, you pick one, you pick the left one and you watch as a tear forms, the slow hesitating path down the inside of your cheek, until it falls into the groove of your lips and you can taste it, salt pain. And that's it. That's the only tear you've given yourself in the last five years. That's all. You've maxed out.

Because the last time, they came in buckets.

You were at the Marquette Mall waiting for your mom to come out of her hair appointment and some kids with Redmen jackets walked passed. You thought nothing of it, but when they were further down with their backs to you, one of them started walking just like you do. You're not sure if they were laughing, because you couldn't see their faces, but it just took over, an anger, a fear, and this devastating sadness, like a toothache in your skin, a body nausea, and your eyes wetted, so you ran to the bathroom and when you run your cerebral palsy shows even more, which just pushed it all out, all this water you didn't even know you have in you coming out of your eyes and nose and mouth.

It wouldn't have affected me like that if earlier in the day, I hadn't heard Dad yelling about our neighbor, Ms. Randle. She constantly complains about kids putting rocks on her lawn. Nasty Bitch apparently accused my Dad of child abuse, telling a neighbor my parents caused my "leg injuries," throwing me down stairs as an infant. After mom told him, Dad slammed a cabinet so hard dishes broke. He never loses it like that, punching walls. But he did that night. I was in my room, overhearing, holding it all in. I was fine, until the Mall. A one-two punch. When I got to the mall bathroom, I went in a stall, sat on the edge, and pulled the toilet paper to blow my nose, but the paper stuck, so I ripped it out and kept ripping until the entire roll was unwrapped in my hands, on the floor, in my lap, wrapped around my fists like a mummy, and the funny thing was it felt like I had enough tears to use it all.

After that, I went on a drought. Never cry. If you do, it shows they can get to you. And now, after this little cry in the mirror, the drought is back officially. Time to move on, I say, okay, I've understood, all right, I understand why they stare and why I'm picked last. So what if I can't dribble a basketball between my legs because I can't spread my feet far apart.

I say so fucking what.

Your bed has always been there for you, always. It's gotten you through homecoming pep rally weekend TV nights with Andy Kaufman Fridays and danceless school dances. That bed's a safe haven, especially with the headset nearby, and especially with Lou. "Perfect Day" calms and "Heroin" shuts it all out and "For Your Eyes Only" (with the vocals) and finally "All Time High (from *Octopussy*)" lullabies.

You wake up later with your shirt sweaty and you don't change. You go to school like that and feel great, normal. In the cafeteria, Hollow says, "What's up, J-J?" You say, "Jack shit," and he pats you on the back and everything's back to being all cool.

You think of the little things that make life worth living. Like Shelley at the clinic. And seeing Hollow holding hands with his Shelley. And playing HORSE with Craig and Antony, how you three never tire of saying, "I've got whore, what you got?" "No, man, you've got whores, not whore," and you win by banking a shot left-handed, because Hollow can never make that shot, so everybody decides to play a game of P-R-O-S-T-I-T-U-T-E, which means you can shoot all night until the lights cut off. And then sitting on the court at Miner's after dark gossiping as the headlights go by and by on US-41 in a serene rhythm.

And the coolest memory of them all, the one that always keeps you hanging in, and that's Lucky.

Lucky is a dog.

The best thing ever would to be a dog, wouldn't it? Dogs rule. Although some don't. Like Rottweilers. But generally you have to admit they do. Especially Lucky. Lucky was my Dad's old German Shepherd, back when Dad was with mom, when he used to only drink, before the methadone and all that, and that dog was an angel. I think there are angels in the world, but they're really rare. And they're hardly ever human. Sometimes they're in the air. Like I've seen angels, and I don't talk about this with people, but I saw one once at the top of my stairs in our old house in Palmer, before we moved to Negaunee. It was one of the few nights when I was left alone, because my mom used to be paranoid about leaving me, even though she understands C.P. I guess when you have a kid born premature weighing under four pounds you tend to worry and it's hard to let go. But I was alone and it was a violent July thunderstorm. I heard a metallic knock outside, which alarmed me because our door is wooden. I knew ghouls are afraid of light, so I turned on every one in the house. Even the corded pantry light bulb and bathroom nightlight. From outside, the house must have glowed. I turned up the TV so I had company, Johnny Carson interviewing Matthew Modine, who is one of my favorite actors, and they're talking about his role in *Vision Quest*, but there's no clip, so Matthew talks about how he grew up as youngest of seven in a Mormon family. He dropped out of BYU, and I have this little revelation, because I keep hearing this, but the best people, the people who succeed are the ones who drop out, and then the lights went out. It was like this was planned, like God was trying to create the scariest night of one kid's life, and He was succeeding. It went from glowing neon white to a black as dark as the pit of my stomach. No light was coming in from the windows or nothing, just the occasional flash of lightning. It was blind man black, and I lost it, yelling, for mom, going "Hello?" to the house, "Hello!" Nothing answered. If someone was outside, they would have knew where I was. I wanted to get to my bed because as long as there are no air pockets monsters can't get you, even if you're an adult. Feeling my way to the banister, listening for any killer's footsteps, I saw it above the stairs and it didn't scare me at all, because it was an angel and I will argue to my death with anyone who doesn't believe me, but it was glowing like nothing from regular life, like a peaceful electromagnetic field, and it was there. No tricks about it. Floating light the pure color of halos. I felt calm, like prayers were landing inside my chest. Then all the house lights came back on. And at the same time the phone rang and I jumped out of my head. It was like the time I sat by Goofus during a Miner-Modeltowner game and he let loose with his Goofus yell when I wasn't prepared. Scared the death out of me. Well, the phone did that. I rushed over and it was mom asking if I was all right, saying she'd be home in a bit. I told her I saw an angel and she said, "You did?" in this voice only moms have.

One time Dad hid in mom's closet. They were watching *Halloween* and he had a knife—my Dad, not Mike Myers. A dull butter knife, but it was a knife, and he opened the door, coming out with his arm raised with fake psycho face. Mom threw a Stephen King book at him, *Misery*, which banged against the closet door and then a lamp, knocking it over. A piece broke. The lamp was a wedding gift from grandma who died in '77 from "complications." I didn't go to the funeral. I didn't want to see her dead. Well, mom couldn't stop shaking. Dad opened his arms to hug her saying, "Kath," but she ran to my room, locking my door behind her. And she held me, woke me up and squeezed. I asked what's wrong and Dad came to the door with this soft voice he didn't even use with me when apologizing. He was saying, "Kathy, come out here, please, Kath, please." Mom tucked in closer and I got scared because this was when their marriage was falling apart, when the tensions were thick as grandma's beef stew, so it was really a wrong move on Dad's part, actually *the* wrong move, and I could feel change in my stomach. Mom didn't go to the door and Dad never even knocked, just left. She put her hand through my hair, combing it with her hands, fixing it, and then looked at me with seriousness, saying I had to be her strongman now. I had to protect her, because my father was leaving and she predicted it. She knew. She knew he was leaving before Dad even knew. He went to Vallejo, where he knew no one. Then Florida. Mom always told me that there was nothing more dangerous for my father than loneliness. She told me one time and I'll always remember it, "He doesn't know what to do when he's by himself." I wasn't alone. I had me. I had mom. I had Lucky.

Before the mine polluted the cricks, Dad and me used to fish in Palmer. By that old waterfall right when you're leaving on the way to Suomi, after the sharp curve where the speed's ten mph. We'd pull off, get out, and walk through swampland meadow with half-dollar size holes in the grass where you could see miniature streams flowing underneath. Walking was difficult, because my feet would sink. We'd get to this hill. And let me tell you, this dog had bad hips. For German Shepherds, it's common. It's a genetic defect, normal in that breed. So we bonded right there. Lucky used to look at me so deep. Like we were connected. Lucky would stop at this hill so I'd have to stop because she'd be in front of me blocking the way and then she'd run down to the bottom to check and make sure it was safe. She'd run back up and guide me down. Now that's a dog. A godsend. Two years ago, she died, a year and three-fourths ago. Late November. I remember petting her and feeling what I thought might be a lump on her neck. I told Dad and he took her to the vet and seven months later she was gone. They gave her five weeks. She lived seven months. She died in Dad's lap. She was in spasms and her head was limp, tired, her legs kicking and Dad was alone with her in the leafy backyard, mom gone to Iron Mountain. Through the window, I watched my Dad. Bawling. I'd seen but never heard my Dad cry and there he was, full beard, looking old when he always comes across as the eternal twenty-two year old. Looking weak, and this was the first time I ever saw my dad look weak, with Lucky in his hands, holding her close, cradling her, petting her. Gently I opened my window because I wanted to hear, needed to hear, everything, and when the window slid open, I could make out Dad's words: "You were good, so so good, you always were" and it was like he was talking to me, whispering in my ear. His tears slid down landing on the fur until there was only a limp small body in my Dad's hands, so small, and then Dad wipes his sleeve on his nose and saw me in the window, his face so wet and hurt, just a hurt, his cheeks red, eyes sore, and that's how it felt to me when Dad left.

No one driving by our house would have known this was going on. I kept staring. But I didn't cry. Maybe because I knew that dog was an angel and could never die.

I tell Hollow this on the way to Bill's, on the way to Rock. But in shorter form. All these old memories drift through my head, but I skip details, because I can see it all and that's what matters. Hollow gets the idea. He listens well. There's a pause, the drive, the dullness of life coming back, and then Hollow says, "Was that the same dog that ate your mother's parakeet?"

"What's your point?" I say.

"Well, I guess even angels get hungry." Then Hollow tells me his mom bought a birdcage yesterday from an antique shop near Koski's Korners. She hasn't bought a bird yet, but plans to soon, before Hollow leaves for boot camp.

And then we're there. Bill's. Rock. He's cooking. Stew. Venison. It smells better than home. The pot is gigantic. He lets it simmer, been "for eight hours." In a half-hour, we eat. I tell him why we came. "For my stew?" No. I want one more tattoo. He says, "They're addictive, aren't they?" I say it's not really a new one; I just want him to finish the last one. He squints and says, "Didn't your father say no?"

"I don't want the girl's name."

He says, "How quickly we move on."

Hollow mumbles that "this is more important," but we ignore him because he's being shy, standing away, as if crow-eyed Bill intimidates him.

I say I'm not moving on and start to say, but then Bill interrupts, asks if I called her. No. He says to. Says she's out west, "waiting for some young man to sweep her off her happy feet." If women have happy feet, they don't need to be swept away. Bill's body lightens when he says this, like he's remembering something good, what I call 'a helium memory,' the type of memory you wish you could fly away with. He says she visits Michigan a lot because her parents are, and I talk over him this time and keep going, saying, "Actually it is about moving on." Bill puts out bowls and glasses, a comedic mix of cups— coffee, Dixie, tea, basically the first things he lays his hands on. As always, dinner's going to be informal. Bill's doing all this to keep his hands busy, so he can avoid eye contact. Bill's big into avoiding eyes, but when he does look at you, he looks into you. Hollow's buried away somewhere in the house, snooping, gliding by shelves in slow motion, like he's memorizing each artifact, and I wonder if it's not a ploy to make his way to the tattoo breast photos. I drop my voice and say to Bill, "I have a strange request." Hollow reappears, his supersensitive hearing intact.

"Okay," Bill says pretty vacant, no feelings, because he's probably gotten strange requests his whole life, like Linus blankets on triceps, eagle tattoos on asses, swastikas on foreheads. Bill owned tattoo parlors in Tucson, Hayward,

Cheyenne, and Gainesville. That's how he met my Dad. They were two Yoopers in Florida. Two Yoopers that loved pavement freedom, Pompano Beach, broad hurricane-escape freeways, Key Largo, philosophizing in the armpits of overpasses to weather out flash Everglade rain showers. They hit it off like Sid and Johnny. And now here was his best friend's son in front of him asking, no, begging for a tattoo.

"I don't have any money," I say.

Bill groans. "Oh, so you want a free meal and a free 'too too." He laughs, but friendly, old, from a real Marlboro Man. I say it's a continuation of the last one. He says he gave the last on the house, so this one might as well be too.

"That mean you'll do it?"

He says, "Do what? What tattoo you want? A different girl's name? Because I'd agree with your ol' man about that."

I say no. I tell him Hollow's going in the Navy and Bill tells us he was stationed on the USS Finback. A Sonar Tech. The most important job on the sub. Without sonar, they'd run into mines, land, other subs. Stationed in Norfolk. Me and Hollow act surprised. Bill says he has an Associate's. From Edison Community College. Fort Myers. Florida. We didn't know he had an education, now did we?

We act interested and then get back to what matters. I want him to give me the name of a city right underneath the lady burning in hell on my arm. He goes, "What city?" And then adds, "Negaunee?" and this gives him and only him a real laugh, "You don't want Negaunee on your arm!" His eyes light up and his face is, for a moment, shiny. Then, late, Hollow laughs.

I say, "Nooo." I say that this is the fun part, the crazy part, the strange part. I say I want him to give me the city name. He asks what I mean and I tell him. I want him to put a city name on my arm and I don't want him to tell me what it is while he's doing it. He says I must be crazy, but in a nice way and I tell him I'm serious. He asks why I'd want to do that and I tell him I have to get out of here. This will make me go, push me. Somewhere. He interrupts, says, "Weren't you going Northern?" I tell him how I can't afford it and need to get away. He asks why, says the U.P. is scenic, uncrowded, with hunting, no crime, "Where else can you leave your doors unlocked? You can't do that in Florida. Even if you're in the car!"

"Weren't some camps broken into?" Hollow asks, "Last month. On Dead River."

I start to tell Bill, but before I get into it he says he understands. To himself, he says, "A city," and laughs. His laughter turns into a smoker's cough and he lights a cigarette near where all the mechanic parts are lying with dishrags so oily you can smell fume and Bill goes, "What city you want?" I tell him that's the point, he has to come up with it and he says, "Then what? You want 'Miami' on your arm the rest of your life?"

I shout out, "No, don't tell me the name!" He shakes his head and I say, "Just do this, okay. Give me a tattoo, any city you want, and then, here's the thing, I'll move there." He turns off the stove, pours stew. I say, "But what I want you to do is I want you to think, because, you're like fifty, right?"

"Forty-seven."

Bill's serious now. I feel bad about asking his age so I cover by saying, "My Dad trusts you and says you're great and told me he's moved to places because of you, because you were there." Bill turns away when I say this. "And, I just want you to think what place it was that you were at that you had the best time of your life, like over your entire life. Where were you when you were the most happy and then I want you to put that city on my arm and what I'll do is I won't look and you don't tell me and then I'll have it covered and when Hollow gets on the bus to leave for boot camp . . ."

Hollow interrupts softly, "MEPS."

"MEPS. When he leaves for MEPS, I'll take the bandage off and find out where I'm going."

Bill says, "And what if you don't like the place?"

I say, "I haven't been anywhere. Only Michigan and Wisconsin. That's the same state! So I haven't really been anywhere, ever. I'm ready to go. Some place."

"Someplace special," Hollow mumbles to himself from the shelf room.

I go on, "It don't matter. Wherever you think. If it was the place where you were most happy, then it must not be that bad a deal." Bill's thinking, and I like this, I like this whole event. I like the feel in the room in my skin in the air. Cold fresh air comes through an open window like angel breath and everyone's alive. This is the best thing I've ever done, I'm thinking. More people should do this, I'm thinking.

Bill says, "I'll give it some thought" and opens the fridge, ducks his head inside.

Hollow and me watch TV. Donahue. The topic is politics and science. Hollow says, "If there's one thing I hate, it's politics and science."

We switch the channels, but it's static. Bill says, "I cut the cable," so we go back to Donahue. It comes in clearly so you can see Donahue's snowy hair perfectly. Two Senators sit by Phil and there's so much gray on the stage, it's like America's dying. They talk about Reagan. Hollow yawns and says the word "yaaawn" while he does it.

Hollow says, "Donahue sucks when he's sitting at the table. I like when he runs around." "When he spazzes out." "He does cocaine." "What?" "I like when the guests don't suck." "They always suck." "Why doesn't he interview Lou Reed?" "You see that video where his head gets peeled off?" "Whose head?" "You see the interview with the people who were walking in the snow and their feet froze off?" "No." "Oh, it was weird. Their feet froze off."

We sit down for dinner. Hollow lip-smacks like an orphan. Bill says, "You boys aren't afraid of eating Bambi, are you?" He tells us he's writing a cookbook for deer meat and how hunters park in front of his yard despite the new "No Trespassing" signs and how he shot his latest buck in the stomach and had to follow the blood trail mixed "with intestinal matter." Bill enjoys ruining the meal and hopes we find it tasty all in one. He says he could shoot an eight point right off his back porch.

After we eat, he takes us behind his house where a hooked deer hangs with its insides carved out. Trying to avoid it, I look at a whittled sign saying, quote-unquote, Your Heart Beats Even When The Kill Isn't Your's, Cause Your's Is Out There. Bill is so apathetic about the gutted deer it's obvious he's trying to play the role of hunter. He shows us a faded tattoo on his calf of Ted Nugent. Alongside it says, "Moter City Mad Man." I look close to see if "Motor" is misspelled and it is. But I don't tell him. I'm sure he's heard it before. People either ask questions too often or not enough. On his other calf I notice an intricate design with broad swirling loops of the letters "F.B." Hollow asks if that's his initials and Bill says, "My first name is Bill," like Hollow's an idiot. So I ask and Bill says polite it stands for "Fred Bear." Hollow asks what that means but Bill ignores him. I tell Bill I love Iggy Pop and he says, "Hmm" like he doesn't know the name or if it even is a name. I tell him Iggy's from Ypsilanti and he says, "By Detroit, right?" I say yeah and that I like MC5 too. He says, "Mmhmm." And says, "Bob Seger's from Detroit" and adds "Michigan anyway."

Hollow adds, "Madonna's from Michigan."

Bill says, "She's Italian. What's her last name? Guccione?"

"Yeah, something like that," Hollow says.

We stare at the woods with the sounds of bugs and distant birds. The beautiful fading dusk.

Then it's time for my tattoo. I say, "But don't tell me, whatever you do."

Bill says, "Man, I've been thinking about this and it's tough."

"Well," I say, "Do not tell me."

Bill says, "But what if my favorite place was where I met my wife?"

And I say, "Please don't tell me."

Bill says he won't, but then continues, "But what if the best time of my life was when I first met my wife and we would go out to the clubs and laugh and . . . that was a different time . . . it's not like your wife is waiting there." I look at Bill and he looks at me and underneath that scruffed leathery skin and tired drunkard body, he has child's eyes. He says, "Or maybe she will be," and gives a little hmph. I nod. Bill pulls out a chair, gives me the tattoo.

He works on my arm and Hollow comes over to see what city it is and I tell him he can't look either. I almost make Bill screw up by jerking to make sure Hollow doesn't see. So Hollow watches Donahue. We try to have a conversation, but nothing comes out. Bill's concentrating, I'm thinking, Hollow's bored.

All I know is Bill gets done quick and that scares me.

Chapter 45: antony

the gun, that weight, that cold weight, like evil ready to cry out. holdin a gun is like holdin death. you can put power in your hands. i feel both good & sick. i turn off the light switch & jus hold it, the dark. my hearin, all my senses, heightened, so i hear my ma put the oven on upstairs, hear tracy stretch, myself breathe

i promised no onell make me look bad again, as long as i live. never. Never

but i got a feelin inside i never felt before. cradlin the gun like a dead bird in that dark of my room, i feel it, somebody, watchin. i dunno if its God or hollows brother or my grandpa or what. but someones there. lettin out a slow breath of air, i flick the light back on

hollow leaves tomorrow, manana, so we decided, or craig decided, to do this shit tonite. craigs grabbin his rifle out "from under lock & key," as he put it. then we cruise to Js, then hollows wholl be sleepin but craig said hollow aint got a screen door so its cake to bust in. & thats that

to keep my mind off my mind i finish the mix tape for tonite. all the best shit wit Comptons Most Wanted kickin it off. its set for that tune. side a, song 1. "Driveby Miss Daisy." song 2 is Young MC "Bust a Move." song 3, P.E. "She Watch Channel Zero?!" for craig. Terminator X samples slayer

i got so many thoughts bout this i cant put it in words which is strange cuz im a rapper & thats what we do. its like Christmas & goin the dentist & your 1st bobjob & detention & free tix to a N.W.A./Beastie concert all rolled in 1 thick fatass joint called life

finishin the tape feels good & bad, like an accomplishment you dont care bout, so i grab my slick rick tape to get me in the mood & throw it in droppin on my bed but the song that comes on is like violins & cellos & shit my grandma would listen to but then a voice starts singin "amazing grace" & it must be that jim neighbors guy which at 1st had me wonderin what was goin on but then i jus sit back & listen cuz his voice aint that bad & i lie there on my bed bitin my fingernails thinkin

thinkin quietly it dont get more fucked up than this. it jus dont
til the phone rings

. . .

. . .

Js father Died. fuckin almighty. in arizona. thats what i heard. mesa. Js ma called for my ma. im goin over craigs. (to me right now everythin looks like a gun)

see if he knows more details
i think he was beaten to death
im not sure
outside a bar
i heard he was beaten to death
i dont even know what to say
Jesus Christ
whats goin on

Chapter 46: Cräig

For the last thirteen hours, I've had *Reign* on loop. Side A. Flip. Side B. Flip. Side A, flip. Side B, flip. Side A, flip, Side B, flip, A, flip, B, flip, A, B, A, B, AB, ABA-BABABABABABABAB. Angel of Death Piece by Piece Necrophobic Altar of Sacrifice Jesus Saves Criminally Insane Reborn Epidemic Postmortem Raining Blood Angel of Death Piece by Piece Necrophobic Altar of Sacrifice Jesus Saves Criminally Insane Reborn Epidemic Postmortem Raining Blood Angel of Death Piece by Piece Necrophobic Altar of Sacrifice Jesus Saves Criminally Insane Reborn Epidemic Postmortem Raining Blood Angel of Death Piece by Piece Necrophobic Altar of Sacrifice Jesus Saves Criminally Insane Reborn Epidemic Postmortem Raining Blood Angel . . .

In my beanbag I fell asleep to Lucifer's lullabies.

In an hour and thirty-one minutes, we head out.

Today is god's birthday. Philgod. Anselmogod. I saved *Cowboys* as the final album to play before leaving. It's time. Under the lights we stand tall no one touches us.

First, a hit of Cat, first.

To stop my leg shakingshakingshaking.

To get my head to stop envisioning the Jason 3-D eyeball popping scene.

To calm down, I dial 900 numbers, 900-SEX-SEXX, which I guessed would work and did. I charged a hundred bucks, actually more. $3.99 a minute with a $9 connection fee and a six-dollar first-time user fee. But the chick was breathy-voiced as an asthma sufferer and I love that. Every time I was gonna release the white, she calmed me down, was like, "I haven't told you the best part yet, what I'm gonna do to myself," and oh god. When they do that. And her voice, gentle chick angelic like god with tits and she was it, man. It. I don't care if she was Tennessee fat, I'd marry her, felony record and all. Only reason I hung up is I had to get showering or Antony'd kill me instead of Corthead, so my parents will get the biggest bill ever from Prairie Entertainment, and this is money I do not have. Or my parents. That's gonna catch dad's attention when he does the old phone bill. How do you explain $3.99 a minute for 60 minutes, maybe 70, 75? Or 80? Combine that with my bond being set at $3000 for the trophy incident and my parents putting up the money, and, well, they're gonna crucify me. Way before the juvie court trial will.

What's funny is I still haven't sold a grave. And I never will.

To relax more, I turn up the stereo and carve a swastika above my ankle, but I think I put it backwards. I did it before I showered, wisely. Blood feels good. Slayer good. I'd carve 'Slatanic Wehrmacht' in my leg but all those letters hurt like hell. Take a paper clip, unfold so the pointy end is a Swiss Midget Army Knife needle and go to town forth and back until blood comes like pretty red paint. It's like itching a scratch not there 'cause it's deeper than skin. It's under the heart, like I'd have to stick that needle paperclip straight in my chest deep as death to get it out. I don't go anywhere with my parents anymore 'cause I'm sick of them and don't know why, just sick. A brick. Thick. You ever clenched your fists and flexed until your ears pop? Today I mirror-flexed so hard my nose bled. Shaking. Blood, good blood. Even my spit in the sink was goobered red. Like KISS. I left it there.

I put all these pins in my feet, like twenty I got from my mom's sewing kit, wanting to walk on fire. That's the thing, you can put pins in, anyone can, but to walk on them, that's what I care about. They fall off or go too far in, hit bone, Christ!, pain is a matter of how hard you clench your teeth. It's for coming unglued my body is rattling atoms explosion-waiting. Propped my foot up to heal, icing it, took the ice rack out the freezer, stuck my foot directly on it for the duration of "Cemetery Gates," then put the ice rack back. I hit the bench in my basement to calm down with weights. Doc says I'll have an aneurysm if I keep clenching like that, it's bad for my brain, why I'm headache crazed. Doing dumbbell curls gives me a shot of testosterone. I pace around the house shirtless bedroom to bathroom to basement walking passed the gun cabinet. I open it, pick one up, bring it upstairs, sit on my bed, and try to see how many ways, how many angles you can put a gun to your head. First, I turn on all the lights—the overhead bedroom light, my side desk lamp, the hallway light. To make it bright as possible 'cause with the gun I feel more afraid of the world, like ghosts suddenly exist. And I don't want anyone to bump me, especially anybody dead. I put the gun in the wide-open O of my mouth, bumping a tooth. Shot of ache. I feel to see if the tooth chipped, keeping my index finger straight and swiveling my head, beaver-faced. After that, I'm more careful. I put the butt of the gun on the floor. I put the butt of the gun between my legs. I put the muzzle to my cheek. I put the barrel to my forehead. I put it to my closed eye. I hold the gun straight up looking through the barrel like a telescope. Back to my mouth. There is something intimate about that final position, the end of the gun going deep, tasting it, tonguing metal, I go too far in, vomit, but not full vomit, just where you catch yourself but it's still in your mouth, where you can faintly taste it. Yank the gun out, shake my head, put it back in again, nice and slow. How come when people in movies put guns in their mouth it doesn't make them puke? Instead I put the barrel to my forehead, comfortable, lean forward, rest like that, thinking. Flicking the safety off and on at random, off and on until I discover a rhythm, off and on with the clicks of the safety until I play the theme from the Muppet Show. At this point, if my parents had been home, I almost might have went upstairs, tried talking. Tell them I need help. Tell them I'll go back to the counselor. But they were gone Presque Isle. That's life. Since I'm alone, I decide to handsome Saturday afternoon tired howlllllll

More lifting.

Dumbbell rows. Five sets of twelve reps. Fifty-five pounds. But the pinch comes, the headache beginnings. So I stop. Sit there. think.

Bobbie

Bobbie will not call back and see she keeps me sane keeps calling me insane called called called called called called called called until she called back with a restraining order Stegnowits warning scares me none none none nonenone o none

,Gone

I had to go to Doc Cox at MGH, that's the guy's name so cut 'im a break, he said I have to quit lifting. That's like asking Helen Keller to quit kicking. She can't; it's in her blood. It's the squats, I squeeze my head too tight, I can't think, the veins bulge the migraines come from punches to the face shock my skull blow a vessel in my head a migraine coming like rain on my dirty horizon better down two or three aspirin 'cause this or four 'cause this one's gonna mess with me tonite phone rings can't turn my head to the side I headbanged so bad a couple nights ago I gave myself whiplash serious can only look straight ahead pick up the phone I'm gonna be a real leper tonite with this fiasco goin' down hello and all these ailments and impalements did I hear J's dad died?

Damn.

God damn.

my body and brains turning inside out like the monkey in *The Fly* I'm growing faster than it'll allow eat all the time carrots whole grape bunches six packs Mountain Dew Fritos pies honey roasted peanuts in bed containers of O.J. Rocky Road chocolate cake I want to be big enough to kill anyone in the room I want dad old dad to come back hover over me try to hover over me close to my face thinking I'm afraid and then just unleash un-un-violence a release an art Pantera cover thrash ask PhilChrist I wish I was born June 30 I know I could kill anyone in the room now! 'cause I'm alone. but I could kill anyone at Ish High in the football locker room hell damn all I can think is "I am sick of your bullshit I never would have had you if your mother wouldn't have just let me get an abortion" quote-unquote to face all I think is "Unloading My Fist in your Face!" pleasure? except well not saying we'll drown Lake superior slowdeath the day immense it's decaytime like the whole town's watching me so let's give them something to watch band-it starve my head ex-amined bitchonthewall I leave MT hostiletime Cra:igy hi break don't let 'im push you stand up that were me I'd nail em in the nose eyes tears wrists teachers pethouse pentup merrily hatelife infestation : C Whitesnaked ItookCat man I took sum metha-C mixed with tab for my head a rrrriot of torsos a Pattycake ah steroidsscumbag highschoolgun's'd tellyoubout the catgun? whorerhard lone ly Ness tiredas E vil Bobbiecall, girl! catnight Bobbiesquit armCO holic killstop alcotease they'relllike whoyou? antonycomesover New rap e focuss onme fckedup wodka youready4dis pai painpai hellp 'n g Crayg? dah-runk dreamschange: babies rain from Heallvens slapon concrete i in a boxin matchmeadow out'side Antony gainst the ref swings me the crowd rushes fightall the stage's a fist then fists clouds break thru rip crashface minefists overthen fetuses form the stars fromthestars comedown likelight like zygote-soft' scream without parashoes chutes hit Earth flat tenbloddy

bold bloods y umbilicalhung meround mypast hurts Helladder999 4yohroatom
aged tomtombomb-junk pigfcknpong O o deth-aag b o 999 6066ie, ipredict-
mydeath

iwant you to come

I want you to

Iwant you to

I want you

I want you

I want you

Iwant you

I want

I want

I want

I want

I want

I want

I want

I want

I

I

I

I

I

I

I

I

I

I

I

I

I

I

I

I am the world's forgotten boy.

Chapter 48: Hollow

That meditative state of riding, in Craig's car happy taking me out for one last time before I go. Go, free, I'm naturally high but with a dank smell of faint smoke in the car. With Antony front passenger side, I'm stuffed in the back, my knees pressed high against the seat, feet hovering off the floor. Driving over railroad tracks, my head bumps the roof. I figure we're going Big Boy because that is the only twenty-four hour place. An annoyed chorus says, "What you doing, man?" when my window comes down, the night air cold, sobering, a rare perfect cool where shorts feel comfortable in the brisk U.P. night. Independence Day is in less than a week, so Marquette County is packed for Pioneer Days, and I wear a generic camouflage T-shirt an Army recruiter gave me as a last ditch effort to have me be all that I can be.

And, all that I can be is silent when Antony mutters that we are doing a driveby.

McDonald's?

No, a driveby driveby.

I am like cool after that we can rob the Co-op. We ride and I look for laughs or are they serious? It hits me they might be when Antony says, "On Cort's ass." Antony's Tiger D cap cocks to the side 'like Flavor.' I lean over the back seat so Craig and Antony are on each side, my head poking between in the middle. Craig looks vicious-faced. "If you guys are serious, pull over," I say meekly. They squirm and the big thing for you to remember is this is happening, happened, I am antsy, mad, they see, and finally Craig drives slowly on the edge of the road, a smoke of dust behind us. Not stopping he turns down the Slayer, always Slayer. He owns two hundred tapes, $2000 in tapes. Antony says to put in some mix tape of his but Craig ignores him. I say, "You guys kidding or what?"

Craig pulls down a side road, tightly wooded. Antony, in front, has his jacket on his lap. In the shade, the dark of Antony's lap, I see what looks like metal, a barrel, sticking out of . . .

"Antony, what is that?"

"Huh?"

"That!"

"Wha?"

"A gun?"

"No."

"Why's it in the car for?" I look to J.

Craig goes, "Act cool, act cool, act cool."

"He's straight and narrow like a straightened arrow," Antony says, "I told you."

"Cool," Craig reemphasizes.

Antony ejects Craig's tape.

"Whatchou doing!" Craig says, grabbing Antony by the wrist. They struggle over the tape, it falling to the floor.

Usually J would be the one to tell Craig to shut up, to grab Antony by the back of the neck, but instead he is in the back with me, no movement, a non-blinking carcass. "This isn't the way to Marquette," I sound whiny. Why did I get in in the first place? Because they basically kidnapped me, Craig hobbling for some reason, busted in my house with cheers of Big Boy fish and chips and chocolate shakes 'on J.' At the time, I was down in the basement with my mother, chasing from room to room a bird I had let out of its cage. Laughing, Craig grabbed my arms and Antony and J clutched my legs as they dragged me off announcing, "We're going Big Boy," and we're not.

Liar, hell, if anything we're heading to Big Bay. I should have known when J didn't agree and my mother said "Take care guys" as we left not knowing they had a gun in the car and are nuts and here I am in a red shit Chevy. I could jump at the tracks, risk a broken leg, hitch home, but for God's sake, I'm going to boot camp! And, that's what they want, me to get injured, not be able to go, end up rotting here. I should be asleep right now, resting.

I can see J's eyes, half-closed, red. Pot? Crying? Antony says Cort moved, he moved, he doesn't live there anymore, here anymore. Craig disagrees, says,

"No, he didn't, no, not yet, you're wrong." Matt Cort's father was laid off at the Empire, but he has so many points built up he's bumping off someone at the Tilden Mine, so they're moving closer to it, to National Mine, out of Negaunee Township.

"You have to drive. J can't," Craig says to me, "Look, here is the deal, we planned this. Ditch me and Antony at the graveyard, okay. From there, boom, it is a straight shot home through the caving grounds. No one will follow us through there."

That sweet smell of smoke is still faintly in the air. Antony adds, "Afterwards, the streets will be packed with cops"— "Yeah, all three" Craig interjects, laughing – "So, we have to get all us off the streets in minutes. So you take the car back with J, and me and Antony go through the woods, you two are home in minutes and don't worry about me and Antony." I do not understand a word of it. Antony adds "We'll take the guns with us. Cops pull you over, you didn't do a thing." J's silent, sucking it all in, an immobile suckerfish, forehead pressed against the car window. Antony goes "No one's in Cort's house." Craig goes, "That's what you want to believe, believe it."

Craig continues, "We need you Hollow." Craig says, "You didn't know what was going on. You're innocent." I say, "There's a word for if you do this and it's an illegal word and then I'm in, I'm in with this and I'm not going to be, because I'm going in the military. Tomorrow!" Craig orders Antony, "Tell him quiet down or one of these neighbors is gonna get our license down." Craig has a gun between his legs. Antony has a gun across his lap. In the distance, I see lights, but can't tell if they're from a house, like they're floating in the woods, a far off specter. We could scream a good minute-and-a-half and no one would hear. Antony rolls his window up and we dart down another dirt road, bumping up and down, ducking to keep from knocking my head on the car ceiling, and suddenly we're slightly to the left of nowhere and I mean nowhere. Antony cranks the stereo bass and Craig immediately turns it down even softer than it was before so that now you can hear a wind, the crickets, something out there making a hideous scraping of wings tree branch arms scraping car sides. I've lived here eighteen years and don't know this road. I heard a senile man lived in this area that walked around Ishpeming everyday, he never spoke, and I remember once driving by and Antony saying "Look at the crazy bastard," and J said, "Let him alone, his wife died." But now J's silent as the moon. That's all I know. On this old hell road, I expect the decrepit cracked guy to appear, a real horror movie move, pop up in front of the car, headlights hitting him, then the car hitting him, but instead, and this isn't any better, Craig pulls over, kills the lights.

"Just," Craig faces me, says, "Do this for me, for us. This once. Please."

The woods wait for my reply. Antony rests his hand on the gun, without thinking, not warning me, just casually, absentmindedly. He could also shoot me absentmindedly, and that idea leaves, because they're my cousins, relatives, family. I think, "I hate these people." That sits heavy. I think how I didn't choose them. I was born into it, a million locations in the world, Barbados Laos Maine. I could've ended up in Hong Kong, Quebec, Butte, but I'm here, born here, in Ishpeming Negaunee Palmer, growing up with these three. With them, I've never been able to talk, about Shelley or my brother or anything. Other than laughing over local car accidents, stealing construction signs, smashing North Road streetlights, pointing at police and running, making fun of Winnie Karpinnen's Men At Work eye by singing 'Who can it be knocking at my door?' I feel like being a male is nothing but emptiness and nausea and I'm so glad I'm going in the service and getting away from this isolated shit life, and it's a realization. I say, "Craig," my voice cracks in half and I could cry, "Craig . . . I'm. I am . . ." And, I rub my hands through my hair, my short hair, remembering my shoulder length hair freshman year, but it's gone now, for basketball, for the service. I look out at the black hole sky and back at Craig and say, "I'm going in the Navy tomorrow. Today." I look at my wrist, at a watch that's not there. "I'm not going to screw that up."

Antony lets loose, "Hollow, this isn't . . . I'm doing this for a reason."

"We have reasons," Craig says, like that explains everything, like that sentence means something.

"Because he hit you?" I say, "With the bat?"

Antony continues, "Craig was telling me how in psychology you need to do symbolic things. This is very symbolic."

Confused, I say, "Did you even hear what I just said?"

Craig speaks to Antony, not me, goes, "No, we understand, and tonight you're not going to do anything wrong."

Antony speaks to me, says, "This is planned, all of it." Except this, this isn't planned.

I say, "I want to go home, now, please. Guys," like a real teacher's pet coward.

Antony bangs his fist on the dashboard and goes, "I'm . . ." Antony looks down at his shoulder, a glance, supposed to be unnoticed, a reflex on his part, then at me. Antony continues, "I changed. Am changing, back. Tonight.I'm . . ." He looks at J and goes, "You get it, right?"

Craig says, "Don't hit my dashboard."

Antony continues, "Right?" Craig shakes his head yes. I look at J so everyone looks at J and J's got this great indifference, a nursing home stillness, his arm bandaged, some city waiting underneath to burn into his future, an idiotic idea, really, but he's numb to life. I wonder when that happened, that unfeeling, at birth? J looks hard, hardened, dull, and even dead. J has so much innocence in him at times I wondered if he'd ever grow up. I look at Antony and, even at sixteen, Antony has that unemployed uncle look. I'm categorizing each of them, my head is doing this, I look at Craig and Craig looks strong, lost, and controlled, like he knows what he's doing and Craig goes, "This is a one time thing. Me and Antony are doing a one time thing. Where everything's cleared and cleaned and; look, I don't want to explain. I don't have to explain." He looks at Antony, "I've already explained," and turns away to look outside at the world that's waiting for people who make the right choices, just waiting with every dream you could ever imagine, but Craig goes right over it with, "This is for Antony. This is so Antony can sleep, and doesn't have this weight, weighing." Antony straightens his D cap, facing it forward, normal, but pulled over his eyes, deep, and we all sit. Craig looks at me, then at Antony, then J, then the seat, then me, the seat again, holds his stare there. Antony gazes at the dashboard where he punched an indentation. If we keep going, if we don't turn right now, we'll end up like J, this zombie, the voice of reason, silenced. I thought I knew . . . I can't even explain. Time passes. Time sits there, empty, ticks of moments, where we could be in a corner booth at Big Boy, remembering, reminiscing, eating, goodbye-ing. Instead we trap ourselves in a Chevy, rolled tight windows steaming from our breaths, my shirt humidity-damp under my arms, all of us lost in our minds, thoughts struggling to be put in words, and I wish I could think straight, but I've clicked off inside, sick-numb.

Antony breaks the silence with "Let's do this," like we're heading into the armpit of battle.

Making a fist, as if crushing her name in it, Craig says through gritted teeth, "Bobbie," like a thrash metal singer, exaggerated. During the diversion of Craig's speaking, J sneak-rolls down his window and the night air for the first time tonight seems uncomfortably cold. Craig says, "I'm gonna put . . . Okay, I'm gonna . . . see her fu-, face. I'm gonna . . . That fuck-ing, that house . . . is, her. And Charles. Fuck him!" He gets controlled again, lucid again, still-quiet, demonstrating how he even controls his insanity. I want to say, 'Who's Charles?' but before I can, Craig says, "This is the last time I ever say either of those names. Ever again."

Antony says, "Amen-motherfucks-let's-do-this." They don't acknowledge me. I'm third string. Like I'm not there. But I am. J takes off his cap, wipes the perspiration off his forehead, wipes his eyes.

Craig turns the key to the car but doesn't realize it's already on so the engine gives a high pitched grind. He mumbles, "Matt Cort. Matt Cort. We're doin' this," but he doesn't look at me when he says 'we.'

Antony goes, "We know we know, let's go."

I say, "This isn't my car. What am I going to tell the cops?"

Antony goes, "There aren't going to be any cops."

I go, "J's gotta get home."

Craig explains, aggravated, like it's obvious, "Drop him by the clinic, right by the clinic." All eyes on Craig, J holds his cap out the window, and drops it. No one notices this, but I do. I look out the back window, but the cap has already disappeared into the night. I want to say something, but Craig continues, "J cuts through the woods. Boom, you're on 41, get the hell back to Ishpeming."

I go, "That's far."

J goes, "No, it's not." This is the first J has talked.

Then I see it. J shuffles, readjusts, and it's the first sight, my first, of the gun, his gun, a third gun, J's, between his legs, a glimpse, metal, black, there. J looks out his window at eerie nightfall, night that has long fell, shadows of a million hiding spots.

So this is what I do. It's the sanest thing and the best thing I've ever done. I run.

My thumb goes to my nose, unhurried, wipes, hand comes down on the door, faked calm. I yank. The door handle. It doesn't budge. J turns to me. I flub around, frantic, lean up front, fists clenched, in case a gun is raised, then both my hands search for the nail-like doorknob, to pull, unlock, with my whole body I ram the door as far as it opens. It ricochets back, chops me in the leg, but I'm gone, stumbling, running, gone.

I run like insanity.

They want insanity. Insanity's the big tough thing, they got it. Antony, acting crazy, acting, reciting raps about killing bitches and taking niggers out and he does it with his pretend lunatic eyes when he couldn't shoot someone if he was in the middle of a war. And, Craig, running around like a nutcase lifting screaming headbanging and that's what every kid does nowadays. Then J. Punk T-shirts with photos of gaunt white juveniles in alleys under the words 'Do The Retard!'

If they want insanity and they want to run for their life, through woods, some U.P. jungle, then that's what they can have, count me in, that's what I want too, the woods, fairy tale forest, sure. I run. Legs pump. A car door opens and slams behind me and there's madness madness madness in branches one knocks me on my ass I plummet down hit my back moss-wet bouncing up continuing running lightning lighting up the sky no rain no way they can keep up with me doing varsity cross country while Craig stands in fat kid huddles I will kill myself before I let him get his hands on me again at a dangerous pace no concern for my body this is how Craig must feel all the time faster than I can control up a hill down one giant basketball step track leap sprint breathing like a fugitive leaves crunch snap twigs breathing breathingbreathing grunting eye shielding then clawing up another hill my hands tear into dirt like a four legged animal raving spitting and panting I hear them, on my heels, Craig and Antony, and then, it's sudden, a small bluff, I'm in the air, floating, falling, a heap of sticks, dry leaves, a hard fall, grass snakes slither away, more scared than me, and there's the harvest moon. My breathing's too loud, I hold it, listen, with my body, to hear, nothing, wind, nothing.

Alone, bruised, I get up, and walk in the direction that feels like home.

I think. I think of the citizens of Ishpeming, of Negaunee, Gwinn, Palmer, Suomi, all the elderly that frequented St. David's Episcopal before it was torn down. And, my Grandma, how she bakes fresh blueberry pies backyard-picked for new neighbors, even the scary hairy ones with dirt-white vans and pay-by-month rent contracts. And, Charles Asgard, who always picked me for games so I never had to sit out at Miner's. And, the memory of the only valentine I ever got, delivered in eighth grade homeroom, from Shelley, reading "To the nicest guy in the school," and she was the only girl to ever give me a valentine, and now, too late, I don't want to leave her, but have to, want to take her with me, somehow, now, but can't, too late, and how many times do people feel love too late? And, my parents, how they get more excited for Christmas than I do. And, how my cousins are only a small part of the Upper Peninsula, a microscopic part and a part that can easily be forgotten.

While walking I listen for footsteps. The heavy footfalls of Craig. The only person who knows these woods as well as me. At the end of a darkened marsh of Cattails, I see him, an awaiting shadow, a waiting shade, a breathing scarecrow, to my left, soundless, following me, my imagination. I wonder if when I get back he'll be at the top of my parents' driveway hill. If he'll have the shotgun at his side. If I've made a mistake. If I can just get away, in what? Six hours. 0800 military time. Monday. How strange it will be in the house, rushed, my parents talking about Craig over scrambled eggs with cheese, asking if I said bye, how nice it was he spent a final night with me. Then I thought about the future. What is life like on a submarine? How hot is Florida in July? How will it feel at Marquette's Greyhound Station with the freedom that is the weight of a duffel bag in hand? All I have to do is get through this forest, walking, until I get to the abandoned trains that have been on the tracks for years, unused, sitting like an extinct industry, cobwebbed, ore pellets heaped inside, rain falling again and again leaving the ground stained orange-red, and I climb, over protruding pipes, my hands covered with a deep dirty blood ore red in the night. This means I'm close, to home.

It's been a long walk when I hear a gunshot. In my mind? I imagine J trying to drive a car for the first time, how dangerous it must be, how he has slow reaction to get his feet to the pedals, how cerebral palsy affects muscle coordination, how the messages in the brain are not making it to his legs, and how he'd always been afraid to drive, but now maybe he was going to learn fast that he could, how easy it was, like riding a bike, finally overcoming that fear, just in time, to escape, and he could get a used car and drive to whatever the new city was and he could think about it from the graveyard to his house where he'd park the Chevy, hoping no one would notice, note the time, but a neighbor would look out their window nonchalantly and see a silhouette walking with what they'd describe as a limp, see some unknown car on the street, and if J ended up staying in Ishpeming, things could get hairy, hectic, bad. And, if he ended up leaving, there would be a warrant out for his arrest but he would be on the other side of the country, because I snuck a peek at what Bill drilled into his arm; I know the city. I'm sly that way. There's no way I was going to be there for the duration of that tattoo with only one TV channel and not get a shot of what the tattoo was. And, Bill was done really fast, so I'm almost one hundred percent certain J is heading to L.A.

I hope he likes California. Mexico close by. Tijuana.

J and Tijuana.

And a girl lives there. L.A. I have a feeling she lives there.

Then Craig and Antony in the cemetery, running like a gazelle and a chimp, a cheetah and a loon, over tombstones as if there were no bodies underneath decaying in vacuums of peace. Both of them running side by side, follow the leader, Craig limping, Antony ahead of Craig, a pair of troubled buddies, bonding the only way they know how. Craig having to piss and Antony telling him there's no time, to wait until they were in the caving grounds where no one would be. Jumping the barbed wire, Antony getting his sleeve caught, ripping his shirt, cutting his wrist, feeling it throb and the feeling is good. Craig taking this opportunity to urinate on SARAH ROPOCH's grave, 1922-69, Beloved Wife And Mother, laughing while he shook dry, invincible with his shotgun and recent memories of how it feels to put a bullet through glass, through wood, so effortless, the fractioned movement of a finger, how he aimed directly at the bedroom, right at the level where a body would be sleeping, where he estimated the head would rest, how Matt Cort had not moved yet, and when Craig pulled the trigger he almost shot Antony in the ear, Antony wacking at the side of his head, to get the feeling back, the blood pumping so fast he felt like he had to fight to get all that energy out, and the sound, the blast, like fireworks, unexpectedly like Pioneer Day fireworks. Antony said he could feel the bullet pass his ear, Craig telling him that was bullshit until they noticed the slow flow of blood on Antony's neck, then the quick drive away, Craig flooring it and lights in the neighborhood flicking on, driving like raw mad boys hitting a post office mail collection box, letters flying, envelopes falling, massive confetti, how that wasn't the plan, the smell of recently fired gun in the car on hands shirts and how they forgot about that, about clues, about rolling down windows, about the smell thick gunpowder sulfur in the air in the nostrils imbedding in the car seats, and again, even the smell, like firecrackers, like joy, misleading. Antony squealing, "I can't hear. I can't hear!" Craig laughing, not holding back, openly laughing at Antony.

But now Antony could hear. He could hear the graveyard, its stillness, the patience of phantoms behind each elm. He could see its Greek statues like horrible lifelike stunned cadavers watching over the necropolis of their fellow dead. A stone white Christ stood fifteen feet away that Craig stares at, another quick snort of Cat for courage making Jesus' carved eyes move in his mind, eyeing him like God would, and the night's sleep deprivation. While Craig gets a good sniff, Antony takes out his ever-present matchbook and eyes a collection of dry leaves. Lighting the match, he turns the book upside-down and lets all the matches catch fire, tossing them flaming into the leaf pile, which burns at a gentle leisure rate, spreading, a virus of lava. What if it kept going? Forever? What could be more majestic and immaculate than a full cemetery ablaze? Maybe an entire town. And, again, the running, through the caving grounds, a desert of woods, the magic of utterly forgotten land, with small pockets of city emerging like a museum of past lives, an abandoned house to their left unremembered, not even boarded. Craig's father's stories echo in his mind about this area, fishing, hunting, dating, walking, running on a once active street, now weeded, overgrown, unusable. Craig tells Antony to stop, listen, and this thrills the both of them, adds to the adrenaline, makes this real, guns ready, safeties off, the both of them susceptible to tripping at any second in the dimness, maneuvering, Craig pretending he's his father twenty years ago, Antony imagining himself as a gang member, included, believing in, taking side paths, remembered paths, like they've done a hundred times before, but rarely in the dark, and how they'd still end up in hell, because of the landmarks, they would lead them and this would be the halfway point, Hell, how when they got there Antony would see it first, point, and whisper the word in a respectful tone, "Hell."

"We're home," Craig'd say, hushed.

They'd dare each other to get close to the edge. Closer. Craig would be tempted to push Antony in, or pretend to, scare him, tackling him, man hugging him. And, it would sink in what they had done, how they had another year to go at Ish High and then what, sell more cemetery plots or put away more IGA bottles or join the Marines, which neither of them could handle, or get a midnight shift at the water sewage treatment plant or go to Marquette for unemployment checks next to the Touch of Finland store and what will happen when they get arrested? If they find out who did it? Is that possible? In the dark, in the quiet they would be forced to realize they had ended a part of life, their childhood, the most important part, forever gone now, exiting with gunshots, how they'd look into the hellhole in the darkness and it would seem less frightening, almost promising and one of them would make a casual comment that they should jump in, that they might as well, that they could go out like a bang, they could do it together, on the count of three, and they'd think about this staring into the abyss, tonight the pit looking like the sky, how Craig would throw his gun into Hell on a whim, a gentle sway and then release from his hand, and the vanishing without making a noise as if the bottom were quilted with pillows feathers how easy it was how easy it'd be to do the same thing with themselves how no one would ever find them and how cool that would be to just disappear to really get the town up in arms and how if they did do that if they did jump in maybe it would be all for the better and maybe with certain people doing something like that maybe in all truthfulness it would be for the better, for the world, maybe it would be,